THE
MISSING

THE
MISSING

LISA
CHILDS

ZEBRA BOOKS
KENSINGTON PUBLISHING CORP.
www.kensingtonbooks.com

ZEBRA BOOKS are published by

Kensington Publishing Corp.
119 West 40th Street
New York, NY 10018

Copyright © 2022 by Lisa Childs

First Printing: November 2022
ISBN-13: 978-1-4201-5458-0
ISBN-13: 978-1-4201-5459-7 (eBook)

10 9 8 7 6 5 4 3 2 1

Printed in the United States of America

Chapter One

The sensation of someone staring at him pulled Elijah Cooke from his state of oblivion. He didn't want to regain consciousness, though, because along with consciousness came all the memories. . . .

As a kid, finding that body twenty-five years ago in the ruins of what had been his family home and business: Bainesworth Manor. And then, just a few weeks ago, another body turned up on the grounds of Halcyon Hall, which was what he and his brother had turned the old family business into—a posh spa for the rich and famous.

But would anyone want to check in again after what had happened tonight? After Elijah's own cousin had tried to kill him, the sheriff, and one of those rich and famous guests?

He flinched as he remembered the blow from the butt of the weapon and then the gunshots.

"Hey . . ." someone murmured to him. "It's okay . . ."

He forced his eyes open, then squinted and grimaced at the glare of the overhead lights. Blessedly, a shadow fell over him, partially blocking the light. Was it a blessing, or another damn curse? Like anyone who had anything to do with Bainesworth Manor was rumored to be . . . cursed.

He peered up . . . into the face of an angel. Her features

were so delicate, her eyes so big . . . her hair so bright and blond. He must have died. But how the hell had a Bainesworth made it to heaven?

"Good, you're awake," a husky female voice remarked.

And he realized his angel was the devil. "How the hell did you get in here?" he murmured.

Edie Stone chuckled. "Security at this podunk hospital isn't like what you have at the hall. Though I hear that's not all it's cracked up to be."

He flinched, and not just because of the pain reverberating inside his skull. Had David crushed it with the butt of that gun.

"Is everyone okay?" he asked. "Holly? Olivia? Deacon?" He couldn't ask about David, not after what he'd done, after he'd tried to kill Deacon, who was the sheriff now, and abduct the man's daughter. And poor Olivia, the guest, had gotten caught in the crossfire of it all, just as Elijah had. That wasn't all the man had done, though; he'd confessed to other murders, his own brother and the woman he'd once loved.

She chuckled again. "I'm the reporter. I'm the one who's supposed to ask the questions."

"Right now you have more answers than I do." He had no idea what had happened after David had struck him.

"Your cousin is dead," she told him.

Pain gripped his heart, contracting it. David hadn't been just his cousin; growing up, he'd been his best friend, the one with whom he and Deacon had found that body all those years ago. "And the others?" he asked anxiously.

"They're all right. Better than you, actually." And she reached out, her fingertips skimming along his jaw before she jerked her hand back.

His skin tingled from that brief contact. Maybe he was just getting his feeling back from being frozen. How long had they been out there before help had arrived? But help had arrived; that was all that mattered. A ragged sigh of relief slipped out through his lips.

"I answered your questions," Edie said. "Now you owe me some."

He shook his head and grimaced at the pain shooting through his skull. "No."

"What are you doing in here?" a familiar voice asked.

"Checking on your brother, of course," Edie replied. "I've been so concerned about him."

His brother, Bode, snorted. "Yeah, right. Get the hell out of here before I call security on you."

She laughed, and the sound quickened Elijah's pulse. "What? You're not strong enough to get rid of me on your own?" she teased the personal trainer.

And a smile twitched at Elijah's lips.

"Out!" Bode told her.

And Elijah flinched.

"Careful," she said. "You're going to hurt your brother's head. He has a concussion, you know."

"How do you know? You're not next of kin. Nobody better have told you anything."

"Why?" she asked. "Worried I'm going to learn all your family secrets?" She walked toward the door then, but she stopped before she opened it and turned back to flash a cocky smile. "You should be worried."

"Out," Bode said. But it was much softer now. And probably not just in deference to Elijah's concussion, but because he was worried.

Elijah was, too. Edie Stone wasn't going anywhere, even though she finally stepped out of the room and closed the door.

His brother's breath shuddered out with relief.

"Don't be too relieved. She'll be back," Elijah warned him.

"I'm relieved you're alive," Bode said.

He lifted a hand to his pounding head. "Am I?"

His brother chuckled. "I feel your pain. Or I felt it myself not that long ago. Lucky for us we were born with thick skulls."

Elijah chuckled, too. "Yeah, lucky . . ." That was something he rarely considered himself, but he had survived. "Is David really dead?" Not that he doubted Edie. She had no reason to lie to him.

"He's dead," Bode confirmed. "Even though I know you guys were close, I'm not sorry—not after what he did."

Panic gripped Elijah's heart. "Are Olivia and Holly really all right?"

"Yes," Bode assured him.

"And Deacon?"

A smile curved Bode's lips. "Since he got to kill the bastard who's made his life miserable, he's probably better than he's ever been."

Elijah wasn't so sure about that. Deacon wasn't like David; taking a life would affect him. How hadn't it affected David that he'd killed his own brother and the woman he'd loved? How had he done that and continued on as if nothing had happened? What was wrong with him? What was missing?

He jerked, startled when he realized what else was missing. Or rather who else . . .

"Where's Adelaide?" he asked with alarm and concern for Bode's baby, his niece. He knew her nanny only worked during the day. "You didn't leave her with Grandfather and his nurse?"

"No wonder they want to keep you overnight for that concussion," his brother mused. "You must have been hit really damn hard to think that I would leave my daughter with Dr. Frankenstein and Igor."

Another chuckle slipped out of Elijah's lips and reverberated inside his cracked skull. He winced. "So where did you leave her?"

"Boardinghouse," Bode replied. "With Rosemary and Genevieve. Of course, then I had to tell them what had happened. That reporter must have overheard and beat me to you."

"Damn it."

Bode sighed. "She won't be the only reporter covering this. Maybe we should get ahead of it, do some damage control."

"Let Amanda Plasky handle it," Elijah advised. It was better that someone without Bainesworth or Cooke blood in their veins handle the press. "And focus on Adelaide."

"I will," Bode assured him. "It's a tragedy that her mother is gone, that she'll never get to know her." Adelaide's mother, Erika Korlinsky, whose body had been found a few weeks ago at the hall. Tears filled Bode's pale blue eyes as he continued. "She won't get to help pick out her prom dress or wedding gown." He sucked in a shaky breath. "But at least it's over now, right? David must have killed Erika, too."

Remembering his cousin's last words, his last confession, Elijah shook his head. Then he had to close his eyes for a moment until the room stopped spinning on him. "No, he didn't."

"What do you mean?" Bode asked. "Of course he did. He was obviously batshit crazy."

Elijah winced again. He hated that word, hated more that it could be applied to so many of his family members. "He admitted to Warren's death and Shannon Howell's."

Would Deacon ever forgive Elijah for that, for suspecting

him instead? At least the sheriff knew the truth now, and so would the rest of the island soon enough; Elijah would make certain of that. He owed his old nemesis that much and more. Deacon had saved his life, and Olivia Smith's for certain. There had been no way for him to save David, no way for anyone to save David. He'd been too far gone.

How had Elijah missed it all these years? How had he missed how unstable his cousin had been?

And what else had he missed?

"So?" Bode persisted. "Just because he didn't confess to it doesn't mean he didn't kill her. Or maybe that kid who kidnapped the Walcott girl, maybe he did it. Either way, it's over, Elijah. We don't have to worry about anyone else getting hurt. It's over."

Elijah wanted to believe that almost as desperately as his brother did. But he had a feeling it was far from over . . . and there would be more bodies.

But he kept his fears to himself. He didn't know who to trust anymore. David had been more than his cousin; he'd been his best friend.

And a killer . . .

How many other secret killers did Elijah know? And would one of them kill again?

Too bad they were keeping Elijah Cooke overnight at the hospital and had transferred him to a private room. If he'd still been in the open area of the ER, Edie Stone would have been able to hear all of his conversation with his brother, who was also his business partner, in the "House of Horrors," as the Bane Island locals called Halcyon Hall. They would never forget its past as a hospital for the criminally insane and an asylum for the young women whose families had committed them to the place. But even with her ear pressed against the door, she could hear only the rumble of their deep voices through the solid wood. She couldn't discern any of their actual conversation.

"What the hell are you doing here?"

The question drew Edie's attention to the woman standing in front of her in the corridor. She'd expected to find a nurse or a security guard objecting to her blatant eavesdropping, but she didn't recognize the blond woman who was glaring at her through heavily lashed eyes. Obviously, the woman recognized her because she continued, "What kind of parasitic reporter are you that you're so desperate for a story that you're harassing Dr. Cooke while he's in the hospital?"

Edie shrugged. "The usual parasitic kind," she replied, and she finally recognized the woman's snippy voice. The last couple of times she'd called Halcyon Hall she had been transferred to this woman—instead of the person she'd requested: Dr. Cooke. "You PR types generally don't have a problem dealing with us if you want us to promote something."

Despite how late at night it was, the publicist for Halcyon Hall still wore her business suit. And despite how cold it was outside, she wore a short skirt and high heels with it. How hadn't she slipped in the parking lot or lost a shoe in the snow that had been falling heavily?

"I want to promote the truth," the woman replied, "while you're only looking for scandal."

Edie shrugged again. "When it comes to Bainesworth Manor, I don't have to look very hard."

The woman, who'd identified herself during their last call as Amanda Plasky, sniffed. "The spa is called Halcyon Hall. It hasn't been Bainesworth Manor for more than forty years. Why are you dwelling on the past?"

"I'm not the only one," Edie said. All the locals refused to call it Halcyon Hall as well. While the building and grounds had been totally renovated after decades of neglect, its new façade hadn't fooled any of them into forgetting what it had once been—a psychiatric hospital that had carried on archaic practices long after they'd been deemed dangerous.

Lobotomies weren't the only horrible things that had happened there, though. Children had been taken from their mothers, whose families had committed them to the facility. The girls had either been pregnant at the time or had been impregnated by someone at the hospital, and then their babies had been stolen and sold. And Edie needed to find them, needed to find the truth.

"Some people need to move on," Ms. Plasky said. "Like you, right now. You need to leave."

"We're not at Halcyon Hall right now," Edie pointed out. "I have as much a right to be here as you do."

"Not with Dr. Cooke," Ms. Plasky said. "You have no right to be anywhere near him. And if you persist on harassing him, I will report your behavior to the police."

Edie smiled at her. "I'm going to report to the police right now. I was just on my way to check on the sheriff, his daughter, and Miss Smith."

"You're harassing them, too?" she asked.

"I'm an equal-opportunity harasser," Edie said with pride. People had learned over the years that it didn't matter to her how rich or powerful they were; she wouldn't be swayed from reporting the truth. The truth was too important to Edie. "But they're actually friends of mine."

"Yeah, right, like anyone would trust you enough to

befriend you," the woman replied as she pushed past Edie to open the door to Elijah's room.

"Ms. Plasky," he said, his deep voice containing a note of surprise. Clearly he hadn't been expecting her and didn't consider her a friend or he would have used her first name.

Edie chuckled, and the woman quickly slammed the door shut on her. Knowing she wouldn't be able to overhear their conversation, she stepped away from the room and headed down the hall to the other room number she'd bought from the receptionist in the hospital lobby. She probably could have just called Olivia or Deacon and asked them where they were, but she'd been paying for Elijah Cooke's room information anyway, so she'd had no problem forking over a little more cash to the young woman. With most of the small island off the coast of Maine shut down for the winter, there were few places for employment or for visitors, like Edie, to stay. The hotel had temporarily closed, as well as many of the shops, bars, and restaurants in town.

So Edie, determined to learn the truth about the twisted history of Bainesworth Manor and the Bainesworth family, had checked into the local boardinghouse. To investigate fully, she needed to stay on the island, especially when the only way onto and off it was the four-mile-long, rickety bridge the state police often closed when the weather made it too dangerous to use.

The bridge wasn't the only dangerous thing about Bane Island; so many terrible things had happened here, long ago and more recently. Like the tragic events of this evening . . .

David Cooke, Elijah Cooke's cousin as well as the contractor who'd renovated the hall, had abducted the sheriff's daughter and one of the guests at Halcyon Hall. And he or his brother had been trying to kill the sheriff . . .

What a mess. . . .

And a great story, but not one Edie wanted to tell. Not when she knew and had come to care about so many of the people involved. She wanted to give them time to deal with everything that had happened and to recover fully. And even if they did, she wouldn't tell their story . . . unless they authorized her to share it.

Instead of barging into Olivia's room, as she had Dr. Cooke's, she lifted her hand and knocked on the door first. Only silence greeted her; no one called out through the door, no one turned the knob to open it. It was late, and Olivia was probably exhausted. So Edie turned to leave, but before she'd taken more than a step down the hall, the door rattled and opened behind her.

She turned around to greet Olivia with a smile, but a state trooper in her drab beige uniform was the one who opened the door. The female trooper turned back toward the room occupants and remarked, "Remember what I said. You're off this case. You're not allowed to investigate."

Had Olivia Smith, the pop singer AKAN, become an amateur sleuth?

But it was a man who replied to the trooper. "Remember what I said—you need to focus on the Cookes. David wasn't the only killer in that family."

Edie had just been alone in a room with Elijah and Bode. Was one of them a killer? Both? She shivered at the thought.

"David claimed he didn't kill Erika Korlinsky," Deacon continued. "And I believe him. I believe her killer is still out there, probably working and living at the manor. That's why I found her body there."

"I am going to speak to Dr. Cooke next," the trooper assured the sheriff. Then she turned back to Edie and stared pointedly at her when she continued, "But whatever I discover won't be a matter of public record until the investigation is closed."

"I'm at a disadvantage here," Edie said. "You seem to know who I am, but I don't know you."

"You don't need to know me," the trooper replied, but the nameplate clipped to the pocket of her uniform jacket gave away her identity: Sergeant B. Montgomery.

"You don't want the credit when you catch Erika Korlinsky's killer?" Edie asked her.

"I don't do this to get credit," the woman replied. "I do this to get justice for the victims."

Edie had more in common with the trooper than the woman would probably ever acknowledge. She wasn't looking for scandals to report; she was looking for the truth, and for justice as well.

"If that's really what you want, Sergeant Montgomery, focus on the Cookes," Deacon Howell advised again.

"Sheriff, you're off this case," the trooper reminded him before she walked away.

Edie stepped inside the room and closed the door before she asked Deacon, "Are you really?"

His daughter jumped up from the chair next to Olivia Smith's bed and grabbed her father's arm. She was tall, like him, and with the same dark brown hair and eyes. "Please, Daddy, stay away from the hall. I don't want to lose you." The teenager turned back to the woman in the bed. With her slight build and the dark circles beneath her hazel eyes, Olivia looked fragile, but Edie had already figured out that the pop singer was tougher than she looked. "I don't want to lose either of you," Holly told the woman.

Deacon smiled and assured her, "Yes, I'm really off the case. You don't have to worry."

His daughter hugged him. "Thank you . . ."

He clasped her close to his chest, to his heart. Even Edie, a newcomer to the island, knew how strained their relationship had been ever since Holly's mother died two years before. Apparently it hadn't been a suicide, as so many had thought, or Deacon's fault, as some others had believed. Shannon Howell's lover, David Cooke, was actually the one who'd killed her.

Feeling as if she was intruding, Edie backed toward the door. "I should leave you guys alone," she said. "I just wanted to make sure everyone was all right."

Olivia Smith chuckled. "Yeah, right. You wanted to get the scoop."

"Just on your well-being," Edie said. "I'm not going to write anything about you guys."

She knew Olivia had come to the hall to escape from the media and a stalker. Fortunately, the stalker had been stopped, but the media was probably just stalled. While a couple of pictures had already been released of the pop singer, revealing where she'd been hiding the past few months, reporters had yet to descend on the island—probably because of the weather. So Edie would have had the exclusive story had she cared to pursue it.

"I'll be old news soon anyway, since I'm retiring now," Olivia said.

Holly gasped. "I know you're staying on the island, but I thought you'd keep writing."

"Writing," Olivia said. "But I'm not going to perform anymore. I'll leave that to better singers."

"But you're so good!" Holly gushed. The sixteen-year-old had worked part time at the spa where celebrities—like

Olivia—sometimes checked in for treatment—either from stress or their vices. Olivia had checked in because she'd thought the hall's security would keep her safe.

It hadn't.

Deacon Howell had. "Remember, honey," he told his daughter, "we want Olivia to stay."

"Yes, of course," Holly said. "But I love your singing."

Olivia reached for the girl's hand and squeezed it. "I'll still sing for you. In fact, I've been working on some new material. . . ."

Certain now that she was intruding, Edie turned toward the door. "I'm glad to see you all survived," she murmured. "I should get back to the boardinghouse before the roads get too bad. You know how much Evelyn worries about me. . . ."

Deacon chuckled. "My last visit there I believe your land-lady actually confessed to putting arsenic in your food."

Edie shrugged. "Yeah, poison . . . that's our love language."

Olivia laughed, and as she did, her shoulders rose, as if a burden of unhappiness had just fallen off her. "You're the best. Please be careful out there."

"Always." Edie nodded and stepped into the hall, but before she could pull the door closed behind her, Deacon followed her out.

"Liar," he admonished her.

She held up her hands. "What?"

"You're not always careful or you wouldn't even be here on Bane Island, poking and prodding into the history of the manor."

She shrugged. "True. But you're not one to talk about lying. There's no way you're really going to stay out of this investigation."

He shook his head. "No. I meant it. I'm done."

She narrowed her eyes and studied his face. She couldn't

believe he would abandon his search for the truth any more than she would abandon hers. "I heard you claiming David Cooke didn't kill that personal trainer whose body you found at the hall."

"Erika Korlinsky," he said.

"Did you know her?" She wondered because he'd seemed intent on making sure Edie knew her name.

He shook his head. "No. But she was more than a personal trainer. She was involved with the younger Cooke brother. She was the mother of his child."

"Oh . . ." Sympathy tugged at Edie over her loss, and Erika's baby's loss; now the child would never get the chance to know her mother. Edie understood that all too well; she'd never really gotten to know her own mother . . . even though the woman wasn't dead. "So you're not going to go after her real killer?" she asked the sheriff.

"I'm going to trust that the trooper will do her job," he said.

"But you're the sheriff," she pointed out. "Isn't solving crimes on Bane Island your job?"

He shrugged now. "Sergeant Montgomery took me off the case," he reminded her.

"And you're really going to let that stop you?"

"I have too much to lose," he said.

"The election?" she asked. "Political backing? Money?"

He shook his head. "I'm not on the Bainesworth payroll like my father was. And if I lose the election, I don't even care, not after nearly losing Holly and Olivia tonight. They're what matters most to me, and they've been through too much for me to put them through any more."

"So you don't want to lose them . . ."

He shuddered, as if horrified at the thought, or perhaps

the memory, of how close he'd actually come to losing them. "I don't want anyone I love to get hurt any worse than they've already been," he said. "Don't you have anybody you care about, Edie? Anyone who cares about you?"

She thought of someone; not the family whose DNA she shared, but of the woman she'd thought was her mother. The woman who'd raised her for the first ten years of her life . . .

She shook her head. "No . . . I don't have anyone." *Not anymore . . .*

"You still have a lot to lose," he said. "You really need to be careful if you're going to keep going after the Cookes."

"I'm not going after them," she said. "I'm not even going after a killer. I'm going after the truth. I want to know what really happened to the women whose families committed them to the manor. And I want to know what happened to the babies some of them had while they were there."

Deacon sighed. "All that happened nearly half a century ago," he said. "You're not going to find any records from when the place was the manor, and you're not going to find anyone who wants to go on the record about what happened back then. If that stuff was out there, James Bainesworth would have been more than shut down, he would have been sent to prison."

But as Deacon had admitted, his father, who must have been the sheriff then, had been on the Bainesworth payroll. Had he destroyed those records? Or lost the evidence?

"I'm not going to give up until I learn the truth about what happened then," she vowed.

"I'm more concerned about the murders," Deacon said. "Hopefully Sergeant Montgomery will be able to find out who murdered Erika Korlinsky and that other woman I found at the manor. . . ."

"What other woman?" she asked with sudden alarm. She'd thought everyone had survived tonight. "Did another body turn up?"

"I'm talking about the one I found twenty-five—twenty-six—years ago." He shuddered again, as if that memory horrified him. He must have been just a kid when he found it.

"The manor was abandoned then," Edie said. She'd been researching it for a few weeks, so she knew that part of its history, that it had quickly fallen to ruin when the state shut it down nearly half a century ago, long before Elijah Cooke and his brother, Bode James, renovated and reopened it as the posh spa it was now. "How do you know that death had anything to do with it?"

He shrugged. "I don't. I just don't like coincidences. She was blond, like Erika Korlinsky, like Shannon, like Genevieve. . . ."

She narrowed her eyes again as she tried to figure out what his angle was. "You said David Cooke killed Shannon. And that groundskeeper abducted Genevieve, so what does being blond have to do with anything?" She reached up to touch her own short bob. "I'm blond, too."

"Exactly," he said. "And blondes do not have more fun at Bainesworth Manor—or Halcyon Hall, as they call it now. You really should stay away from there."

She sighed. "That's not a problem since I can't get past their security system."

Deacon chuckled. "And that was when that idiot Warren was in charge of it. Now that he's dead, it'll probably be even harder for you to make it onto the property."

"What about your father . . . ?" she mused.

Deacon's entire body tensed. "What about him?"

"You just said you're not on the Bainesworth payroll like he was," she reminded him.

"*Was*," Deacon stressed. "He's not now. As sick as he is, he's of no use to them anymore."

To express her glee, she wriggled her eyebrows at the sheriff. "And that's what might make him of use to me," she said. "Maybe he'll want to unburden his conscience. . . ."

Deacon shook his head. "He'd have to have one to want to unburden it," he said. "I doubt you'll get anything out of him but frustration and disappointment."

Which was obviously all the old man gave his son.

"I'm sorry," she murmured. She knew how hard it could be to get along with family, especially when you'd never really connected with them. But would she have been able . . . if circumstances had been different? She'd had no control over those circumstances, though, which reminded her so much of the situation in which those young women committed to the manor had been. . . .

Helpless.

Hopeless.

Deacon sighed. "I moved back here to make peace with my father before he died," he admitted. "It didn't take me long to realize that wasn't going to happen—not while he's alive. He's already lived longer than his oncologist thought he would, so I guess I was right about him. He did make a deal with the devil."

"I don't think he'd have cancer then."

"I wasn't talking about the devil," Deacon explained. "I was talking about James Bainesworth."

She nodded with sudden understanding. "Just like everybody else on the island does when they talk about the devil . . ."

How hard must it have been for Elijah to grow up here . . .

where everyone believed he was the devil's spawn? And why had he returned here after he'd left?

Deacon had come back to make peace with his father.

Had Elijah come back to make peace with his grandfather? Or to carry out the devil's legacy?

Chapter Two

With a sudden pounding on the door, the pounding in Elijah's head intensified so much that a groan slipped out between his gritted teeth. *Damn!* He'd just given away the fact that he wasn't really sleeping. He'd just been pretending so that his visitors would leave him to rest.

But his brother and the hall publicist had insisted on staying until the doctor came to check on Elijah, so they could confirm for themselves the extent of his concussion and whether or not he would be fine.

Amanda Plasky didn't bite back the curse that slipped through her lips. "It better not be that reporter."

"It better be the doctor," Bode said as he got up from his chair to open the door. Now he groaned. "Trooper Mont—"

"Sergeant," she corrected Bode, her voice cold.

Elijah opened his eyes and focused on the female officer. Her eyes, the dark blue of deep water, were as cold as her voice as she stared down his brother, despite being a few inches shorter than the personal trainer.

"Sergeant," Bode obliged. "This isn't a good time to talk—"

"You keep saying that," she interrupted him again. "But

I'm actually not here to talk to you. I need to take your brother's report about what happened this evening."

"He has a concussion," Bode said. "He needs to be resting—"

"And he shouldn't talk to you without his lawyer present," Amanda added.

Elijah groaned again. He just wanted this over with, so he could put this entire evening behind him. "I'll talk to the sergeant," he said. "I don't need a lawyer."

He'd done nothing wrong, or at least that was what he wanted to believe. But how had he—a psychiatrist—not seen his cousin for the psychopath he'd been? Could Elijah trust his judgment of anyone anymore?

"Elijah, this is a bad idea," Amanda warned him . . . as if she believed he might have something to hide.

"I agree," Bode told him. "You need your rest. You could have died tonight."

"I do need my rest," he agreed. "So I need you two to leave. I'll tell the sergeant what happened tonight, and I'll sleep better having this behind me." He doubted that, though; he doubted he would ever sleep without reliving moments of this night . . . of how he'd thought he was going to die . . .

That someone he'd loved and trusted was going to kill him . . . as well as two innocent people. Elijah wasn't sure how innocent he was . . . because he should have known.

"Her report can wait," Amanda insisted. "You need to sleep."

"And I will . . . when this is over," Elijah said. "I can't wait to get this behind me. . . ."

"Are you sure?" Bode asked, and he stared intently at him with the eyes they'd both inherited from their grandfather.

Hopefully that was all they'd inherited from the narcissistic bastard.

Elijah nodded.

And Bode did as well. "Okay, we're leaving, Amanda," Bode told the publicist. When she opened her mouth to argue with him, he reminded her, "I'm the one who hired you . . ."

So he could fire her.

Elijah doubted his brother would actually carry out that threat; Bode had touted the publicist as one of the best in the business and her willingness to work with them as a victory. She had managed—so far—to stifle any news reports about all the bad things that had been happening at the hall. But he suspected that, after tonight, that would no longer be possible. Even Amanda Plasky wasn't that good . . .

And he suspected Edie Stone was better.

"Elijah, I can stay . . ." Amanda offered.

He shook his head. "I would prefer that you don't," he said. When she grimaced with a flash of hurt, he added, "You need to get back to the mainland before the bridge closes again." If it wasn't already closed. "We're not your only clients, and you have your own life to think of. You don't want to get stuck here on the island." And she would be a hell of a lot safer anywhere but Bane Island and the hall.

"It's sweet of you to worry," she said, and she leaned over his bed as if she intended to kiss him.

But he caught her shoulders and held her back. Unlike his brother, he would never make the mistake of getting involved with an employee or a colleague. The situation at the hall was messy enough without making it messier. "Have a safe trip back to the mainland," he told Amanda.

And finally she straightened up, turned on her heel, and headed toward the door. "Good-bye then."

A slight smirk curved Bode's lips, but he refrained from teasing Elijah about the publicist's obvious interest in him. "I'd better go get Adelaide from the boardinghouse," he said, "or that reporter will probably start trying to get a statement out of her."

"Since she hasn't spoken yet, that would be quite the feat," Elijah said. But he wouldn't put it past Edie Stone to accomplish it; he wouldn't put anything past Edie Stone.

Before Bode could follow Amanda out the door she'd left ajar, the sergeant sidestepped into his path. "I do want to speak to you," she told him. "You have yet to answer all my questions about Erika Korlinsky's murder."

The color receded from Bode's usually healthy complexion, leaving him deathly pale. "Unlike my brother here, I think I'd better have a lawyer present for that discussion."

"Why?" she asked. "Do you have something to hide?"

Elijah had once wondered about that himself, but he'd seen his brother's reaction to the DNA confirmation that the mother of his child had been the body the sheriff had found on the property. Bode had been too shocked and devastated to have been responsible; he'd really believed she'd left him, that she'd left the island . . . just as their mother had so many years ago.

In reply to the sergeant's question, Bode shook his head. "No. It just seems as though I am your number-one suspect—"

"With good reason," she interrupted. "You had an intimate relationship with the deceased. And she was leaving you. Maybe she was trying to take your child with her, and you weren't going to allow that to happen. . . ."

He shook his head. "Like I said, I'm not having this discussion without a lawyer—one who can hopefully point out to you that this case should be closed."

The sergeant lowered her blond brows as she furrowed them beneath the bill of her trooper cap. "Why?"

"Because her killer is dead," he said. "Either Teddy Bowers or David Cooke must have been responsible for her death."

"Why?" she asked again. "What was their motive?"

Bode shrugged again. "I don't know . . . they were both crazy."

Elijah flinched at that word again.

But his brother didn't notice as he continued, "They didn't need a motive."

While his brother hadn't noticed his reaction, the sergeant had because she was focused on him now. "Is that true, Dr. Cooke? Do people generally kill with no motive?"

"My area of expertise is addiction and post-traumatic stress disorder," he said. "I'm not a doctor of criminal psychology."

"You're not like your grandfather?"

God, he hoped not, but he clenched his jaw to keep that from slipping out.

She continued, "Although your grandfather didn't treat just the criminally insane who'd been committed to Bainesworth Manor."

"I thought you wanted my statement about what happened tonight," Elijah said. "Because that's all I'm prepared to discuss."

"You don't want to give me your opinion on who killed Erika Korlinsky?" she asked, but she turned her attention back to his brother, staring at him pointedly. "The sheriff is convinced it wasn't Teddy Bowers or David Cooke."

Bode snorted. "Of course he is. He has a grudge against Elijah. That's why Deacon Howell shouldn't be investigating anything that has to do with Halcyon Hall."

"He isn't," the sergeant said. "I am."

Some of the tension eased from Bode's muscular body then. "That's good. That's good."

"But I tend to believe what Sheriff Howell has told me," the sergeant continued. "He's certainly been right about other things."

"Oh, fuck . . ." Bode murmured. "He's gotten to you with all his wild accusations."

"What do you think he's told me?" she asked. "About how you must have been the last one to see Erika Korlinsky alive?"

Bode tensed. "Her killer is the last one who saw Erika alive."

The sergeant nodded. "Exactly."

Elijah's skin chilled, as if he'd been plunged back into that cold cabin, back into the nightmare from which he'd just recently regained consciousness. And now the person he was at risk of losing was his brother . . . to prison. "Bode, get out of here," he advised him. "Clearly Sergeant Montgomery has already made up her mind." She was as convinced as Deacon that Elijah's baby brother was a murderer.

While Elijah might have once had his doubts, he didn't anymore. And his niece couldn't lose her father after already losing her mother. Adelaide was only four months old, so she wouldn't even remember Erika. And if Bode was imprisoned for her mother's murder, he could spend his life behind bars.

Bode hesitated for a moment, as if he was worried that Elijah still suspected he could be guilty, and he wanted to convince him that wasn't the case.

But Elijah pointed toward the door. "Go, pick up your daughter. You need to focus on Adelaide right now," he said.

"She's your priority." And Elijah's, too. He wanted to make sure the baby girl didn't lose her only living parent.

Bode nodded and stepped around the trooper to open the door all the way from the crack Amanda had left it.

"I will need to speak to you again," the sergeant warned him.

"The next time my brother speaks to you, he will have a lawyer present," Elijah said. And if that lawyer couldn't protect him from being railroaded, Elijah would have to find another way to save his younger brother from prosecution.

And maybe that way stood just outside the door, leaning against the wall of the corridor. He'd been worried that Amanda might try hanging around, but she wasn't the blonde in the hall.

Wearing a long, black wool jacket over faded jeans, a thick sweater, and tall, black boots, Edie Stone stood outside his room. She'd obviously been eavesdropping because a slight smirk curved her lips. She was infuriating and determined. She claimed she just wanted to learn the truth . . . would she? Would she find out who really killed his niece's mother so his brother didn't get arrested for a crime he hadn't committed?

"I'll get rid of her," Bode assured Elijah.

And the sergeant arched a brow. "Are you making threats against Ms. Stone?"

The color drained from Bode's face again. "God no, I just don't want her harassing my brother. He needs his rest. In fact, I think your report should wait until he's out of the hospital."

Elijah had wanted to get it over with, but clearly the state trooper had an agenda that had less to do with closing tonight's case than working on another one. "Yes, Sergeant," he said. "I would prefer to talk to you when my head's not pounding."

But it wasn't just his head pounding now; his heart was pounding, too, as Edie Stone continued to stare at him with that little smirk on her mouth, like she knew he needed her help. Probably because she had overheard what the trooper had been saying to his brother.

Would she help him . . . if Elijah asked?

"I'll get the doctor for you," Bode told him, then he turned to the sergeant and carefully spelled out his intention, "just as soon as I get Ms. Stone to leave you alone."

"I don't want her to leave," he said.

"What?" Bode asked. "You can't actually want to talk to *her.*"

"You won't talk to the police, but you'll talk to a reporter?" the sergeant questioned him.

And he found his own lips curving into a smirk. "Maybe her mind's a little more open than yours."

The trooper sucked in a breath, clearly offended by his comment. "I need your witness statement about what happened tonight."

He nodded and then flinched as pain reverberated throughout his skull with just that slight motion. "And I'll give it to you," Elijah promised. "Tomorrow."

Her lips tightened with disapproval, but then the trooper conceded, "Fine."

"Since I was knocked unconscious tonight, my statement will be the shortest anyway," he pointed out. "So it's not as if I'm going to tell you anything the sheriff, Ms. Smith, and Holly Howell haven't already told you."

"Then you will confirm that David Cooke denied involvement in the murder of Erika Korlinsky?"

He wished David was responsible. God, he wished it was

so, and that the case could be closed. But maybe he actually had something in common with Edie Stone, or at least in what she claimed to want, because he wanted it, too: the truth. He wanted to know who was really responsible for the murder of the mother of his niece. Risking the pain, he nodded again.

"Okay," the sergeant said. "We'll talk tomorrow."

"Now who's making a threat?" Bode murmured.

The sergeant didn't say anything as she walked past him. But she paused beside Edie Stone. "I don't want false information getting out about an ongoing investigation," she said.

Edie held up her hands. "My interest isn't in an ongoing investigation," she said. "My interest is in the investigation that should have been done years ago, the investigation into what happened at Bainesworth Manor before it was finally shut down."

"It was shut down over forty years ago," the sergeant said. "It's no longer any threat to the public."

"Tell that to Erika Korlinsky," Edie remarked.

"Her murderer is the threat," the sergeant pointed out with another pointed glance at Bode. "That's the investigation that concerns me."

"Her murderer is dead," Bode insisted. "You can close that case. You can—both of you—stop harassing my family." He started to close the door to Elijah's room, shutting him inside alone.

Earlier, that was all he wanted, but now he didn't want to be alone. He wanted her. "Wait," he said. "I do want to talk to Ms. Stone."

Bode's forehead furrowed. "I'm going to get that doctor. You're obviously not all right."

"Are you saying he has to have a brain injury to want to

talk to me?" Edie asked in her usual infuriatingly smart-ass style . . . which amused Elijah more than it should.

Just like she fascinated him far more than she should. Before his brother could close the door tightly, she slipped through the opening and walked up to Elijah's bed. That slight smirk slid away as she leaned over and peered down at him. "Are you okay?" she asked. "Because your brother is right, you must have taken a hell of a blow to the head to want to talk to me."

He grinned now. "Must have . . ." he murmured.

"So I'd better make this quick before your brother comes back with the doctor and kicks me out of here," she said.

"If the sergeant hasn't already arrested him," Elijah remarked as fear for his brother's future gripped him. His brother's and his niece's . . . and even his own. He was finally getting to know his younger brother, to have a relationship with him.

Edie glanced at the closed door. "She does seem to have her mind pretty well-made-up."

"What about yours?" he asked.

She shrugged. "What about mine?"

"Do you think he did it?" he asked.

"Do you really want my *opinion*?"

An opinion wasn't going to help him; only the truth could do that. So he shook his head and groaned as his vision blurred.

"You really are hurting," she murmured, and her hand brushed along his jaw. "I should let you rest." But her hand still cupped his jaw, and she continued to stare down at him. "But I'm too curious . . . if you don't want my opinion, what do you want?"

"The same thing you claim you want," he said. "The truth."

She sighed. "Be careful what you wish for," she warned him. "Sometimes the truth hurts."

"If that's the case, why are you so determined to get it?"

She shrugged. "It's better than living a lie."

Elijah wasn't sure what he was living: a lie or a nightmare.

An unending one—the same one he'd been having since he'd been with Deacon Howell when they'd found that body nearly twenty-six years ago . . . lying in the ruins of what had been Bainesworth Manor.

So badly decomposed but for the blond hair.

He shuddered.

"You're cold," Edie said, and she reached down to tug the blanket up over his hospital gown. "You're probably in shock, and if I were a better person, I'd leave you alone. I wouldn't take advantage of you in your weakened state."

A chuckle slipped out of his lips now. "You make it sound like you're about to seduce me."

She wriggled her eyebrows at him as she leaned closer. "What would you do if I tried to . . ."

He grinned at her teasing, tempted to admit that he might give in.

Then she continued. ". . . seduce the truth out of you?"

"I can't give you what I don't know myself," he admitted. And maybe he needed to find it out on his own instead of involving someone he couldn't trust. Hell, after learning what David had really been, Elijah would be a fool to trust anyone.

And, as Amanda had warned, the last thing he and Bode needed right now was bad press for the spa; they had too much invested in it—too much money, time, sweat, and now blood. He didn't want his brother getting accused of something he didn't do, but he also wanted to make sure that if he was, they would have the funds available to defend him from those charges.

"If all you're looking for is dirt on Bainesworth Manor, I can't help you," he said. "It shut down years before I was born. I don't know anything about it."

"Your family ran it," she said.

"My grandfather."

"Then let me talk to him," she said.

He shook his head. The last thing he wanted was her anywhere near his grandfather. "No. Letting you back in here, thinking that you . . ."

"That I what?" she asked when he trailed off. "Why did you want to talk to *me*?"

He sighed and murmured, "It must be the concussion." That had had him considering for even a moment that he could trust her to help him. She obviously had no interest in anything but her own agenda. "This was a mistake. You need to leave."

He expected an argument from her, or at least some more witty banter. But she just ran her fingers along his jaw once more, making his skin tingle, his pulse quicken. If only he could blame that reaction on the concussion, too. . . .

But she got to him . . . in a way nobody had in a long time, if ever.

What the hell was it about her?

Her brow furrowed as she stared down at him, as if she was wondering the same thing. Then she pulled her hand back to her side, turned, and walked away from him. Without a backward glance at him, she opened the door and stepped out into the hall.

When the door closed behind her, he expected to expel a breath of relief that he hadn't made another deal that he'd come to regret . . . like the one he and Bode had made with their grandfather.

But instead he held his breath until it burned in his lungs along with the doubts that burned in his mind. Should he have asked her to help?

Edie's hand shook as she pulled the door shut behind her and stepped into the hall outside the room. This had probably been her best shot at getting information out of Dr. Elijah Cooke, or at least befriending him enough that he would let her inside Halcyon Hall so that she could dig through old papers, so that she could try to find the records from the past, from Bainesworth Manor.

But with the pallor of his skin and the dark circles rimming his pale blue eyes, he looked like death or close to it, too close for her to push him over the edge. He was in pain. And so she relented.

For now.

She would try again, try to get through to him that the only way she was going to leave him alone was when she learned everything she could about the manor. And even then . . .

She wasn't sure she was going to want to stop talking to him, goading him, challenging him.

There was something about Dr. Elijah Cooke beyond his obvious good looks, beyond even the intelligence. Hiding beneath his chilly, prickly exterior was a wounded soul. Tonight, maybe because he'd been physically wounded, that emotionally wounded soul had been visible and vulnerable. Too vulnerable for even Edie to exploit. She would have felt no better than his grandfather, who'd exploited those young girls.

So she forced herself to walk away from his room, down the hall toward the front doors of the small hospital. Bane Island was pretty self-contained, with its own grocery store, pharmacy, bars, churches, this medical facility—albeit small—and the spa. Not that Edie would ever settle down in a place like this.

Or in a place like anywhere . . .

After spending her first ten years on the run, she always got an anxious, restless feeling whenever she stayed anywhere too long. She had that feeling now, but it wasn't because she'd spent the past few weeks on the island. It was because of her stalled investigation.

She couldn't help those women—women like her landlady's sister—if she couldn't find out the truth. She'd had an opening with Dr. Elijah Cooke, but instead of taking it, she was walking away.

Was she getting soft? Sentimental? That wasn't Edie Stone. Hell, maybe, like Elijah Cooke, she just needed some rest. The past week or so had been crazy on the island. Hell, it had been crazy since she'd followed Judge Whit Lawrence here three weeks ago. She'd intended then to do an exposé on the budding politician, but she'd wound up finding a bigger story here on the island.

Bainesworth Manor.

This could be the biggest story of her career, like the exposés that had been done on the convents in Ireland and Spain, where young, unwed pregnant girls were sent to have their babies and forced to give them up for adoption . . . if either them or their babies survived the primitive conditions. To find an operation like that in the United States, a private one that had exploited and profited off the young women and their families . . .

This story could be her Pulitzer. But it could also be so much more . . . for so many people who didn't know the truth about their own lives.

She hesitated at those doors for a moment, staring at the parking lot, where snow swirled around the streetlamps, dimming the light in the lot—casting wavering shadows all over it. Edie wasn't scared of venturing out into the blustery weather and the darkness; she was afraid she was walking away from an opportunity she might not have again.

Talking to Dr. Elijah Cooke, one of the few remaining descendants of the Bainesworths who had built the manor all those years ago when they had settled on this remote island off the coast of Maine. Would he let her close enough to talk to him again?

She started to turn back, but then she remembered that his brother had just gone to find the doctor who was treating Elijah. He had probably returned to Elijah's room, and he wasn't about to let her back inside with them. He wasn't about to let her get to the truth about the manor, or about what had happened to that personal trainer whose body Deacon had found.

The woman had been involved with Bode James; she'd been the mother of his child.

He had to be responsible for her death, no matter how much Elijah clearly did not want that to be the truth. A twinge of sympathy struck her, but she ignored it, just as Elijah was purposely ignoring the debts his family owed to those girls who'd been mistreated at the manor so long ago.

Edie stepped closer to the lobby doors until they swished open and cold air swooshed in, striking her with such force and frigidity that she sucked in a breath as if she'd been slapped. Then she held that breath, bracing herself as she walked out into the cold. Her boots slid on the snow-covered asphalt as she started across the lot toward where she'd parked her Jeep. The snow must have been falling hard, or the lot had yet to be plowed, because the snow was deep in some spots. And underneath it was a layer of ice that had her slipping and sliding as she rushed toward her Jeep. She hadn't parked far away; the lot wasn't that big. But the few feet farther from the hospital she was, the darker it became . . . so dark that she felt as if she couldn't see.

She fumbled inside the deep pocket of her coat, trying to find her keys. If she clicked the fob, the lights would come on, but before she could find them, other headlamps came on directly in front of her—the high beams so bright that they blinded her. She squinted and looked away, but then the engine revved. And the vehicle—which she couldn't even see for the brightness of those lights—headed toward her. She turned to run, but it was too slippery and the vehicle was too fast.

She couldn't get away from it; she could only try to get out of its path as she leaped into the darkness and hoped that it wouldn't follow her, that it wouldn't run her over.

She struck the ground hard, so hard that the breath was knocked from her lungs, leaving her gasping and unable to breathe . . . while oblivion threatened to claim her.

Had Edie Stone been hit? Gloves tightened around the steering wheel, jerking it to the left to send the vehicle careening out of the lot. The driver couldn't risk staying to watch, to see if she got up from where her body had flown.

Was she dead or just hurt?

Death would have been best for everyone. Then the reporter would no longer pose a threat. But even if she survived, maybe she would finally get the message that she needed to back off. She needed to leave Bane Island before she wound up dead . . . if she wasn't already.

Chapter Three

Maybe the concussion had done more damage than he'd thought . . . because the minute she'd walked out of his room, Elijah had regretted sending Edie Stone away. When the door had opened again just moments after she'd closed it, he'd chuckled and said, "I must be irresistible since you just can't seem to stay away from me. . . ."

He knew the truth, though, that Edie Stone's only interest in him was so she could get to the truth. Or what she thought the truth was . . . about the manor, about his family . . .

Unfortunately, she was probably right.

"I hope you've mistaken me for Amanda and not that reporter," Bode said as he stepped back inside Elijah's room. "I'm glad to see she's gone."

He wasn't. "I have no interest in Amanda Plasky," he reminded his brother.

"You should," Bode said. "We're going to need her more than ever now."

"You were the one who just about threatened to fire her," Elijah pointed out.

And Bode groaned. "I shouldn't have done that; that was stupid. But the trooper and the reporter rattled me . . ." His voice trailed off, and he uttered another groan.

"Are you okay?" Elijah asked with concern.

Bode shook his head, but then he chuckled. "You're the one in the hospital. The one who could have died tonight, and you're worried about me."

"I'm your big brother," Elijah said, but guilt made his voice gruff. "Even though I haven't always acted like it." He hadn't been there for him like he should have been, but Bode was eight years younger than Elijah, so they hadn't really grown up together. Not like Elijah had grown up with David . . . only to have the man nearly kill him tonight. David had always been there for him, defending Elijah from the bullies he'd been too small to fight himself. He hadn't had his growth spurt until he'd left for college. And once he'd left, he'd sworn that he would never come back, and he probably wouldn't have if Bode hadn't swayed him with his plans for the hall.

If he hadn't pointed out how they could make something good of something bad . . .

How they could make amends . . .

Bode sighed. "Maybe we should have tried reconnecting as brothers before we leaped into becoming business partners," he admitted. The beginning of their partnership had been rocky, with both of them vying for control over the other.

"You were the one who was hell-bent on starting the hall, on coming back here," Elijah reminded him.

"Eventually you agreed to it," Bode reminded him. "Despite all your arguments against it, all your gloom and doom prophesies about how cursed this damn place has always been."

"Bane Island . . ." he murmured.

It was there. Right in the name. The name their great-great-grandfather had given it after his boat had crashed on its rocky shore nearly two centuries ago. The bane of his existence, yet Elijah James Bainesworth hadn't left the island. He was even buried in the small family cemetery on the property of the hall.

"You should have listened to me," Elijah said.

Bode sighed again. "If I'd known then what I know now . . ."

"Would you have decided against it? Would you have left it in ruins?" Elijah asked. Because he knew that he would have . . .

He never would have risked coming back here had he known that more women would be hurt. Killed.

Bode shook his head. "I can't undo the past, and I wouldn't want to," he admitted. "Because if I did, I wouldn't have Adelaide."

A smile tugged up Elijah's lips at the thought of his sweet little niece. She was just a baby, and Elijah had never been interested in babies before. It wasn't as if they could talk or really communicate, but somehow Adelaide did. Somehow he was able to see the sweetness in her, the goodness. Maybe she was the hope for the future of the Bainesworth descendants.

"I can't lose her," Bode said, his voice cracking with emotion.

"You won't," Elijah said, and he reached up to grab his brother's hand to squeeze it reassuringly. "She's safe with Rosemary and Whit and Genevieve."

"Tonight," Bode said. "She's only with them for now." He glanced at his watch. "And I've left her for too long."

Elijah peered around his broad-shouldered brother at the closed door. "You were going to get the doctor."

"He left for the night already," Bode said. "He just gave the nurses instructions to keep checking on you, to wake you up every hour, to make sure that you're able to wake up, and that you're not having any swelling on the brain." His lips curved slightly. "I could have told him that your brain can't swell any more than it already is."

"Calling me arrogant again?" Elijah asked, but he was smiling, too.

"You were the one saying how irresistible you were when I walked in," Bode reminded him.

Elijah groaned. "I thought you were Edie Stone."

"I'm glad I'm not," Bode said. "I'm glad she left. The last thing we need is her digging up dirt on the manor."

"What if she found out the truth?"

"We know the truth," Bode said with a groan.

"What do you mean?" Elijah asked. He wasn't sure what they were talking about now. He'd been thinking about Erika's murder, but he suspected that his brother had been talking about the manor.

"Our grandfather did things he shouldn't have done," Bode replied.

And Elijah groaned now. "Not to hear him tell it . . ." Every time Elijah had tried asking about their grandfather's past, about their past, he'd shrugged off the questions and had just parroted back Elijah's reason for wanting to open the spa. *I just wanted to help people. . . .*

"It doesn't matter anymore," Bode said. "Whatever the hell happened back then happened a very long time ago."

But had the wounds ever healed? Were there people still hurting because of what Dr. James Bainesworth had done? Or, worse yet, was the old man causing more pain again? More deaths?

The way Erika had been murdered . . .

"Erika just died," Elijah reminded him. Needlessly. Even though the young woman had seemingly left the island a few months ago, just a couple of weeks after the birth of her daughter, she hadn't been dead that long. Where had she been in the months since she'd left Bode? Or had she never really left? That was clearly what the trooper and the sheriff believed. "And you're going to be blamed for it if the truth doesn't come out."

"And you think Edie Stone is interested in solving that murder?" Bode asked.

Elijah shook his head.

"No, she's not," Bode said. "She's just interested in salacious headlines. In selling stories, in gaining interest in herself. I just told you that I can't lose my daughter. And I meant I can't lose her because I can't go to jail, Elijah . . . not for something that I didn't do." He glanced at his watch again. "I have to go. I have to pick her up now." His voice cracked again, as if he was panicking at being away from her, or maybe at the thought of being away from her for a life sentence. His life.

Elijah sat up and swung his legs over the side of the bed. "I'm going with you."

"To the boardinghouse?" Bode asked, his brow furrowing.

He nodded and tried not to flinch at the pain radiating throughout his skull. "And then to the hall." He couldn't call it home; it would never really be home to him. They hadn't grown up there, in the ruins of the manor; they'd grown up in a modest house on the island with an uncle and aunt, David's parents, after their mom abandoned them.

"But the doctor wanted to keep you overnight."

"So the nurses could wake me up and make sure I had no swelling going on," Elijah said. "You can do that. I can stay at the cottage with you and Adelaide." He wanted to be close to her, too, wanted to ensure that she stayed safe. Especially after tonight.

After Elijah had nearly died, had nearly left his brother and his niece alone, he wanted to be with them both as much as he could. He didn't want to be alone.

Bode's little stone cottage was the most comfortable place on the grounds of the hall. He'd made it a home for his daughter, had even finished decorating it for her first Christmas, just a couple of weeks away. Maybe there, with his family, Elijah wouldn't feel as alone and vulnerable as he'd felt tonight, when his best friend had nearly killed him.

Maybe that vulnerability was why he'd nearly confided to a reporter, why he'd just about asked Edie Stone for help. And that would have been a mistake. Bode was right. They couldn't risk bad press now, not even for the truth.

Bode studied his face for a long moment before he nodded. "Yeah, let's bust you out of here. I'd rather have you with me, too," he said, with genuine concern and fear in his silvery-blue eyes. "I'd rather be the one to make sure nothing else happens to you."

"David's gone," Elijah reminded them both. Their cousin couldn't hurt him now.

"But if you and Deacon Howell are right, Erika's killer isn't gone," Bode pointed out, and he shuddered. "Which means he's still out there. That he might come after someone else next."

Who?

One of them?

Adelaide?

Or another blond woman . . . like Edie Stone?

Panic pressed on his chest at the thought of her being hurt. Or worse . . .

That was an even greater concern than Bode going to prison for a crime he hadn't committed. It was someone else dying.

"Come on," Bode said. "Let's get you out of here. Let's get you home." In one of the drawers of the bedside table, he found the bag of Elijah's clothes and helped him into the bloodied pants and shirt. "Didn't you have a coat? You're lucky you didn't freeze to death."

Bode nearly had a few weeks earlier, when the groundskeeper had knocked him out with a shovel and left him lying unconscious in the cold. Elijah shuddered at the memory, at how he'd nearly lost his brother. He never wanted to find anyone like that again.

Edie had had her breath knocked out of her, so much so that she couldn't get it back, and her head grew lighter and lighter as she slipped in and out of consciousness.

She was aware of the cold as it seeped through her coat and jeans. Her hands were already frozen, the skin bare and bitten from the snow in which she lay. As her head grew heavy, her face sank into the snow, too, and the coldness of it bit the already chafed skin on her cheek.

She moaned, and tears of pain sprang to her eyes. She blinked her lashes, which were already laden with snowflakes, and tried to force back the tears. She couldn't cry now. She couldn't give up.

She had to get up.

Or she was going to freeze all over and die here.

Just as the person who'd nearly run her down had intended.

No. They weren't going to win. They weren't going to end her investigation. They weren't going to bury the truth, and her along with it. She wasn't going down without a fight.

She braced her frozen hands against the ground and

tried to push herself up. But her hands were numb, offering her no support, and she sank back into the snow with another moan of pain and frustration. She wasn't sure how long she lay there before she heard the footsteps and a faint rumble of voices as someone joined her in the parking lot. She could only hope that the people she heard weren't the driver and an accomplice, checking to make sure that she was dead.

"Oh my God . . ." a deep voice murmured. A familiar voice.

And then a strong hand closed around her shoulder, rolling her over, and she stared up into his handsome face, his pale blue eyes narrowed with concern.

With horror . . .

That she'd been hurt. Or that she'd survived?

"What are you doing?" another voice asked.

And she raised her gaze from Elijah's face to his brother, who stood behind him. "What does it look like I'm doing?" she asked, her voice scratchy from the cold and emotion.

"Passing out in the snow," Bode James replied.

"What the hell happened?" Elijah asked. He moved his hand from her shoulder to her upper arm, and then his other hand snaked around her waist, as if he intended to lift her.

But wasn't he hurt, too? Just a short while ago she'd left him to rest, and she'd been convinced that he was going to spend the night in the hospital. And that maybe she would have a chance to see him in the morning, before he checked out.

Instead, she'd been the one who'd nearly checked out. *Permanently* . . .

"Someone ran me over," she murmured.

And Elijah's hands stilled against her. He glanced over his shoulder at his brother. "I don't know if I should move her. She might have broken bones. Go. Get help!"

But Bode hesitated a moment. "What do you mean? A car hit you?"

She wasn't sure that it had, or if she'd jumped far enough away to avoid being struck and it was the impact with the ground—not the vehicle—that had rattled her so much. "A car came at me," she said. "Someone tried to run me down."

"Are you okay?" Elijah asked. "Where do you hurt?"

Her lungs burned from the cold air, from the panic that gripped her. But she forced that aside to focus on the rest of her body. Her skin was cold anywhere it had been exposed, but it might not have been frostbitten yet. She needed to get up, out of the snow. So she reached out and gripped Elijah's broad shoulders. He wasn't wearing a coat, just a shirt, and she could feel the cold of his body through the thin material of it. "What—what are you doing out here?" she asked.

"He checked himself out AMA," Bode answered for him.

Elijah turned back to his brother and repeated, "Go! Get a doctor for her!" And, his voice gruff with concern and urgency, he added, "Now!"

And Bode turned so quickly that he nearly slipped on the snow. He steadied himself and rushed off toward the hospital.

"I don't think anything's broken," Edie said. Any pain she felt now was more from the cold than an injury. Maybe her heavy clothes and the snow had protected her from the worst of the impact of hitting the ground. "I can move." She tightened her grip on his shoulders and pulled herself up. He didn't straighten away from her, though, and their faces nearly touched, the white clouds of their breath merging with their closeness. Then he stood up from where he'd been crouched over her, his arm around her back lifting her completely out of the snow.

"I'm fine," she said. And she wriggled enough so that her

boots touched the ground, her legs shaking for a moment before her knees locked and held. A breath of relief escaped her lips. "I'm fine," she repeated.

"Someone really tried to hit you?" he asked almost doubtfully.

"There were lights and a revving engine and the vehicle came right at me."

"Maybe the driver didn't see you," he suggested. "You're wearing dark clothes."

Irritation burned inside her, like the cold burned her exposed skin. Her hands tingled from it, or maybe from the contact with his cold body. "Did you miss the part where I said it had lights? Bright lights? Shining right in my face. Blinding me . . ."

"So you didn't see the driver? You didn't see the vehicle?" he asked.

She emitted a small growl of frustration and shook her head. "No. I didn't see anything, but they sure as hell had to have been able to see me."

But since they hadn't stopped, they weren't likely to come forward now. And she couldn't identify who it was or what they'd been driving. The only person she could be certain hadn't tried to run her down was Elijah because she'd left him lying in his hospital bed right before it had happened. He couldn't have beaten her out to the parking lot, out to his vehicle . . . if he'd even had one in the lot. He'd probably arrived here in the back of an ambulance, not on his own, not with the extent of his concussion. He really shouldn't have checked himself out of the hospital.

His tall body shuddered as he staggered back a step from her. Either he was freezing or dizzy or, more than likely, both.

"You shouldn't be out here," she said. "You should be

back in that bed." And she started tugging him toward the light of the lobby doors just as Bode James hurried out with a nurse at his side.

Bode had left his brother's room well before she had; he'd had time to beat her to the parking lot and to his vehicle. But had he had time to try to run her over and then return to his brother?

The nurse reached out toward her, trying to check her over, but Edie stepped back behind Elijah. "Dr. Cooke is the one you need to take care of," she said. "I'm fine."

And she was now, as the fury starting to bubble inside her warmed away the cold. She didn't buy Elijah Cooke's excuse that the driver might not have seen her.

She didn't believe that vehicle had come toward her accidentally. The driver had intended to run her down.

To scare her away?

Or to kill her?

Evelyn Pierce didn't care how late it was. She wasn't going to be able to sleep, so she paced the hardwood floor of the parlor.

The sheriff, his daughter, and that guest from the hall, Olivia, had come in a while ago, looking bedraggled and beat up from their close call hours earlier at the manor. She and Bonita kept warning everyone to stay away from that place, that it was cursed and brought nothing but pain to anyone who went there. But, just like Rosemary Tulle, they hadn't listened to them, and they'd nearly paid the ultimate price.

Her heart raced as she thought of how close they'd come. But they were fine.

She pressed a hand to her heart, trying to slow it down,

trying to reassure herself. She'd known the sheriff since he'd been a little boy peddling his bike all around the island, even where he shouldn't have . . . like the manor. And since he'd come back to Bane, he'd helped her find Bonita every time she'd gone missing.

He was a good man. And he'd been through so much. They all had. He, and his daughter, and that female celebrity . . . the one who sang the sad songs that Genevieve had played for Evelyn.

But they were fine.

Holly was going to bunk with Genevieve again, while Evelyn had made up one of her last remaining rooms for Deacon Howell and Olivia. Because the sheriff's house had been damaged in an explosion a day before, they'd had no place else to go. Evelyn was glad that they were here, that they were safe.

But that damn, stubborn reporter had gone out and hadn't come back. Edie hadn't gone to the manor, though, or at least Evelyn hoped that she hadn't. Evelyn suspected, instead, that the woman had gone to the hospital . . . because of the man, because Edie had probably overheard what he'd said when he'd left his child here with Rosemary. Rosemary had been Evelyn's first boarder this holiday season, when she'd come here to find her daughter, who'd gone missing from the manor. Genevieve had been found—fortunately.

So many had gone missing from that place, according to Edie, who was researching the former psychiatric hospital. But that hadn't been news to Evelyn. She knew that; her own sister had gone missing from that place. Because the woman who'd returned . . .

Evelyn glanced at her sister, who, even though she was in her early sixties now, sat on the hardwood floor with her legs crossed as easily as she had when she'd been a teenager. Her hair was white, like Evelyn's, but her face was nearly free of wrinkles, making her look younger than Evelyn even though she was five years older. And the look on her face, one of such wonder and awe, made her look like a child, too, as she stared at the baby that Rosemary rocked in the chair next to the hearth.

The baby . . .

Bonita thought it was hers.

Had her sister really had a baby all those years ago during those long, horrifying months when their parents had committed Bonita to the manor? Evelyn had never known the truth of what had happened to her once-vivacious sister there because Bonita had never really come back to her, not the Bonita Evelyn had known. This woman was more like Evelyn's child now than her older sister.

When once Evelyn might have sought Bonita out for comfort, when they were kids, Bonita was now the one who frequently crept into Evelyn's room and into her bed at night, when nightmares awakened her. She had a lot of nightmares.

Fortunately, Bonita had not seen the man when he'd dropped off the baby. He'd called Rosemary to ask her to watch his child, and so Rosemary had waited at the door for him, sparing both Evelyn and Bonita from having to meet him. He was from the manor.

He was one of them. A Bainesworth. And even though she hadn't seen him, Evelyn had heard what he'd said about what had happened, about who was hurt. . . .

Another man from the manor. And that was who Edie had probably rushed off to see. Because that other man was the one who ran the place . . . just like his grandfather once had.

Sure, they claimed it was different now. That it was some fancy spa that helped people achieve total wellness of the mind and body. Evelyn suspected it was the same as it had always been—because it was the same family running it and because women kept getting hurt there, or worse.

And so she paced, not just because she knew the man was coming back for his child, but because she was worried that Edie might not come back. Edie Stone.

Her lips curved into a smile as she thought of the reporter. She wanted to not like her—because of what she did, because she was so determined to dig up the past—but it was hard not to like Edie. She was so . . .

Edie.

Lights glinted off the glass of the front window of the parlor as a vehicle pulled into the driveway. The rumbling engine startled the baby, who awoke with a cry.

"Shh . . ." Rosemary murmured. "It's probably your daddy coming back for you. . . ." And there was a wistful regret in her voice. She'd enjoyed holding the baby, maybe because she hadn't been able to hold her own child when Genevieve was a baby. At just sixteen years old—like Bonita had been—Rosemary had given her baby to her mother to raise, only realizing recently what a mistake she had made.

Just like Bonita and Evelyn's parents had made a terrible mistake when they'd committed their rebellious teenage daughter to that horrible place nearly fifty years ago.

At least Rosemary had her daughter back—fully— while a part of Bonita had remained forever in that house of horrors.

Bonita's eyes, blue like Evelyn's, but always so cloudy-looking, widened with horror. "Who? Who's come for my baby?"

Evelyn shook her head. "I think it's just Edie. It sounded like her Jeep, and it pulled into the driveway." Hopefully the man would not feel comfortable or welcome enough to do that—because Evelyn didn't want him here. While she hadn't been able to refuse the innocent child's presence in her home, she believed only the child was innocent. No man from that place, from that family, could be innocent.

"And this isn't your baby," Rosemary said gently to Bonita.

The young woman was a psychologist, who, for some reason, had taken a job at the hall; that was how the man knew her and why he'd trusted her with his baby. Evelyn trusted her as well to handle her sister with care and understanding. Rosemary knew, better than anyone, the devastating loss Bonita had suffered.

If Evelyn's sister had really had a child . . .

"You said your baby was a boy," Rosemary reminded her. "This is Adelaide. She's a little girl."

And she was only three or four months old, whereas if Bonita had had a child, hers would be in his midforties now. Old enough that that groundskeeper who'd abducted Genevieve could have been her grandson, just like he'd claimed, before Bonita had killed him.

"She's not my baby . . ." the older woman murmured, and those bleary blue eyes clouded even more with confusion.

Evelyn's heart ached for her sister, ached that she couldn't help her find what she was missing. But it was more than a baby . . .

It was herself.

And Evelyn suspected Edie was still missing as well. If Edie had pulled into the driveway, she would have come inside through the unlocked kitchen door. But footsteps pounded across the front porch. Heavy footsteps . . . like the ones a big man would make.

Her heart started pounding like those footsteps. Rosemary was busy with the baby, so Evelyn had to answer the door. She had to get to it before Bonita did, and Bonita was already jumping up from the floor. Evelyn rushed into the foyer, but before she could get to the door, it opened.

She released a ragged sigh of relief when Edie stepped inside the door . . . until she saw that Edie wasn't alone. Two men stood behind her, and from the paleness of their blue eyes, Evelyn knew immediately who they were. Men from the manor.

And Bonita must have known, too, because the minute she stepped into the foyer, she started screaming with terror.

Chapter Four

Screaming jerked Elijah awake, and he nearly tumbled off the edge of the couch on which he'd been sleeping. He opened his eyes to blinding light, then squinted to peer around him, and just as he had every time he'd been awakened over the past few hours, he floundered for a moment while he tried to figure out where the hell he was and what had happened. This light wasn't the small beam that Bode had shone in his eyes over and over last night. This was warm and bright sunshine pouring through the windows of the stone cottage, and the screaming that had awakened him subsided to soft cries, and he realized it was Adelaide.

Not that woman from the night before.

His head pounded and he flinched with pain—not because of his concussion but because of that woman's fear. Of him . . .

Of Bode.

She'd been terrified of them just because they looked like him, or at least what *he* must have looked like nearly fifty years ago, when she'd been at the manor. *Grandfather* . . .

Not wanting to traumatize her further, he and Bode had taken Adelaide and rushed out of the boardinghouse. They'd left so quickly that he hadn't even had a chance to say hello to Rosemary or good-bye to Edie. Rosemary he would see again because he'd hired her to work at the spa.

But Edie . . .

He should have stayed and made sure that she'd told the sheriff about someone trying to run her down. She'd refused to let the nurse check her out at the hospital, and she'd also refused to call the police or even notify their security guard. Maybe she'd realized that he could have been right, that it could have been an accident that the vehicle had nearly struck her. Maybe the driver just hadn't seen her.

Would Elijah see her again? *Should* he?

"No," Bode said, startling Elijah again.

Had his younger brother read his mind?

But Bode wasn't talking to him. He had his cell pressed against his ear while he juggled his daughter in his other arm. He'd just stepped through the archway that led down the hall to the bedrooms. Adelaide must have caught sight of the Christmas tree twinkling in the corner of the room because she fell silent while her father continued speaking. "Tell the trooper she'll have to come back another time to talk to Dr. Cooke. He's still recovering from his concussion. And unless the sheriff has a warrant, don't let him inside the hall either."

Elijah ran his hand over his face, over the stubble on his jaw, and groaned. He was never unshaven, never so disheveled and unkempt as he was now. He needed to shower. Badly.

"Good morning, sunshine," Bode greeted him as he slid his phone back into the pocket of his track pants. "Did you sleep well?"

"With you waking me up all night shining a light in my eyes?" Elijah asked. "I should have stayed at the hospital."

"Probably," Bode agreed. "But since you kept waking up

with reactive pupils, I don't think you'll have to go back—
especially now that our crazy cousin is dead."

Elijah shuddered as the events of the previous evening
rushed over him again. "I wasn't the one David wanted to
kill." He'd not been the target, just collateral damage in his
cousin's quest for vengeance against the sheriff. "Is Deacon
here?" he asked. "Was that security you were talking to?"

"Yeah . . ." Bode said with a sigh. "Deacon drove Olivia
Smith here to pick up the things she'd left in her suite."

There had been no time last night, when they'd all left the
grounds in ambulances. "You can let him in," Elijah said. He
was willing to let go of the resentment of his old school bully.
When they were growing up, Deacon had hated him—hated
that Elijah was smarter than him. And that might have been
Elijah's fault—because he'd made sure Deacon was always
aware of how much smarter than him that Elijah was.

But apparently he hadn't been as smart as he'd thought or
he would have seen the truth about his cousin, his former
best friend. Deacon had always seen it. So Elijah owed the
sheriff an apology—for the distant past and the not-so-
distant past.

"They said that he wasn't actually trying to get inside,"
Bode said. "He was just dropping off Olivia and Holly.
Holly's vehicle is here, too. They'll leave in her car."

And probably never come back, if Deacon had his way.
Apparently he hadn't even wanted to come inside, but then,
he never had actually *wanted* to come here, especially when
they were kids and Elijah and David had cajoled him into
riding their bikes out to the ruins of the manor. That was
something Elijah had regretted ever since, with every nightmare he'd had after that day, after they'd found that body.

Elijah forced himself up from the couch. And as he
surged to his feet, Adelaide squirmed in her father's arms,

almost as if she was reaching out to him. Elijah ached to hold the baby, to cuddle her until she cooed at him like she was cooing at her dad now. But he had other obligations. Other apologies to make . . .

"I need to go up to the main building," he said. "I need to talk to Olivia and Holly."

"Don't apologize," Bode told him, as if he had read his mind. "It opens us up for liability in case they decide to sue us over what happened last night. And it isn't as if you had any way of knowing what David was going to do, that he was going to abduct Holly and Olivia."

"But *I* should have known," Elijah said. "*I* should have known how dangerous he was."

Bode reached out and grasped Elijah's shoulder, squeezing it. "You're a psychiatrist," he told him. "You're not God. You couldn't know what was in David's heart."

"No, I'm not God," Elijah said. He only hoped that he wasn't the devil, like everyone thought their grandfather was, like that older woman had thought both he and Bode were the night before.

She'd been so terrified of them.

A pang struck his heart, making him flinch again. With pain.

With regret.

For all the pain his family had caused. That was how Bode had convinced him to come back, to renovate the manor and build the spa with him. He'd wanted to make amends for all the bad that the Bainesworths had done here on the island. He'd wanted to make it up with good.

Their plan hadn't worked.

"I need to talk to Olivia and Holly," he insisted.

Bode sighed but reached into his pocket and pulled out a key ring. "Take my vehicle."

"Won't you need it?" Elijah asked with a glance at his niece. Her rosebud lips parted as a little bubble slipped out of them. He smiled at her—at her cuteness.

"Her nanny should be here soon," Bode said, "and then I'll run up to the hall."

Bode was speaking in literal not figurative terms. The personal trainer didn't just preach his fitness regime; he religiously followed it himself, making daily runs around the property despite the frigid winter weather.

"Be careful," Elijah advised.

"Like I said, we're all safe now," Bode insisted, and Elijah wondered who he was trying to convince—Elijah or himself. "David's dead. Everything will be fine."

"You also turned away the trooper," Elijah reminded him. "But she's going to come back."

Bode groaned. "I know, but it doesn't matter. I didn't do anything to Erika, so I can't be arrested." He glanced down at his daughter. "I can't be taken away from her."

No. He couldn't be; it would be devastating for the baby, who clearly loved her father. She'd already lost her mother; she couldn't lose him, too. But she might.

Innocent people were often arrested. And knowing how all the locals felt about the Bainesworths, Elijah worried that Bode might be tried and convicted—not on any evidence circumstantial or otherwise, but on the basis of his genes and what a jury of his peers might believe about him just because he was James Bainesworth's grandson.

Elijah squeezed his brother's hand as he took the keys from it. "Thank you for watching out for me last night," he said. And now it was his turn to watch out for Bode, to make sure nothing happened to him.

Bode shrugged off his gratitude with a grin. "Just what brothers do . . ."

Maybe other brothers, but not them. They'd never been close. Being so much younger than Elijah, Bode hadn't really grown up with him and David. And then they'd been apart for so many years when Elijah left for college. Even after starting the spa together three years ago, they hadn't been close . . . until recently.

Until Elijah had nearly lost Bode when that grounds-keeper attacked him and left him for dead. Maybe it was nearly losing his brother that made Elijah appreciate and respect him. And now he had to protect him.

"I'm going to find you a good lawyer," he promised. "We'll make sure you have representation before you talk to the trooper again."

"You really think I need it?" Bode asked, and his blue eyes narrowed as he studied Elijah's face. "You don't still have your doubts . . ."

Elijah shook his head. "Of course not. I just don't want her railroading you. It's clear her mind is made up and you're the only suspect she'll consider." Unless Elijah could come up with other suspects. He couldn't do that alone; he worked too hard to always see the good in people . . . even when there wasn't any, like with David. He needed the help of someone more cynical than he was.

"The trooper's mind is made up because your old friend Deacon Howell made it up for her," Bode said.

Elijah sighed. "Deacon's not the only one who holds a grudge against us," he said.

"If you're talking about that old woman last night, her grudge isn't against *us*." But clearly, from the gruffness of his voice and the grimace on his face, it had affected Bode, too, that she'd been so terrified of them. Because of *him* . . .

Dr. James Bainesworth.

"Security wasn't the only call I took this morning," Bode said with a sigh.

"I thought I heard you talking to someone else," Elijah said as he tried to recall the murmur of voices. Voices. So it must not have been a call. "Or was someone here?" Because one of those voices had been female, and Adelaide was too young to talk.

Bode's face flushed a bit. "Heather came by to check on you."

Elijah snorted. The young personal trainer hadn't come to Bode's cottage to check on him. "Yeah, right . . ." He hoped that his brother had learned his lesson about getting involved with an employee.

As if he'd read his mind, Bode said, "I sent her away so she wouldn't wake you up. The call was from someone else. Grandfather wants to see you."

Elijah's stomach tensed with that sucker punch of dread that always hit him whenever he had to visit his grandfather—their not-so-silent partner in the spa. James Bainesworth had only agreed to let them renovate the manor if they included him and allowed him to live out the rest of his life on the property.

He'd already been in his mid-eighties when they'd made the deal with him. So the rest of his life hadn't seemed like much, but it had already been four years since they'd made that pact . . . with the devil.

"I have other people I need to see first," Elijah said. Hopefully they wouldn't be as upset at seeing him as the lady from the boardinghouse had been the night before.

Moments later, when he caught them in the reception area of the hall, they didn't scream with terror. In fact they actually looked at him with concern. "Are you all right, Dr. Cooke?" Olivia Smith asked.

She had a bandage on her head and her own share of bruises and scrapes, but she seemed genuinely worried about him. And Elijah felt even worse over what had happened to her, and especially to Holly.

The dark-haired teenager stood close to the former guest at the spa, as if protecting Olivia from him. Or maybe it just looked that way because Holly was so much taller and broader than the petite pop singer. Maybe Holly was the one actually seeking protection *from* her because Olivia had protected her last night. She had willingly put herself in grave danger to try to save the sheriff's daughter.

David had been armed and much stronger than either of the women. Elijah was lucky David's blow to his head hadn't killed him. "I'm fine," he assured her. "I'm more worried about you and Holly." He focused on the teenager again, but she wouldn't meet his gaze.

Her skin was pale, leaving just the dark circles beneath her dark eyes as the only color in her face.

And despite his brother's warning regarding liability, Elijah was compelled to apologize. "I'm so sorry about what happened," he said. "I'm so very sorry. . . ."

Olivia reached out and clasped his forearm. "For what? You found us. You saved us."

"*Dad* saved us," Holly said, her voice and eyes hard with indignation. Clearly her loyalties had changed; when once she'd rebelliously embraced everything her father hated, like the hall, like the Cookes, now she appeared to hate it, and them, as well.

While Elijah understood, he also regretted that he was losing one of the few locals who hadn't hated him. But he was compelled to agree with her. "Yes, he did, and he saved my life, too."

"And yet you wouldn't even let him inside today," Holly said. "Not that he even wants to come inside this place."

Elijah understood that as well. Deacon had lost too much here. His wife just a few years ago, but even before that—when they'd found that body all those years ago—they'd lost the innocence of their youth. Too many times over the past few weeks when Deacon had been investigating the spa regarding Genevieve's disappearance and the body he'd found while searching for her, Elijah had caught Deacon staring at the space at the bottom of the stairs where he'd found that first body. So badly decomposed that it hadn't even looked real . . . like it had never been an actual person. . . .

Who had she been?

Elijah glanced to that spot now where he'd found Deacon sprawled across that corpse, and he couldn't suppress the shudder that came over him. That memory had haunted him for years, just as he suspected that it had Deacon.

Olivia must have noticed his reaction because she mused, "It's almost like you don't want to be here either."

He didn't. Thinking that he could change anything, that he could have somehow made amends for the atrocities that had once happened here—that had been arrogant on his part, just as arrogant as Deacon had always thought he was.

"I wish you would stay at the hall," he told Olivia, "but I understand that you probably want to return to your real life."

Holly tensed again. "This *is* her real life," she said. "She's staying on Bane Island with me and Dad."

Elijah emitted a slight breath with his surprise. He'd realized that something was going on between the celebrity and the sheriff, but he hadn't realized how serious it had become. So serious that she'd decided to remain on the island. So serious that she'd risked her life the night before to save his child.

"Please know that you're welcome to stay at the hall as long as you'd like," he said. "No charge."

"She's staying with me and Dad," Holly answered for her again.

"But the sheriff's house—"

"Yes, your cousin blew up our home," Holly said, and she shuddered now. "We're all staying at the boardinghouse until our place can be repaired."

That was what Edie had said last night; that she would tell the sheriff about what had happened at the hospital when she saw him at the boardinghouse. She had already realized that was where he would have to stay after his house was damaged. Had she talked to him about that parking lot incident? He wanted to ask, but he didn't want to upset Holly and Olivia any more than they already were.

Edie would have plenty of opportunities to tell the sheriff about that incident. Deacon and his daughter and Olivia would be staying at the boardinghouse for a while because Elijah's cousin had been one of the few contractors on the island. David had taken over the business from his dad when Elijah's uncle moved to Florida with his wife some years ago. Elijah's aunt and uncle had raised him and Bode more than their single father had. His dad had been too busy running fishing charters off the mainland and trying to find his runaway wife.

Last night, after returning to Bode's cottage, Elijah and his brother had called the aunt and uncle who'd raised them. They'd broken the news that they'd lost both their sons. Either they hadn't believed them or they'd been too upset to talk . . . because they'd hung up on them. Elijah would have to call them back, would have to ask about funeral arrangements. . . .

About the estates of Warren and David, and about David's business.

Could his employees continue it? Could they take on projects like fixing the sheriff's house?

Instead of warning Holly that it might take a long time for her home to be repaired, Elijah focused on Olivia. "You're going to stay in the same house where the reporter is staying?"

Olivia smiled, as if his concern amused her. "Edie isn't interested in writing about me," she said.

"Do you really believe that?"

She nodded. "She's become a friend, and she's been good to me. I trust her. You could, too . . . if you wanted to learn the truth."

"He already knows the truth," Holly said. "That my dad's right. He's always been right. This place is cursed." She urged the other woman, "Please, let's get out of here and never come back."

"You're quitting?" Elijah asked the girl who'd worked at the hall on the weekends. He'd been aware that she'd only applied to spite her father, though, and he'd probably only hired her for the same reason.

She snorted. "I don't ever want to come back here."

So he didn't bother offering her the counseling that he had intended to. Ever since her mother had died, she'd needed it, and after last night, she more than likely needed it even more. But he was clearly the last person from whom she would accept any help. And that was all he'd wanted to do when he'd started the spa with his brother—help people.

Now he risked losing the spa and maybe his brother, too, if the trooper refused to look for any other suspects for Erika's murder. He wasn't comfortable looking at people like they could be killers, and obviously—after missing the fact that his cousin and best friend was a killer—he wasn't good at it.

"You really trust Edie Stone?" he asked Olivia.

She nodded. "Yes, I do. You could trust her, too," she urged him. "I believe she'll only print the truth."

"He doesn't want the truth getting out," Holly said. "It would destroy the hall."

Elijah had worried about bad press before, had worried that any coverage bringing up the horrific past of the manor would affect the future of the spa. But there would be no spa without Bode. As the former fitness guru to movie stars and other celebrities, he was the draw for their exclusive clients. And if he was in prison . . .

The business would suffer, but Bode's daughter would suffer even more. And that wasn't fair. The child had done nothing to deserve it, had done nothing but be born with Bainesworth blood in her veins. Were they all cursed?

Was there any way to reverse that curse? To bring them good fortune instead of bad?

Edie had waited out the morning in her attic bedroom, listening for the sound of doors opening and closing and of cars starting and driving off, before she'd ventured down both flights of stairs to the kitchen. She hadn't wanted to have to answer any questions the other boarders might have about the night before, about the coincidence of her arriving back at the boardinghouse at the same time as the Cooke brothers. She'd even changed her mind about telling the sheriff about the parking lot incident because she'd known she wouldn't have been able to answer any of his questions about it. She hadn't seen or heard anything that would have been helpful in identifying the car and the driver.

And maybe Elijah had been right.

Maybe, because of the heavily falling snow and the darkness, the person just hadn't seen her. She snorted at the thought of that—knowing damn well it hadn't been an accident. But it didn't matter what it had actually been, a murder attempt or a warning to scare her off. Neither one had worked. She wasn't going anywhere . . . except out of her room now that all the other boarders had left the old Victorian house.

Maybe it was hypocritical of her to avoid answering questions when she was so pushy about getting people to answer her own questions. But she hadn't become a reporter because she liked talking about herself. She never wanted to become part of the story. But last night, when she'd walked through the door with the Cooke brothers, she had felt as though she'd become part of the problem. She shouldn't have let them near the house, near Bonita.

Poor Bonita . . .

Evelyn stood at the sink, washing up the breakfast dishes. She was alone, which was rare. Usually her sister was at her side or, when Edie was around, hiding somewhere behind Evelyn.

"Is she okay?" Edie asked. She didn't have to say more; Evelyn would know who she meant.

The older woman glanced over her shoulder at Edie and nodded. "She's sleeping. It was a rough night."

"I'm sorry," Edie said, her heart heavy with guilt over her part in the older woman's terror.

"I'd like to blame you for this," Evelyn said. "But I should have said no when Rosemary asked if he could bring his baby here. I shouldn't have let him anywhere near Bonita."

Edie closed the distance between them, joining Evelyn at the sink. She picked up a towel and bumped her shoulder against Evelyn's as she reached for a wet dish. "It was a sweet thing you did," she said as she dried the plate, "letting Rosemary watch his baby while he checked on his brother."

"Did he really almost die?" Evelyn asked, and she sounded almost regretful that he hadn't.

Elijah Cooke really had no friends on the island, at least not among the locals. "He took a really bad blow to the head," she said, "and has a concussion. He should have stayed in the hospital."

But he'd looked fine last night . . . with that silky black hair of his and those arresting blue eyes. He was such a good-looking man, even better-looking than his famous brother in Edie's opinion. Maybe what she found the most attractive about him was the intelligence in those pale eyes and in the way he bantered with her. Elijah Cooke wasn't the uptight scholar or the entitled rich guy she'd expected him to be. He was much more down-to-earth than she'd thought, but maybe that was just because he'd gotten knocked down so hard the night before, when his own cousin had nearly killed him.

"He shouldn't have come here," Evelyn said. "I think he looks even more like his grandfather than the other one does."

"You've met James Bainesworth?" Edie asked with surprise.

She'd thought only Bonita had been committed to the manor. Not Evelyn . . .

Evelyn shivered and shook her head, and a lock of white hair fell into her eyes. While her hair was white, there were few lines in her face. "I never spoke to him, but I saw him from time to time around the island."

"Have you seen him lately?" Edie wondered. He was the man who could answer all her questions, who could tell her where all the bodies were buried and where the babies were.

But maybe he wasn't the only one . . .

She remembered what Deacon had said last night about his father, about the former sheriff being on the payroll for Bainesworth Manor.

"Nobody's seen James Bainesworth in years," Evelyn said. "Maybe his grandsons have locked him up like he locked up all those girls all those years ago." She shuddered again. "It would be good if they have. Poetic justice and all that."

Edie bumped the older woman's shoulder again, leaning against her slightly, offering her support. Evelyn stiffened; she wouldn't take it. She was too used to being the caregiver to accept any care for herself. Maybe that was why she and Edie got along so well; they were very much alike. So they understood each other.

"What about the sheriff's dad?" Edie asked.

Evelyn shrugged. "Sam Howell has probably seen Bainesworth. Those two used to be thicker than thieves." Her pretty face contorted with a grimace of revulsion. "Though I'm not sure how much the old sheriff gets out now because of the pancreatic cancer. Maybe there is karma after all."

Edie sighed. "I don't know. Maybe karma is just something people bring on themselves." Manifested of their own guilt.

"Exactly," Evelyn agreed. "Karma gets them as punishment for the horrible things they've done. Or, in this case maybe, in addition to looking the other way all those years, it was also all the drinking that Sam Howell did."

Had he done all that drinking to try to forget his part in the things that had happened at the manor? If so, that must have meant that he had a conscience after all—despite his son's doubts about that. So maybe he was about ready to clear that conscience.

"Where is Sam Howell?" she asked. "Is he living at home yet?" As at the sheriff's home, there had been an explosion at his father's house as well. She didn't know if it had left it uninhabitable like Deacon's was.

Evelyn turned fully toward Edie now, her eyes wide despite the redness and swelling of them. After Bonita had stopped screaming last night, Edie had heard crying, but she'd thought it had been only Bonita. Clearly Evelyn loved her sister so much that she'd cried with her.

A pang struck Edie's heart—a pang of regret for all the pain these women had suffered. Was her being here bringing it all back up again? But maybe learning the truth would finally give them the closure and the peace they deserved. She had to do this for them as much as for all the other women who'd lost their babies, who'd lost themselves all those years ago.

"Why are you asking?" Evelyn asked, appalled. "Are you going to try to talk to Sam Howell?"

Edie nodded. "I want to get the former sheriff to tell me what he knows about Bainesworth Manor, what he knows about the babies. . . ."

Evelyn gasped and glanced toward the stairs, as if worried that Bonita might overhear them. Bonita always talked about her baby, and Evelyn had admitted that for years she'd thought her sister had been talking about a doll. But then that groundskeeper who'd kidnapped Genevieve had claimed to be Bonita's grandson . . .

Had Theodore Bowers been related to Bonita Pierce? Had she actually had a child all those years ago?

Deacon had shared that the state lab had lost the DNA results on that kid, so his relationship to Bonita and to Bainesworth hadn't been confirmed yet. But he'd claimed to be the grandson of Bonita Pierce and old man Bainesworth. No wonder the poor woman had been so terrified when she'd seen Bainesworth's grandsons . . . if they looked as much like him as Evelyn believed they did.

"Edie, I know you haven't made many friends on the island, but you can't be so desperate for company that you'd seek out that man. . . ." Evelyn was obviously trying to tease, like they always teased each other, but there was also real concern in her eyes. "It was bad enough that you showed up last night with those men from the manor. . . ." She shuddered then at just the memory of them.

"I'm sorry," Edie said—with solemn sincerity and no teasing. "I didn't think about how Bonita might react." Or she would have brought the kid out to them and never let them anywhere near the older woman.

"She's not your responsibility," Evelyn said.

She shouldn't have been Evelyn's either; she shouldn't have been so damaged, at a place that was supposed to have helped her, that she'd been left as dependent as a small child.

Blinking back tears that were pooling in her eyes, Evelyn continued. "I should have known when I told Rosemary that it was okay for him to bring his baby here that it wasn't going to end well." She reached out then and grasped Edie's chin, tipping her face toward her. "And it won't end well for you if you won't let your investigation go. These aren't people you should mess with. They're dangerous."

"Sam Howell and James Bainesworth?" she asked. "They're old and dying."

"That doesn't make men like them any less dangerous," Evelyn insisted. "Maybe it makes them even more dangerous because they have nothing left to lose."

"Then they have no reason not to tell me the truth," Edie said. "They should let me know how to find the . . ." She lowered her voice to a whisper and finished, ". . . babies. . . ."

Evelyn shook her head. "You don't have enough money to buy the truth from Sam Howell."

She actually had money—a lot of money—*family* money. But as her family had learned, money wasn't able to buy everything they wanted. It hadn't been able to buy her back even after they'd finally found her. She'd tried to connect with them, but after all the years of distance and lies . . .

That was why the truth was so important to her. And it had been denied too long to everyone affected by the manor.

"I doubt Sam Howell needs money anymore," Edie said. "He can't take it where he's going."

"To Hell?" Evelyn asked. "You might be surprised. Men like him and Bainesworth think they can buy their way out of anything."

"Then I'll give him money," Edie said. It didn't matter to her. "Just tell me where I can find him."

"You really think you can get him to talk when nobody else—not even his own son—has?" Evelyn asked.

Edie nodded. "That's kind of my thing . . ." Because of her reporting, she'd often been called the child that Barbara Walters and Oprah Winfrey would have had if they'd somehow been able to pool their DNA. Edie had taken that as the highest compliment, and a challenge to actually live up to the hype other people had manufactured for her.

That was why she didn't waste her time on the stories that other reporters covered, like whatever the latest celebrity was up to; she felt she had a duty to do better things, bigger stories. And she suspected there might not be a bigger story than Bainesworth Manor and what had happened there all those decades ago.

"Don't you want to know the truth?" Edie asked. "For her? For you? Don't you want to know if you have a nephew out there somewhere? A great-nephew . . . or niece or . . ."

Evelyn sucked in a breath and held it for a long moment, so long that Edie feared the older woman might pass out. Her face lost all its color before she finally, slowly nodded. Then she released the breath in a shaky sigh and said, "I'll tell you where Sam Howell lives. But if anything happens to you . . ."

"You'll throw a party?" Edie teased. "And hack into my laptop to sell my story ideas as your own?"

"I'll hack something," Evelyn replied.

Edie suspected that would be Sam Howell into little pieces, and her heart swelled with affection for the strong, stubborn woman who was Evelyn Pierce.

"I'll be fine," Edie assured her.

Evelyn snorted. "Yeah, because he won't tell you anything that will help you find those babies and those missing women. Probably the only one who could tell you where those bodies are buried is the man who buried them himself."

"James Bainesworth?" Edie asked.

Evelyn nodded. "Yup, the devil himself." Evelyn reached out and gripped both Edie's shoulders now. "Tell me you won't try to see *him*. Tell me you'll stay away from the manor and that monster."

"I won't get into the manor," Edie said. "I've been trying for weeks." She'd made it onto the grounds once—when Rosemary had gone missing from the hall, when the psychologist's search for her missing daughter had nearly cost

Rosemary her own life. But at that time Edie had been so preoccupied with helping search for Rosemary that she hadn't taken advantage of her opportunity to snoop around the hall or to question Elijah Cooke like she'd wanted.

She'd had the chance last night, but instead of taking it, she'd left him to rest . . . only to have him find her in the snow a short while later. Was his brother the reason she'd been there? Was Bode James the one who'd tried to run her down?

Was the entire Bainesworth family as evil as the locals believed they were? Or were they just bearing the guilt of their grandfather's sins?

Chapter Five

"I'm here, Grandfather," Elijah said as he climbed the stairs to the second story of the carriage house James Bainesworth had claimed as his lair—probably because it had the highest vantage point on the grounds of the hall. Not on the island, though.

That was the Bane Island lighthouse, but it had been abandoned long ago because boats rarely tried to approach the island for fear of crashing against the rocky shore as his ancestor's boat had so many years ago. Elijah could see the old limestone lighthouse out of the window in front of which his grandfather had parked his wheelchair. He spent so much of his time in front of that window that the carpet was worn threadbare beneath the tires of his chair.

"About damn time," James Bainesworth chastised him as he turned toward Elijah.

Elijah sighed. "I've been a little busy. . . ." And he touched the swollen bump on his head and flinched.

His grandfather betrayed no concern or sympathy. "You should have known better than to trust those Cookes."

"I'm a Cooke," Elijah reminded him.

The old man shrugged shoulders that should have been frail given his age. But they were still broad and just a little stooped. "You're more Bainesworth than Cooke, thank God, or you'd be an imbecile like those cousins of yours."

Elijah wasn't sure how smart he really was when he hadn't been able to see his best friend for the murderer he'd been. He shrugged now. "I'm not sure which genes would be better to have more of . . ." Because he would really have preferred to have neither.

"You don't want to be an idiot," Grandfather said.

"It's a little late for that . . ." he murmured. And he wasn't just referring to his missing David's true character; he was wondering instead about the deal he'd made with his grandfather.

About his mistaken belief that the spa could somehow make up for the horrible things that had happened at the hall before it had become the hall . . . back when it had been the manor, and this man had run it.

Grandfather uttered what sounded like a low growl, and a grimace of disgust crossed his wrinkled face. "So, what are you going to do about it? Are you going to wallow in self-pity now and let the manor fall to ruin again? Are you just giving up?"

Elijah snorted. "You're a fine one to talk. Isn't that what you did all those years ago?"

"I had no choice!" Grandfather yelled, and he sounded much younger and stronger than a man who'd lived for ninety-two years. "The state shut down the hospital."

And James Bainesworth should have gone to prison then. But Elijah suspected that the man had used all his money to fight his legal problems, leaving none left for the maintenance of the manor. And left to the brutal weather elements on the island, it had fallen to ruin quickly. It had already been old . . . since the original Bainesworth settler had built the manor when his ship had crashed on the rocky shore in the eighteen hundreds. The unrelenting winds and the salt water and the vines and trees hadn't needed much time to break down the structure, to make the stones shift and crumble, the windows crack and shatter, and for the roof to cave in under the weight of fallen trees and snow.

That was how it had already looked that day when he and David had challenged Deacon to ride their bikes out to the manor. The day Deacon had raced them down the driveway and rushed inside before them, only to start screaming seconds later, like that woman had screamed at the sight of him and Bode the night before at the boardinghouse. At the time, still standing outside the building, David had laughed at Deacon.

But Elijah had known, even as a kid, that it would have taken a lot to make Deacon scream like that, especially within their hearing. So he'd beaten his cousin through those broken double doors, and he'd discovered what had had a tough kid like Deacon crying like a baby. He'd seen the corpse . . . and the end of their childhood.

"You have choices I didn't have back then," Grandfather continued, his voice gruff, as if his yelling had strained his voice, "you can protect this place. You can make sure everything ends now . . . that the sheriff closes the case on the dead woman."

"Which dead woman?" Elijah wondered aloud.

The old man's already wrinkled brow furrowed more. "What are you talking about? Did one of those women your crazy cousin abducted die last night?"

He shook his head—though it had been clear that David hadn't intended to leave Olivia alive.

"Oh, you're talking about the sheriff's wife, then," Grandfather said. "That Cooke kid confessed to throwing her off the cliff. She didn't jump."

Bode must have already stopped at the carriage house during the course of his run. He must have filled in their silent partner on everything that had transpired the night before. Or had Grandfather's nurse found out all this information for him? The burly, middle-aged man seemed to spend more time skulking around the hall than tending to Grandfather's physical needs. What did Theo really do for James Bainesworth?

Had he replaced Deacon's father as the Bainesworth henchman?

"No, Shannon didn't jump."

"Cooke killed her, like he killed that fitness trainer woman," Grandfather said. "Those cases are closed, and any investigations should end. You should be able to get back to business."

"We've never not been in business," Elijah said.

And he was grateful that they'd only lost a few guests after the body was discovered. Nobody had canceled any upcoming reservations, not that there were many of those over the holidays. It was the off-season right now; the only people at the spa were ones like Olivia Smith, who'd wanted privacy and peace and seclusion. The pop singer had been hiding from a stalker and paparazzi. He wasn't sure what his other guests were hiding from or looking for.

The guest who'd stayed the longest at the hall, Morgana Drake, claimed to be a medium, looking for ghosts. The older woman wanted to help the lost souls of the girls, who she believed had died at the manor all those years ago, cross over to the other side. How many had there actually been, though? If any?

Elijah would have assumed that it had been just an urban legend that people had died there . . . if Deacon, David, and he hadn't discovered that body over twenty-five years ago.

But whoever she was, her death had happened decades after the manor had closed. She might not have had any relation to the manor and what had happened there.

"Make sure you keep it that way," Grandfather said.

Elijah narrowed his eyes and studied the old man's face. There was something in his pale blue eyes . . . something that looked a lot like fear. "What is it?" Elijah asked. "Are you afraid that if we have to close the spa, we'll put you back in that retirement home?"

Or was he worried that if the authorities kept investigating that murder, they would find out who had actually committed it?

"We have a deal," Grandfather said. "If I deeded over the estate to you and your brother, I had a life lease on it, and that you had to make sure I was well taken care of. Our terms had nothing to do with whether your silly celebrity spa thing succeeded or failed. You're stuck with me, son." And then he chuckled.

And a chill raced down Elijah's spine. He and Bode had definitely made a pact with the devil . . . because he didn't think it mattered how old James Bainesworth was, he wasn't dying any time soon.

It was more likely, with the way Elijah and Bode kept getting hurt, that one of them would die before him.

Or go to prison . . . for something they hadn't done.

Elijah had to figure out who had really killed his niece's mother before Bode was arrested, and before one of them was wounded—*or worse*—again.

Edie knew she'd found the right place when she steered her Jeep into the driveway and she saw the sheet of plywood nailed over the window closest to that gravel drive. She might have suspected that Evelyn had given her directions to a boarded-up and deserted cottage if not for the minivan parked in the driveway, though. A decal in the back window identified the owner as a visiting nurse.

That was how the sick man was able to stay in his home; he had help. One of the rumors that flew around the diner in town, where Edie spent a lot of her time, was that old man Bainesworth had a nurse, too, some big, burly guy who came to town to run his errands for him. What else might the man be doing for the former owner of the manor?

She shivered even before she opened the door of her Jeep and stepped out into the cold. Here . . . close to the rocky shore . . . the wind whipped around, slapping against the exposed skin of her face and neck. At least today she was wearing gloves, but the leather was thin and unlined, like her long jacket. While it was wool, it wasn't thick enough to offer much protection from the frigid wind chill.

She shivered again and rushed toward the cabin. A woman had already opened the door as she approached. The panes in it were covered with wood, like the window that looked onto the driveway, so she would have had to open it to find out who had driven up.

The woman was in her fifties or so and looked as strong and capable and no-nonsense as Evelyn was. Her shoulders slumped slightly at the sight of Edie. She must have been expecting, or hoping, that someone else had dropped by.

Guessing who, Edie said, "I'm sorry I'm not Deacon."

"You know Deacon?"

She nodded. "Yes, I do." And she would let the woman think that he had sent her to check on his father . . . if he ever checked on him. From what Deacon had told her about his dad, it didn't sound as if they had a very close or caring relationship.

"Is he okay?" the woman asked. "We heard the sirens and saw all the lights last night." This boarded-up cottage was so close to the hall that it might once have been part of the property. Had Bainesworth gifted it to him as one of his payoffs?

"Deacon is fine," Edie said, and her teeth snapped together as they began to chatter in the cold.

"I'm sorry," the woman said.

Edie tensed. "That Deacon is fine?"

"Oh God, no," the woman exclaimed. "I'm sorry to leave you out there." She stepped back and beckoned toward her with an outstretched arm. "Here, come inside. You must be freezing."

Edie eagerly crossed the threshold and opened her jacket, but then she shivered as she realized it wasn't much warmer inside.

"Come in here," the woman said as she started down a short hall. "I just filled up the woodstove. It gets really warm near it."

That must be why the hospital bed was in the living room next to that stove, to keep the man lying in it from freezing to death before the cancer took him. While his body was long, it looked thin and frail beneath the blankets covering him. "That doesn't sound like my damn son . . ." he murmured, and he opened his eyes.

Edie crossed the worn pine floor until she stood next to the bed. "Hello, Mr. Howell," she greeted him.

"Who are you?" he asked Edie, narrowing his dark eyes with suspicion as he studied her face. "You don't look like a trooper coming to notify me that my kid died because he couldn't let go of his grudge against those damn Cookes and Bainesworths."

"I'm not a trooper," Edie said. "And Deacon is fine. He and Holly and Olivia are okay."

"Holly?" he gasped the girl's name and jerked upright on his already inclined bed. "My granddaughter was involved in all that commotion last night?"

She nodded. "Yes, David Cooke took her and Olivia hostage. But Deacon saved them. He and Elijah Cooke."

The old man snorted and leaned back. "Of course Deacon did. Damn hero complex of his going to get him killed someday. . . ." He closed his eyes for a moment, though, as if trying to conceal his love for his son and his relief that he was okay. He opened his eyes again and stared at her with suspicion. "He and that Elijah kid actually worked together?"

"That Elijah kid" was nearly forty, like Deacon, but she didn't correct him. "Yes. Elijah figured out where David took them."

The old man snorted. "Makes sense that he would know. He probably told the big thug where to take them. That one was always the brains, the other just the big idiot who did whatever he told him."

Despite the warmth of the woodstove, Edie shivered again. "Are you saying that you think Elijah told David to kidnap Holly and Olivia?"

He shrugged shoulders that were so thin and bony-looking that she half expected them to break through the flannel shirt he wore over a thermal one. Despite lying in bed, he was fully dressed, as if he could get up and move around. Go out . . .

He leaned back on his pillow and closed his eyes, and for a moment she thought he'd slipped off to sleep . . . or death.

And she glanced at the nurse who had walked over to a small kitchenette in a corner of the open living area. The woman appeared to be doing dishes and seemed totally uninterested in their conversation, or the lack of it at the moment. Before Edie could catch her attention, the old man shifted on the bed.

"No . . ." Sam Howell murmured. "That was probably the big one acting on his own, acting out against Deacon. He always hated and resented my son for being better than him at sports and with women. . . ." He opened his eyes again. "So who's this Olivia?" Then his brow furrowed again as he stared at her. "And who the hell are you . . . if you're not a trooper?"

"I'm not a trooper," she said. "I'm a friend of your son's and of Olivia's. She was a guest at the spa. She and your son have gotten close."

"Does she know what happened to the last one who got close to my son? That his wife wound up dead?"

Edie nodded. "Yes, and she heard David Cooke confess to killing Deacon's wife. That's all over now. Nobody will suspect your son of being involved in her death anymore." Edie had an appointment at the diner later this afternoon to talk with the editor of the *Bane Island Tribune*. She wanted to submit a story about what happened last night, but for local publication only. She just wanted to clear Deacon's name for once and for all. She wasn't even going to mention Olivia.

"No one really believed that Deacon had anything to do with his wife's death," the woman spoke up. "It was the Cookes trying to make it sound like he was responsible. But all the locals know not to trust them." Now she narrowed her eyes as she studied Edie as intently as the former sheriff was. "You're not a local, but you look familiar. . . ."

Edie mostly covered stories in written formats, special features in big publications. But occasionally she did on-air interviews or exposés. And usually, because of the content of those exposés or the revelations in the interviews, they were memorable. *She* was memorable.

And the old man chuckled as he recognized her. "You're that reporter . . . the pain in the ass. . . ."

She chuckled, too. "That probably is what Deacon calls me. . . ." It was certainly what the Cookes called her. "But my name is Edie Stone, and your son and I actually are friends now."

"I don't know what my son calls you. He never mentioned you, but then, he never mentions much of anything to me. He didn't even call to let me know what the hell happened last night," he ruefully and resentfully admitted.

Edie swallowed the apology burning in her throat. She didn't think Deacon would appreciate her apologizing for him. She doubted he would appreciate her talking to his father at all.

"I meant you're a pain in the ass to the ones you've brought down. To the important people whose lives you turned upside down." He snorted. "So, what are you doing here, girl? I'm not important. Not anymore."

"Your son told me that you once worked for James Bainesworth."

The old man released a ragged and weak-sounding sigh, as if he didn't have much breath to spare or much left in his cancer-ravaged body. "Of course he did. He'll never forgive me for not being the honorable man he is."

"Have you asked for his forgiveness?" Edie wondered aloud.

The old man tensed, and his dark eyes narrowed in an

angry glare. "What—you think I need to beg my son to forgive me? You think I've been such a terrible father?"

She shrugged. "I don't know what kind of father you
were." But from the way Deacon had spoken about him, she
doubted that Sam Howell had been a very good one. "And I
really don't care."

"Good. Because that's none of your damn business.
You're not going to make me break down and bawl like a
baby like you've made some of those saps you've interviewed."

She smiled at his reference to those saps before shrug-
ging again. "A lot of stuff is none of my damn business.
That's never stopped me before."

"You're really here about Bainesworth Manor," he con-
cluded, and he bristled with irritation. "Because Deacon told
you that I worked for James. So, do you think I'm going to
confess all to clear my conscience before I die? Did you
come to hear my confession, Edie Stone?"

She smiled at his anger and unrepentantly said, "Yes."

"Thought you were a reporter—not a priest."

"Sometimes it seems like I'm both," she said.

She'd had people make confessions to her. Those "bawl-
ing saps," as Sam Howell called them, were people who'd
admitted to making mistakes, to having affairs, to lying.
Then some had even committed more serious offenses, like
the killers who had confessed to her despite maintaining
their innocence to everyone else.

Was this man a killer? Had he done more for Bainesworth
than just look the other way? She shivered again despite the
heat exuding from the woodstove.

"Will you give me absolution, then, if I confess?" he
asked, and while the tone of his voice was mocking her,

there was a solemnness on his face. He apparently knew that he needed it, that he'd done something that needed forgiveness.

"I'm not here to absolve you of your sins," she said.

"So you just want to hear about them?"

"I want to hear about Bainesworth Manor," she said. "I want to find out what happened to the young girls who went missing from that place."

He shrugged. "They ran away."

"I can understand why they would want to," she said, "with the place performing illegal lobotomies."

She would rather run away than have someone mess with her brain, either physically, as they had with the lobotomies, or with drugs and therapy. She'd had enough of therapy when she'd first been returned to her family. It hadn't helped; maybe because even then she'd been more prone to asking questions than answering them—especially about herself.

"But they never rejoined their families again," she continued. She'd checked with them, followed up to confirm that some of them had never turned up.

So had they escaped or had they died? She'd searched all the public records she'd been able to find at the library on the island. Some death certificates had been issued at the manor, and Dr. James Bainesworth had signed them. For accidental drug overdoses.

Suicides. Stillbirths.

But she'd found more articles in the newspaper archives reporting girls missing from the manor.

"Would you go back to the people who sent you there?" he asked.

She shook her head. "No, but are you sure all of them

survived?" Or had too many already died at the manor, so Bainesworth hadn't wanted to report any more?

Any murders.

Sam Howell shrugged those bony shoulders again. "Hard to say. Only safe way off the island is that bridge, and it's not always passable with a car. And if they tried swimming away . . ." He shook his head. "The current might have pulled them under, or the waves might have sent them crashing back against the rocky shore. And if their bodies were swept out . . ."

She shivered again. "That would explain why they were never seen again."

"It would be one explanation. . . ."

"Would there be others? Were any of them murdered?"

Sam shook his head. "No homicides reported."

"Not on the death certificates Dr. James Bainesworth signed," she acknowledged. "But no autopsies were done on them."

"Bane Island didn't have a coroner until a few years ago, and when cause of death is obvious, a doctor can sign the certificate," he said.

"And what about the women who went missing?" she asked.

"Can't do an autopsy if there isn't a body . . ." he murmured.

Was that why those women had never been found? So their real cause of death would never be discovered?

"What about the body your son found when he was a kid?" she wondered.

"He wasn't the only one who found it," Sam Howell said. "Those Cooke boys were with him. They goaded him into going there in the first place. He's always hated the manor.

Thought it was cursed. With the way he finds bodies there, maybe it is, or maybe *he* is. . . ."

Because Deacon Howell had been the one to discover his wife's body and then the most recent body as well.

The personal trainer.

The mother of Dr. Elijah Cooke's niece.

"Had the woman they found been murdered?" Edie asked.

He shrugged again and looked away from her, toward the woodstove. "The body was badly decomposed. I don't remember what the coroner on the mainland ruled it."

But she suspected he was lying.

"We figured it was an overdose of some kind . . . either accidental or on purpose."

"Who's 'we'? You and James Bainesworth?"

"The manor was already shut down then."

"But you still talked to him," she guessed. "Do you still talk to him now?"

He sighed. "Funny thing with a man like James Bainesworth. Once you're of no more use to him, he tends to forget who you are."

"So you haven't seen him since he's come back to the island?" she asked.

"I've seen him a couple of times . . ." he murmured, and a grimace crossed his face.

She wasn't sure if the grimace was because of physical pain from his cancer or if the memory of those times he'd seen his old friend had caused him discomfort. "How could I get in to see him?" she wondered.

He shook his head. "You'd be wasting your time, girl. No matter how close to death old James Bainesworth might be, he knows better than to ask for absolution from his sins. There are too many."

So the former sheriff wouldn't admit to his own crimes, but he wasn't above alluding to the crimes of another man, his old friend.

"I need to talk to him," she insisted. "I need to know what he did with those babies the girls had. I want to see adoption records and—"

Sam Howell chuckled. "I guarantee that *Dr. Bainesworth* was too smart to leave any paper trail. If there had been any physical evidence of what he'd done back then, he would have gone to prison when the state started investigating and shut down the hospital."

That was her concern—that the man had destroyed everything that could have revealed the truth. Tears of frustration stung her eyes, but she blinked them back.

Men like Sam Howell—like James Bainesworth—they would attribute any sign of human emotion to weakness. And Edie couldn't seem vulnerable to them if she wanted to earn their respect and confidence.

"Would you call him for me?" she implored him. "Can you ask him to see me?"

"You think I can get through that switchboard at the hall easier than you can?"

She'd been shut down right away no matter which one of the family she'd tried to reach. "You don't have his direct line?"

"Not anymore. Like I said, I'm no longer of use to him." He gestured at the bed and his frail body lying inside it.

And it was clearly killing him as much as the cancer was that he wasn't the man he'd once been, that he no longer had any importance to people of importance.

To anyone.

"You can be of use to me," she said, trying to appeal to

his pride and his ego. "Help me get onto the grounds. You must know how I . . ." She trailed off at the look that suddenly crossed Sam Howell's face—smug, knowing, self-important.

He'd remembered something that made him useful to her and maybe a liability to the hall.

"What?" she asked. "What is it?"

"You really want to get onto the grounds?" he asked, and it was almost as if he was dangling something in front of her . . . like a string of yarn before a cat. He was trying to get her to pounce on it.

She wasn't about to waste any of her time, and especially not his, trying to be coy. "Yes," she said. "I've tried, but they won't let me through the damn gates."

"You don't have to go through the gates to get onto the grounds," he said, and a slight smile curved his thin lips.

She narrowed her eyes and leaned closer to the old man, studying his pale face. "There is that stone wall on all sides of it, except on the ocean sides where the rocky cliffs drop straight down into the ocean." She'd considered every way to get over the wall or up the cliffs, but it just wasn't possible, especially in this wintry weather.

"You don't go *over* the wall, girly," he said. Then he lowered his voice to a raspy whisper and added, "You go *under* it."

She narrowed her eyes. "Is there a culvert or something that I missed?" It would have been easy enough to miss it with how thick the trees were around the estate and how deep the snow was.

"There are passageways," he said. "Tunnels . . ."

She shivered. "Where?"

"Under the estate."

"But how do I get to them?" she asked.

"Have you seen the lighthouse?"

"I came across the bridge from the mainland," she said. And the lighthouse was on the other side of the island. She'd only seen the top of it rising high over all the pine trees. And from its moss-covered stones and broken and dirt-smeared windows, it appeared that it had been decommissioned long ago.

"Go to the lighthouse," he told her.

"For what?" she asked. "Getting a vantage point isn't going to help me find tunnels."

"Don't go up," he said. "Go down. . . ."

Realization dawned. The tunnel started under the lighthouse.

"The Bainesworth ancestors ran things through those tunnels during wars and Prohibition and maybe during other times as well. . . ."

Women and babies.

They might have gone in and out of those tunnels. Excitement had a shiver racing through her now as her skin tingled. She felt like she had last night . . . when she'd touched Dr. Elijah Cooke's face, when she'd stroked her fingers along the stubble on his strong jaw. She was both thrilled and terrified.

And just as she had the night before, she had the sudden urge to flee. But now she wasn't running away from someone; she was running to . . .

Those tunnels . . . and to the men to whom they would lead her. Not just Elijah but his grandfather.

"How do I find him?" she asked. "Once I get inside the grounds?"

"James Bainesworth?" he asked. His gaze traveled over

her face and he chuckled. "He'll find you once you get there."

She shivered at that.

"But you better be prepared. Warm clothes. Boots. Flashlights," he murmured. "Those tunnels have been closed a long time. I doubt the younger generation even knows they're there."

So she would know something about the manor that Elijah didn't. And maybe she'd have the chance to learn even more . . . if those tunnels really led her inside the property. "Thank you, Mr. Howell," she said.

"Don't thank me, girl," he said. "I'm not doing you any favors, helping you get into that place. . . . In fact, I probably just put you in danger. Grave danger . . ."

Chapter Six

Her Jeep wasn't in the driveway, so Elijah had no reason to be parked at the curb outside the boardinghouse. But he'd driven through town on his way to the old Victorian house and he hadn't spotted her Jeep anywhere along Main Street. With its bright red color, it was impossible to miss.

Edie Stone, with her bright blond hair and larger-than-life personality, was impossible to miss.

Had she left the island?

The snow had let up enough overnight that the bridge to the mainland had probably reopened. But he couldn't imagine Edie leaving, even if her near miss in the hospital parking lot hadn't been an accident. Someone trying to scare Edie Stone away was probably only going to make her more determined to stay.

So where was she?

And why was Elijah so determined to see her that he found himself staking out her home, like a stalker, waiting for her to return? He was even slouched down in the driver's seat of one of the Halcyon Hall SUVs, with its specially for-mulated charcoal paint. It wasn't as if anyone could actually see him through the darkly tinted glass. He didn't want to upset the boardinghouse women again or he would have gone to the door. He would have asked them where Edie was and how he could reach her.

But he suspected from the way the one who'd answered the door last night had anxiously jerked Edie inside, as if to protect her, that they would not tell him where to find their boarder. Instead, they would probably call the police on Elijah.

So what the hell was he doing?

To help his brother, he needed to find that good lawyer he'd promised him—not a reporter. Especially not a reporter who specialized in exposing scandals and taking down the guilty.

Bode wasn't guilty.

Elijah couldn't believe that his brother would have had anything to do with the murder of his baby's mother. Bode, better than anyone, knew how difficult it was to grow up without a mom. At least Elijah had a few memories of their mother; Bode had been so young when she'd taken off that he couldn't have any.

Elijah couldn't blame her for not wanting to stay on the island, though, not with the way everyone hated them just because of who they were related to and not because of anything that they'd actually done themselves. While still in high school on the island, she'd gotten pregnant with him and had married his father right after graduating. Unlike her sister, who'd left for college and never come back. Wanting to be like the aunt he barely remembered, Elijah had graduated early from high school so he could head off to college, too.

And like his aunt, he'd never intended to come back.

He shouldn't have. No matter what Bode had said about having no regrets because of Adelaide, Elijah still worried that the price of their return had been too great, with too many lives lost already. Would there be more?

Would Edie's be one of them?

"Where the hell are you?" he murmured, his breath steaming up the inside of the windows. He'd left the engine idling, but he'd turned down the fan of the defroster. He reached for the control now, but as he did, a tap rattled his side window. He lowered it to see the sheriff's flushed and angry face.

"What the hell are you doing?" Deacon demanded. "Why are you here? Didn't you and your brother upset Bonita enough last night? You want to scare the hell out of her again?"

"I'm sorry about that," Elijah said, and he sincerely was. "That's why I didn't go to the door."

Deacon narrowed his eyes, as if trying to determine whether or not Elijah was lying. Then he nodded. "It's good that you didn't. But they've seen you skulking around out there."

"I didn't get out of the vehicle," Elijah said.

"They recognized that it came from the hall and figured you were *one of the men from the manor*," Deacon said, emphasizing that last part with what must have been an imitation of one of his landladies. "That's why they called me."

Now that his window was down, Elijah could see the side mirror, and in it the reflection of flashing lights on the roof of Deacon's sheriff's department SUV. He was definitely here in an official capacity and not just because he was staying at the boardinghouse himself because that explosion had damaged his home.

Elijah groaned. "I was hoping that they wouldn't see me."

"Then you shouldn't have come here. Why the hell are you here anyway?" Deacon asked.

Elijah uttered a ragged sigh now. "I wish I knew. . . ."

And instead of reacting as he usually did to Elijah, with anger and more resentment and suspicion, Deacon chuckled. "Not totally recovered yet from that concussion, huh?"

Elijah touched the swollen knot on his head and groaned. "I wish I could blame the concussion."

"So I guess you're here for Edie?" Deacon mused with another chuckle of genuine amusement. "She getting to you?"

Unwilling to admit that, Elijah shook his head. "I just wanted to make sure she was okay after what happened last night. . . ."

Deacon's brow lowered beneath the brim of his sheriff's department hat. "What do you mean? Nothing happened to Edie last night."

Elijah gritted his teeth in irritation and shook his head. "She didn't tell you." He'd known then that they should have called the police, or at least alerted security last night. He wasn't sure the small hospital even had security, though.

"Tell me what?" Deacon asked. "What happened?"

"When Bode and I were leaving the hospital, I found her lying in the snow in the parking lot." And he shivered thinking about it now, wondering how long she'd been lying there.

Deacon gasped. "What the hell happened?"

"She claims someone tried to run her down."

"'Claims'?" Deacon asked. "Why would you think she'd lie about it? Edie seems pretty damn honest to me, especially when all she seems to really care about is learning the truth."

That was the other reason he was here—that he might be able to trust her to find out the truth about Erika's murder. After his disturbing visit with his grandfather, he'd returned to his office and googled Edie Stone. And the things he'd found had intrigued him even more.

But Elijah forced himself to focus on the sheriff, who was waiting for his explanation. "She was wearing dark clothes, and it was snowing hard. So it might not have been on purpose that the car headed toward her; maybe the driver just didn't see her."

Deacon snorted. "I've been there, too, with someone nearly running me down in the street. When the vehicle's coming at you, you're pretty damn sure what the driver's intention is. You downplayed it when I told you about that Halcyon Hall vehicle nearly running me over, and you downplayed when shots were fired at Olivia at the hall, claiming it might have been a hunter. Why do you struggle so hard to admit what's really going on? What are you trying to hide, Elijah?"

Elijah shook his head. "I'm not trying to hide anything," he said. "I just don't always want to think the worst in every situation." Not after he'd grown up with people thinking the worst of him just because of who he was related to. Because of things that had happened before he'd even been born.

So he never wanted to rush to judgment about anyone or anything, though maybe that was why people had died, why his own cousin had nearly killed him. . . .

Because he tried too hard to see the good where there really was none.

"Then why are you here checking on her if you don't think someone purposely tried to run her down?" Deacon persisted, arching a dark brow.

Elijah sighed. "You just pointed out that I've been wrong. Someone did try to run you down. Someone did shoot at Olivia. So I could have been wrong last night." And if he was wrong and someone had purposely tried to kill her, she was in danger. "Where is Edie?"

Deacon shrugged. "I don't know. She was still here when

Olivia and Holly and I left for the hall this morning . . ." He trailed off and grimaced.

"Yeah, I know that's not your favorite place," Elijah acknowledged. It wasn't his either. No matter how many renovations he and Bode and David had done to the structures, it still felt the same to him.

Cursed . . .

"No, I just realized where she might have gone," Deacon said. "Last night, at the hospital, I made the mistake of mentioning my dad to her, how he used to be on your grandpa's payroll. . . ."

Deacon's dad had been in his midforties when Deacon was born, so he was close to Grandfather's age. Apparently, Sam Howell had been his enabler, and maybe his enforcer, as well as his friend. All Elijah remembered of the retired sheriff was that he'd usually been drunk and mean . . . even when he was on duty.

"Damn it, Deacon," he said. "Why would you tell her that?" It certainly explained why she hadn't pushed harder to get more information out of him, how easily she'd left when he'd changed his mind about talking to her; she'd found another source of information.

Deacon shook his head. "I don't know what the hell I was thinking . . ." he murmured. "But she'll be fine. My old man can't hurt her. He's at death's door."

"I'm sorry," Elijah said. He knew it was hard to lose a parent . . . even though technically his weren't dead. Just lost . . .

His dad was a lot like Deacon's dad . . . with the drinking. He didn't necessarily get mean when he drank, though, just very honest. The last time Elijah had seen him—four years ago—his dad had told him that if he and his brother went into business with the old man they were dead to him. And so when they'd started the spa, they'd died . . . to their dad. They'd been dead to their mother a long time ago or she wouldn't have just walked out on them. He sighed.

And Deacon echoed the sound. "Yeah, I should probably be more concerned about him than I am Edie. He's no match for her. But then, nobody is." He narrowed his eyes as he studied Elijah's face, as if wondering . . .

Deacon was an observant guy; evidently more observant than Elijah. Did he realize that Elijah was a little too interested in Edie Stone? Especially after what he'd read about her . . .

He understood now why she was so hell-bent on finding out what had happened to the babies born at Bainesworth Manor . . . because she'd once been a baby who'd gone missing.

Where the hell was she now? Still at the former sheriff's cabin? It was close to the hall, between it and the lighthouse near the old pier, so he hadn't passed it on his way to town, which made sense that he hadn't seen her red Jeep.

"Will you call your dad and find out if she's at his place yet?" Elijah asked.

"No," Deacon replied shortly.

Maybe he didn't want to talk to his father, but more likely he didn't want Elijah talking to Edie. "Why not?" he asked.

Deacon stepped back from the side of Elijah's SUV and gestured toward the house. "Because she just pulled into the driveway."

The driver's door of the Jeep was flung open, and Edie jumped out as if she was in a hurry. Then she glanced toward the street and froze.

Elijah started to push open his door, but Deacon pushed it shut again. "The Pierce sisters don't want you here," he said. "If you go on their property, they'll press trespassing charges."

Elijah winced at the sharp jab of pain. He'd done nothing to them . . . nothing to hurt them . . . except exist. "I won't. I just want to talk to Edie," he said.

A husky chuckle emanated from somewhere behind Deacon's broad shoulders. The sheriff stepped back from the SUV and turned toward the woman who'd joined them. "I see you survived," the sheriff murmured. "Is my dad as unscathed as you?"

"Your dad's a sweetheart," she said.

Deacon snorted. "Yeah, right. . . ."

"He was most helpful," she said, and her green eyes were bright with excitement.

Elijah tensed now, wondering what the former sheriff might have revealed about the manor and his grandfather. "What—what did he tell you?"

She shrugged. "It might not matter. I heard you say that you're here to see me. Kind of ironic after all the times I tried to get in to see you that you're struggling to do the same thing here." She glanced back at the house, where curtains swished in one of the windows on the first floor of the turret. "What do you want to talk to me about, Dr. Cooke? Are you ready to bare your soul to me?"

Deacon snorted again. "He'd actually have to have one to bare it, and we all know he sold his to the devil so he could open that damn spa with his brother."

Elijah wanted to deny Deacon's claim, but he'd felt that way himself too many times, not so much that he'd sold his soul but that he'd at least made a deal with the devil. To take care of him until he died.

Only problem was that Elijah hadn't remembered that the devil was immortal. That was why he hadn't died.

"I haven't led the interesting life you have, Ms. Stone," Elijah told her. And he hadn't. He'd worked hard in high school and college and med school, and then he'd worked hard helping other people live their lives without ever really living one of his own. "I don't have anything to tell you."

The excitement in her green eyes dimmed, and her brow furrowed as she studied his face. "Then I guess you really didn't want to talk to me."

"Even if he did, you'd have to wait," Deacon said. "Sergeant Montgomery is this close . . ." He held up his gloved hand with two fingers nearly touching ". . . to putting out a warrant for the arrest of one Dr. Elijah Cooke . . ." He turned toward Elijah then ". . . if you don't give her your statement about last night. She was in my office when Evelyn called, and I told the sergeant to wait, that I was probably about to save her a trip out to the hall when I brought you in for harassing two sweet old ladies."

Elijah groaned over the sheriff's harassment charge and over the thought of having to speak to the sergeant. But maybe it was better—for Bode—that Elijah talked to her in town rather than her trying to interrogate his brother again over Erika's murder.

"Sweet old ladies? The Pierce sisters?" Edie asked, and she snorted now. "One of them routinely confesses to poisoning me and the other one shot a guy claiming to be her grandson. Dr. Cooke here was probably in more danger from them than they were from him."

Befuddled, Elijah stared at her. "And you choose to stay here?"

"Well, the hotel is closed for the season, and you won't let me into the hall." She smiled. "But even if I had other options for lodging, I'd stay here. They're my kind of people."

"Crazy?" Deacon asked with a chuckle.

"Colorful," Edie corrected him. "Interesting . . ."

That described her perfectly. And maybe that was why Elijah was so interested in her. Although, as a psychiatrist, he was interested in everyone—in what made them tick, in what had made them the people they'd become. . . .

Maybe that was why he'd never looked too closely at any members of his own family. Because he'd known there was a chance that some of them could be like *him* . . .

Like James Bainesworth . . .

Although Grandfather insisted that everything he'd done while running the manor he had done only to help people. Maybe Elijah was more like him than he thought . . . because that was why he did everything he did as well.

And to help Bode, he might need to enlist Edie and her relentless quest for the truth. But right now he needed to give his truth. "I'll follow you to your office, Sheriff," he said.

"I'll follow you," Deacon said, and he gestured for Elijah to drive off. Obviously, he wanted to talk to Edie without Elijah overhearing.

She must have suspected the same thing and didn't want to be interrogated herself because she started to back away from the street, toward the boardinghouse. "I have to go, guys. See you both later—"

"Edie!" Deacon called out. "We need to talk about what happened in the parking lot last night."

She shot a glare at Elijah. "You told him? I thought you believed it was an accident, that the driver didn't see me?"

He shrugged. "I don't know what to believe anymore."

Why would someone want to run down Edie? Sure, he hadn't wanted her doing some big feature about the hall's horrific history as a psychiatric hospital, but he didn't want her dead.

"Doesn't matter what anyone believes," Deacon said. "We need to find out what happened."

Edie shrugged now. "Nothing. I got out of the way. I'm fine." She took a big step back. "And you two have a certain trooper waiting for you, and I have a meeting at the diner."

"We'll talk later," Deacon said, his voice a warning to her.

One Edie ignored as she turned toward the house. As she did, the curtains in that front window swished again; the older women must have been watching them, worrying.

Elijah needed to leave, for their sakes and sense of security and, apparently, for his own. But before he could shift into Drive, the sheriff reached into the open window again and gripped Elijah's arm.

"Regardless of how resourceful the Pierce sisters are, you need to stay away from them," Deacon said. "And if you're as smart as you've always told me you are, you would stay away from Edie Stone, too."

"For her sake?"

"For yours," Deacon said.

"I didn't know you cared, Sheriff."

"Neither did I," Deacon said. Then he uttered a heavy sigh and added, "But I appreciate how you helped out last night. How you helped me save my daughter and Olivia."

Elijah swallowed hard on the guilt and regret he felt. "I'm sorry, Deacon. I'm so sorry about David and about . . ." Emotion choked him, but he cleared his throat and finished. "I'm just sorry about everything. . . ."

Deacon studied his face for a moment before nodding in acceptance of his apology. If Deacon Howell could forgive him, and acknowledge his sincerity, maybe the rest of the island might give him and Bode a chance to prove that they weren't like their grandfather or their Cooke cousins.

But the only way Elijah could do that would be if he

could prove that his brother hadn't killed the mother of his child. And his only way to manage that would be to find the real killer. Maybe he could convince the trooper to look for another suspect. But if Sergeant Montgomery wouldn't, Edie Stone might help . . . if he could risk trusting her.

The front door opened before Edie could even cross the porch. Usually she went around to the kitchen, but she'd been in the street with Deacon and Elijah, so she had to pass the front door anyway, just as she'd had to last night when she'd met the Cooke brothers after they'd parked at the curb.

She shouldn't have let them come to the door last night. But she hadn't realized that Bonita would get so upset; she hadn't realized how much James Bainesworth's grandsons looked like him, like the man Bonita feared so much.

The man Edie wanted to meet and interview. She shivered, and Evelyn reached out and jerked her into the house, just like she had last night. "Get in here and close the door. You're letting out all the heat," the older woman admonished her. She trembled, and Edie suspected it wasn't because of the cold any more than Edie had shivered for that reason.

"I didn't open the door," Edie reminded her. "You couldn't wait to get me inside." And away from Elijah Cooke.

"You're going to get yourself killed," Evelyn said, and clicked her tongue against her teeth in a tsking sound. "First going to the former sheriff's house and then talking to that man from the manor. . . ." She shuddered—this time in revulsion.

"Evelyn, you know there's no way that Elijah had anything to do with Bainesworth Manor." Edie felt compelled to defend him. "It closed before he was even born."

"Elijah? You're on a first-name basis with that man?

Which one? The trainer or the . . ." Her throat moved as if
she was struggling to swallow ". . . the doctor?"

"He's the psychiatrist," Edie admitted.

"He's just like his grandfather, then," Evelyn insisted.
"He's running that place—"

"It's not the manor," Edie interrupted her. "It's a spa now."
And instead of being committed there against their will,
guests had to pass an application process and get on a long
waiting list for the privilege of staying there.

"Then why are people still dying?" Evelyn asked. "Why
is it still so dangerous to go there?"

Edie shivered now. "I—I know David Cooke was responsible for a lot of what happened there. And maybe that Teddy
Bowers kid—"

"Not my baby!" Bonita shouted as she stepped through
the doors of the parlor. The front parlor with the windows
that looked onto the street, where the curtains had been
swishing back and forth.

"No, no," Evelyn agreed. "He wasn't your baby."

Usually Bonita shied away from Edie and hid from her
behind her sister whenever she was around. But the older
woman stepped closer to her now, and for once her cloudy
blue eyes seemed a little clearer, a little more focused. Then
she asked, "Are you going to find my baby?"

Edie's breath caught in her lungs for a moment, burning
there, as she dealt with her surprise that the woman was actually aware of what Edie was trying to do. She also held her
breath as she took her time considering how to reply. Bonita
was more like a child than a senior citizen, and Edie didn't
want to make her any promises she might not be able to
keep, especially after Sam Howell had warned her that
James Bainesworth had probably destroyed all the adoption
records, hell, all the records from the manor.

So she chose her words carefully and replied sincerely. "I'm going to try."

Bonita nodded in acceptance, as if that was good enough, as if she understood already that Edie might not be able to bring her baby back for her. Was she even aware of how long ago she'd lost her child, of when she'd stayed at the manor, where she must have been given a lobotomy like so many others had been despite the practice having been outlawed decades before?

In the lids above those cloudy blue eyes were faint scars from where the tool must have drilled through into the woman's brain. Poor Bonita . . .

She seemed satisfied with Edie's answer, though, because she turned and flounced off, humming and skipping, across the dining room toward the kitchen.

Her sister stared after her, bemused, as she murmured, "I didn't know she had figured out why you were here."

"Maybe she's aware of more than we give her credit for," Edie remarked.

"Well, I know that," Evelyn said defensively. "That's why she usually stays away from you. She instinctively knows that you're trouble." Then she sighed and reached out, linking her arm through Edie's to tug her toward the kitchen. "You missed lunch and it's nearly dinnertime. You must be starving."

Edie's stomach rumbled, but it might have been more from nerves than hunger. "Are you afraid the poison's going to start wearing off if I don't eat soon?" she teased her landlady.

Evelyn chuckled as she pushed through the swinging doors into the kitchen. "I have to be more careful now," she said. "What with the sheriff staying here and all. . . ."

Edie nodded and murmured, "We both do."

Damn Elijah for telling Deacon about that near miss in the parking lot last night. She was surprised that he'd bothered because he'd tried claiming that the driver probably hadn't seen her. She knew that it had been no accident. But she hadn't told the sheriff because she didn't want Deacon acting overprotective and watching her too closely. She knew that to get her story, she might have to do some things he wouldn't approve of . . . like trespassing . . .

If only she had time to go out to the lighthouse now . . .

"I'll have to have an extra helping of poison for dinner," Edie said. "I'm meeting someone at the diner for lunch." She would have canceled that meeting with the local newspaper reporter if she thought she would have enough time to get through those tunnels before it got dark. The days were too short this time of year; the sun, if it came out at all, set early.

Evelyn tensed. "Not one of those men . . ."

She shook her head. "No . . ." But Elijah would be in town, meeting with the state trooper. If the sergeant didn't arrest him, maybe Edie would have the chance to question him . . . after the trooper finished her inquisition. "I might be late getting back," she warned her. "So don't hold dinner for me."

"Are you getting sick of my cooking?" Evelyn asked. "I can dial down the poison."

Edie chuckled. "No, I need to buy some things in town," she said. "Unless you have a big flashlight I can borrow and some warmer clothes." Because even if the sun was shining tomorrow, there would still be no light where Edie was going . . . underground.

Evelyn narrowed her eyes and studied Edie's face. "You are definitely trouble." She shook her head. "And I'm afraid you're going to get into more than even you can handle . . . if you keep hanging around with those men from the manor."

An image of Elijah flashed through Edie's mind. The thick, black hair with just a few strands of silver at his temples, the chiseled features, and those arresting pale blue eyes . . .

And she couldn't argue with her landlady. She was definitely going to get into trouble.

Sergeant Beverly Mae Montgomery, or just Mae as her closest friends and family called her, had earned her promotion with hard work and dedication. And by closing the most cases of anyone at the state police post.

She needed Dr. Elijah Cooke's statement to close the investigation into the events of the previous evening and the attempts on the sheriff's life. But the other investigation mattered more to her.

The one into Erika Korlinsky's murder.

Sitting at a table in a small conference room at the Bane Island Sheriff's Department, she watched as Dr. Cooke signed the statement he'd just given her. The one about last night, about his cousin nearly killing him and Deacon Howell and Olivia . . . whatever her real name was.

David Cooke had also confessed to the murder of his own brother and his lover, Shannon Howell. Dr. Cooke's statement, which matched the statements of the other people involved, closed a lot of cases for her. She could have celebrated, but she wouldn't until she knew for certain who had killed Erika Korlinsky.

She had a pretty strong suspect, but she needed evidence to get an arrest warrant, let alone a conviction. But maybe she could get a confession . . . like David Cooke had apparently given before his death.

"I do need to speak with your brother," she told Cooke.

He looked up from the paper, his brow furrowed, as if he

was confused. "Bode wasn't there last night. He had no idea what was going on with David." A muscle twitched along his jaw. "Unfortunately, neither did I. . . ."

"Would it have made a difference?" she asked. "Or would you have protected your cousin like you're trying to protect your brother?"

Cooke's light blue eyes widened with shock. "You think I would have protected David if I'd known he'd killed Shannon, that he was trying to kill Deacon?"

"I don't know, Dr. Cooke," she answered him honestly. "I don't know you. But I have known some people who will try to protect a relative from justice no matter how horrible his crime."

He shook his head. "I wouldn't do that," he said. "I would have turned David in had I known that he'd killed Shannon and that he'd been trying to kill the sheriff."

She almost believed him, but she was compelled to point out, "A brother is a lot closer to you than a cousin, though. So you might protect Bode James."

He shook his head again. "My cousin was closer to me than my brother is." He uttered a ragged-sounding sigh. "David and I were nearly the same age. We grew up together. He was my best friend."

"And you had no idea he was a killer?"

The muscle twitched along his jaw. "No."

"Then how can you be so certain that your brother is innocent?" she asked. "Since you've admitted that you're not nearly as close to him as you were to David Cooke?"

He opened his mouth as if he was going to give her a reason. Then he closed it again and shook his head. And she knew that he had none.

He couldn't prove his brother's innocence any more than she could prove his guilt. At the moment . . .

But she would. "I will need to speak to your brother soon," she said.

"Not without a lawyer," Dr. Cooke said.

She smiled. "I think you know he's guilty," she said. "And that could make you an accessory to murder, Dr. Cooke. So you may want a lawyer next time we speak as well."

The doctor stood up then. He opened his mouth, but he hesitated a long moment, so long that she thought he wasn't going to say anything else, but then he spoke. "I hope that your unwillingness to look at any other suspects besides my brother doesn't cost more lives."

She shivered at his tone and his warning. She wasn't surprised at either, though. Suspects often tried to warn her away from arresting them. But coming from him . . . after all the pain his family had caused . . .

"Are you threatening me, Dr. Cooke?"

He shook his head and uttered a ragged sigh. "God no, I don't want anything to happen to you or to anyone else. That's why I want you to find out who really killed Erika."

"I will." But even as she made the vow, she worried that this case wasn't going to be as easy to close as the other ones. That this case might cost her more than she was willing to give.

Her life?

Chapter Seven

Fury coursed through Elijah, the anger so hot and pervasive that he didn't even feel the bite of the wind or the sting of the hard chunks of snow that whipped against him the minute he pushed open the door of the sheriff's office and stepped outside.

He'd suspected last night, at the hospital, that the trooper had had her mind made up. But now he knew for certain that she wasn't going to look for the real killer of his niece's mother. She was convinced that his brother was guilty and that Elijah was complicit.

An accessory.

He needed to find that lawyer, and not just for Bode now, but for himself as well. The trooper clearly was not going to stop until his brother and probably Elijah, too, were behind bars.

"Why . . . ?" he murmured. Why was she so determined to place the blame on Bode?

"Talking to yourself, Dr. Cooke?" a husky female voice asked. "Maybe you should get some counseling for that. . . ."

The fury inside him ebbed away. . . into amusement.

Edie Stone never failed to lift his spirits even when she infuriated him.

"Hmmm . . ." he mused. "Then I'd better talk to a psychologist, not a reporter."

"Hey, you were the one waiting outside my house just a little while ago," she said.

"Yeah, for Rosemary."

She laughed at his lie. "You can see that psychologist any time; she works for you."

"She works for the hall," he automatically corrected her.

"And you run the hall," she said.

He was the director, but he hadn't felt like he'd actually been running the place lately. More like it had been running him . . .

Ragged.

He uttered a weary sigh.

"I'm surprised you're up for running anything today," she said. "Especially around town. You took a hard blow to the head last night."

"Yes, I did," he agreed. "Maybe that's why I was outside your house earlier today."

"You forgot where you live?" she teased.

His lips twitched with the urge to grin. "Sometimes I wish I could forget. . . ."

Her brow furrowed as she stared at him. "I don't understand why you're here," she murmured.

He pointed toward the sheriff's office behind him. "Here? I had to give my statement about last night to Sergeant Montgomery. But that's not what she was really after . . ."

"I meant on the island at all."

He sighed again. "That's not something I'm sure I can answer." Even for himself, but most especially not for a reporter. He couldn't explain to her about wanting to make amends for what his family had done all those many years ago.

"Can you tell me what Sergeant Montgomery is after, then?" Edie said.

"My brother."

Edie chuckled now, that throaty, sexy chuckle that had Elijah's skin tingling with more than the cold. "A lot of women are after your brother. He's been voted sexiest man alive I don't know how many times. . . ." She uttered a lustful-sounding sigh now.

Something gripped his stomach, making it churn, and he grimaced. Was that jealousy? No. He'd never been jealous of his brother, but for some reason he found himself asking, "Was one of those votes yours?"

She leaned toward him, so close that when she chuckled again the little puff of her breath touched him, making him shiver. "No. I find intelligence far sexier than muscles."

He chuckled.

"Too bad you're not as smart as I've heard," she said. "Since you're standing out here in the cold."

"You are, too," he said.

"But I was just in there," she said, and she gestured toward the diner that was in an old Victorian house right next door to the sheriff's office, so close, in fact, that he had parked there instead of on the street, where snow had been piled too high between the curb and the sidewalk. Her red Jeep was parked in the lot, too, near his SUV. "Want to grab a cup of coffee and warm up?" she asked.

Another way of warming up, with her, flashed through his mind, and he wasn't that cold anymore. He tensed, trying to push those thoughts, that attraction to her, from his mind . . . and his body.

"You must have been at the boardinghouse earlier because you were looking for me," she said. "Why?"

"I wanted to make sure you were okay."

"You didn't believe someone deliberately tried running me over last night," she reminded him. "So what did you really want, Elijah?"

His name on her lips, uttered with that husky voice of hers, had him shivering again. But he also felt a strange chill, as if someone was watching them. He glanced around them, looking for whoever might be staring at them. "Let's get that cup of coffee," he said, and he put his hand at the small of her back to steer her toward the diner.

She tensed. And he wondered if she felt it, too.

"Do you have the feeling that someone is watching us?" he asked, hoping it was just his imagination.

She chuckled. "I'm sure everyone's watching us." And sure enough, when they stepped inside the diner, it was eerily quiet despite how busy it was, as everyone stared at them walking in together. "Their interest must be in you," she said. "They've stopped reacting when I come in here."

And she'd only been here a few weeks, while he'd grown up here. So it wasn't that they were reacting to a stranger; they were reacting to him, as the locals always did, with silent hostility.

But then someone approached. A gray-haired man who looked vaguely familiar to him. "Hey, Dr. Cooke, isn't it?" he asked.

Elijah nodded and braced himself, waiting for the insult, the accusation.

"Do you care to confirm the story Ms. Stone gave me a short while ago?"

"Confirm? What story?" And he realized who the man was—the editor of the Bane Island newspaper, not that much ever got printed in it besides classified ads. Apparently Edie Stone was trying to get something else published in it.

The man, Tom Thiesen, persisted. "About last night,

about your cousin, David Cooke, confessing to killing the sheriff's wife?"

Elijah glanced at the woman beside him, sick that he'd nearly trusted her. "I thought you weren't going to report about what happened last night?" he asked her.

She shrugged. "I'm *not*. I just wanted to make sure that someone did—for Deacon's sake."

"But what about Ms. Smith?" She didn't need any more publicity. Any more stalkers.

"Who's Miss Smith?" Tom asked, his brow furrowing with confusion.

Elijah suppressed a groan as he realized what Edie had really been doing. She'd left Olivia completely out of the story and had focused on only one aspect of it. Deacon's innocence. That was something that he'd intended to make sure the town knew as well.

He owed his old enemy. So he drew in a deep breath and cleared his throat before replying loud enough for everybody in the silent diner to hear, "Yes, my cousin, David Cooke, was responsible for the murder of Shannon Howell. He confessed to it last night."

"Did he confess to the murder of the other woman the sheriff found at the manor?" the reporter asked.

Elijah wished like hell that he had. But he couldn't lie, so he shook his head.

"That's all the doctor is going to say," Edie said, and she grasped his hand to tug him toward a table.

As they moved through the crowd, Elijah heard the remarks.

"Another crazy Bainesworth . . ."

"Sadistic bastard just like his grandfather . . ."

"Thinks he owns the whole damn island just like the old man . . ."

Edie led him toward a booth and shoved him down into the corner of it, as if she was shoving him out of the line of fire. "Wow," she murmured. "You sure have a lot of fans."

He grimaced. "This was a bad idea."

The whole thing. Coming into the diner. Coming into town in the first place. Talking to her . . .

It was a bad idea. She was a reporter, and he doubted he could trust her. Or anyone.

The trooper wasn't the only one who had her mind made up about him and his brother. The whole damn town did; they all believed they were exactly like their grandfather.

Evil . . .

Edie studied Elijah across the Formica tabletop of the booth she'd shoved him into in the farthest corner of the diner. Despite how far from everyone else they were sitting, they could still hear those muttered—and not so muttered—remarks.

"Do you want something to eat?" she asked. "Or just coffee?"

"It's probably not a good idea to eat or drink anything here," he mused. "Who knows what might have been done to it?"

She shrugged. "I doubt you have to worry about poison," she said.

"Not like you do at the boardinghouse?" he asked with a slight gleam of amusement in those eerily pale eyes of his.

She smiled. "Evelyn and I tease each other, but I know

she cares about me." Maybe a little too much. "She'd have a stroke if she knew I was here with you."

"She'll hear about it," he warned her.

She shook her head. "I think Evelyn's too busy running the boardinghouse to listen to idle gossip."

"It's not just gossip," he said. "You are here with me."

"Why are you here with *me*?" she asked. "Why are you willing to talk to me now after turning me away for the past few weeks?"

"I'm still going to turn you away if you try to show up at the hall," he said.

She was definitely going to show up . . . if the former sheriff had told her the truth. Impatience burned inside her to check out those tunnels now, today, but the afternoon had already slipped into dusk, darkening the already dark sky outside the windows of the diner. And the snow was falling again, still, always. . . .

She waved at the young waitress, who'd served her and Tom earlier, and called out to her, "Two coffees please." Then she glanced at Elijah. "Unless you don't drink caffeine?"

"I thought both of those were for you," he replied, but then he grinned, and his eyes twinkled. "Yes, I drink caffeine. I'm not my brother." Then his grin slipped away and he added, "Does that disappoint you, that you're not with the sexiest man alive?"

She leaned across the table and swiped her finger along his rigid jaw. His features were even more chiseled than his brother's, and with those gray strands in his thick, black hair, he was very much the silver fox. "Who says I'm not?"

His throat moved, rippling, as if he was struggling to swallow something, and then he chuckled. "You're trouble, Edie Stone."

She nodded. "So I've been told . . ." He was so fun to

tease that she couldn't resist adding, "Is that why you were looking for me, Dr. Cooke? You want to get into trouble?"

He sucked in a breath, and a muscle twitched along his seemingly tightly clenched jaw. She would have suspected he was unused to women flirting with him if she hadn't seen how proprietary the publicist had acted over him the night before. Amanda Plasky clearly wanted to protect more than the hall from Edie; she wanted to protect Elijah, too.

"I think I'm already in trouble," Elijah murmured.

Before he could say anything more, the waitress approached with the coffeepot. She turned over the cups on the table and splashed some of the steaming brew into them so abruptly that droplets of coffee spattered the tabletop.

"Ms. Stone, you wanting to talk to my grandma about what happened to her all those years ago," the young woman began, then shot a pointed glance at Elijah. "*I* don't think it's a good idea anymore."

"I'll do my best not to upset her," Edie promised. "I'm only trying to help her. That's all I'm trying to do."

The young woman hesitated, shot another glance at Elijah, then shook her head before walking off. And Edie's stomach muscles tightened. She wanted to talk to anyone who'd survived a stay at the manor, who was lucid enough to talk about it, but there weren't many survivors. And most of them didn't want to talk about the past. She hoped she hadn't just lost access to one of them.

"Is that really all you're trying to do?" Elijah asked.

"Honestly?" Compelled, as always, to be honest, she shook her head. "I'd like a Pulitzer, too, and I think this is the story that'll get me one."

His lips curved slightly, as if her answer amused him.

"What?" she asked as she propped her elbows on the tabletop and leaned across it, closer to him. What was it about him that seemed to draw him toward her . . . as if there were some invisible threads stretching between them, like the gossamer threads of a spider's web . . . ?

Was she the spider or the hapless fly?

"I looked you up today," he said. "I found out about your past."

She nodded. "I suspected as much when you said earlier that your life wasn't nearly as interesting as mine." Other people might have been referring to the celebrities she'd met and interviewed, but he met celebrities, too. So she'd known . . .

"That's why you're so intent on finding these babies," he speculated. "Because you were a missing baby once."

She shrugged. "I was just the baby."

"You weren't found and returned to your parents until you were ten years old, and that surrogate your parents hired, the one who kidnapped you, was finally caught. That must have been a tough ten years, constantly on the run, constantly changing names and appearances and identities," he said, his deep voice a low, almost hypnotic murmur.

She could see it in him now, the traits that had made him such a sought-after psychiatrist. His brother wasn't the only draw for the spa. While Elijah's reputation was quieter since people still weren't as willing to admit to issues with their mental health as they were their physical health, Dr. Cooke was every bit as well-known as Bode James.

"That must have been tough," he continued, commiserating in that hypnotic tone of voice, "not knowing what the truth was, so I can understand why it's so important to you now."

It had been tough, and so damn confusing. It had also been all she'd known, so she'd been shocked to find out her mother wasn't her mother at all but her kidnapper.

As if seeing her struggle, Elijah reached across the table

for her hand, but she wrapped them around her mug instead. The warm ceramic didn't chase away the chill she suddenly felt. "Psychoanalyzing me, Doctor?"

"Honestly?" He nodded. "It's an occupational hazard, I guess. Apparently I don't always get it right, though."

"You're really upset about your cousin," she said, and she wanted to turn the tables on him now, unsettle him the way he'd unsettled her. "That you missed it."

He nodded again. "Yes."

"It's making you doubt your own judgment."

"Now who's psychoanalyzing whom?" he asked, his lips curving into that slight, sexy grin.

Elijah Cooke really could be the sexiest man alive . . . at least to her. Her pulse quickened at just the look on his face, in those glittering blue eyes of his. But then his smile slipped away, his jaw going rigid as he clenched it again.

"I'm not wrong about my brother, though," he insisted. "The trooper is. Sergeant Montgomery is convinced he did it, and I don't know how to prove that he didn't."

"That's why you wanted to talk to me," she guessed. "You want me to find the killer? I'm a reporter, not a detective."

"You've done it before," Elijah said. "You've gotten people to confess."

She remembered the high-profile case that had probably caught his attention. A girl and her boyfriend had gone on a van life camping trip, but only the boyfriend had returned in her van with her credit card and cell phone. He wouldn't talk to the police or to his girlfriend's family or even his own. But Edie had gotten him to talk to her.

"He was already a suspect," she said. "The only suspect . . ."

"But there were other killers you interviewed, ones you got to confess to more crimes than they'd been arrested for," he pointed out.

She shrugged off his admiration. "Again, I knew who the suspects were. What about you?"

He tensed, and the color drained from his face. "You think I'm a suspect?"

She shook her head. "No, I don't." She truthfully didn't believe he was a killer. "Who do you suspect, since you're so sure your brother is innocent?"

"*I* have no idea . . ." he murmured. "Bode thinks it was either David or Teddy Bowers."

"I can't interview either of them now," she pointed out. "They're both dead, which seems a little convenient for your brother."

Elijah closed his eyes, as if he couldn't look at her, and shook his head. "Damn it! You're just like everyone else," he murmured, his voice gruff with obvious disappointment. At least it was obvious to her, because her family had so often been disappointed in her. "You've got your mind made up just because of who my grandfather is, Bode's grandfather. . . ."

"Your cousins weren't much better," she reminded him.

He flinched now. "So you think the only people on this island who are bad are my relatives. They're the only ones who could possibly commit any crimes."

She shook her head. "No. I don't believe that," she assured him. "Because I know that even good people are capable of doing bad things."

Like the woman she'd spent ten years believing was her mother. Nobody had ever loved Edie more than she had—not even her biological parents. She had never disappointed her like Edie had disappointed her parents. She'd never been able to live up to their expectations of her and for her.

Elijah finished reaching across the table now, and he wrapped his hand around her wrist. Her pulse leaped at the touch of his thumb, of his skin against hers. But she didn't pull away from it, from him . . . she liked it too much, liked that tingling, pulse-pounding awareness between them.

"You were lucky," he said. "You had two families fighting over you, wanting to keep you."

She narrowed her eyes, wondering at his tone. "What about you?"

He shook his head. "Bode and I were an inconvenience. After our mother took off, our father dumped us on his brother and sister-in-law to raise." He glanced at his watch and groaned. "I need to leave. I need to . . ."

"To what?" she wondered.

"Manage the arrangements for David and Warren."

"Your aunt and uncle aren't coming back for the funerals?"

He shrugged. "I don't know. . . ."

Her heart ached for him. Apparently everyone in Elijah's life had abandoned him when he'd needed them. That was probably why he was so desperate to believe his brother was innocent. But was Bode really not guilty? He'd been the closest to the victim, had had a personal relationship with her, and a child.

Would she, if she tried, get a confession out of him as she had the others?

"Let me talk to Bode," she said. "Let me into the hall."

Elijah shook his head. "No."

And she wondered if he was worried she might get his brother to confess. "But how will I find any other suspects if I can't talk to anyone who knew this woman?"

"Erika Korlinsky," he said. "That was her name. But I suspect that you're not really interested in her or in solving her murder. You're only interested in those other women and the babies." He cocked his head slightly. "You talked to the sheriff's father today. Did he help you?"

She shrugged. She wouldn't know until she found the tunnel he'd told her about whether he'd actually helped her. If she could get onto the property of the hall . . .

"The man I need to talk to is your grandfather," she said.

He shook his head. "Absolutely not." He pulled out his wallet and dropped some money on the table. "And as I told the sergeant, although she took it as a threat, you need to be careful."

She wasn't threatened by his words; she was threatened by what she felt as warmth flooded her with his obvious concern. Dr. Elijah Cooke wasn't the villain everyone wanted to believe he was. He wasn't his grandfather.

He stood up and walked through the diner, and everybody got quiet again except for the muttered insults, and they stared at him with such distrust and hatred that she was worried about him. He was the one who needed to be careful.

She would have jumped up to follow him out, but the waitress returned, blocking her into the booth. "Why did you bring *him* in here?" the young woman asked.

"I am trying to put together a story about Bainesworth Manor," Edie reminded her.

"But he wasn't even alive then . . ." the woman murmured.

"No, he wasn't," Edie conceded. "Yet everybody acts like he's to blame for what happened back then."

"His grandfather did it."

"Before Elijah was born," Edie said. "So he couldn't have stopped him."

"He could have stopped that cousin of his, but he killed, too, if what everybody's saying is true, if the sheriff's wife was murdered, and then there's that other body that turned up out there," the woman persisted. "It's a dangerous place. And he's a dangerous man."

Edie suspected he was in more danger than he presented. Finally, she jumped up and edged around the woman, so that she could follow him outside. But she got there too late; the SUV was gone. He'd already driven off. Back to the hall? Or the funeral home, to make the arrangements for his cousins?

Alone.

Elijah Cooke seemed used to handling things on his own, yet he'd reached out to her. He'd wanted her help, and she had offered him nothing constructive. A pang of regret struck her. She wanted to call him, wanted to apologize, wanted to start over with him, but she doubted that she'd be able to get through to him if she tried calling the hall.

But maybe . . .

Maybe she would be able to just turn up there.

Wanting to buy the supplies she needed before the stores closed, she hurried off down the street on foot. As she passed the storefronts, she noticed a reflection in the dark glass of the windows of the shops that had already closed for the day or the season. Someone was following her.

And as she hurried, that shadow kept pace with her. If she stopped, it stopped. And if she quickened her step, it speeded up, too. Who the hell was following her?

She whirled back, but she could see no one on the street behind her. A door opened with a ding as someone went in or out of a store she'd already passed. Was she just paranoid?

Still feeling uneasy, she turned back around and continued down the street toward the hardware store. Evelyn's flashlights had all had dim bulbs and were cheap plastic. So Edie needed to buy a heavy-duty one, but she wished she had it already . . . as she noticed that shadow again in a window she passed.

Between where she was and the hardware store, there was an alley . . . the darkness of it spilled onto the sidewalk as she passed in front of it. And as she walked through that shadow, someone reached out and grabbed her. And a scream tore from her throat.

"What the hell's wrong with you?" Deacon asked as he jerked his hand from Edie's arm and stepped back. He didn't move far enough away, though, because she easily reached him when she swung her arm and slapped his shoulder.

"You scared the shit out of me!" she yelled at him, her voice raspy from her scream, which had been so loud that his ears were still ringing with the echo of it.

"Good," he said. "You need to be careful."

She glared at him, her eyes still bright with indignation. "I am always careful."

He snorted. "Yeah, right," he said. "I could have pulled you into this alley no problem."

Her face flushed now, and her glare intensified. "I knew you were following me. I didn't expect you to jump out of the alley at me."

"I couldn't follow you and jump out of the alley at you," he pointed out. "When I went back to the boardinghouse to find you, Evelyn said you were picking up some stuff from the hardware store, so I cut through the alley to get to it."

She tensed, and the color that had flushed her face receded now, leaving her pale. "You weren't following me?"

He shook his head, and then he peered around them. People had stepped out of stores, probably because they'd heard her scream. "Who was it?" he asked.

She shrugged. "I don't know. I didn't actually see anyone or I wouldn't have thought it was you." She released a shaky breath. "Hell, maybe I'm just paranoid."

"No, you're not." He pulled out his phone to show her the

surveillance video he'd emailed himself from the hospital. "Somebody definitely tried running you down last night." And he held out his phone toward her. He studied her face as she watched the video of herself walking out of the hospital, into the lot, and the moment the headlights flashed on, blinding her before she turned and jumped . . . just as the vehicle passed inches away from her.

His heart pounded fast just as it had when he'd first seen it, the very obvious attempt on Edie Stone's life.

But she just shrugged. "It wasn't as close as I thought," she murmured.

"If it was any closer, you'd be in the hospital," Deacon said. "Why the hell didn't you tell me about this last night?"

She shrugged again. "You can't see the driver. Hell, with the snow falling, you can't even see the vehicle, and maybe the driver didn't see me."

"You don't believe that any more than I do," Deacon said. "I don't believe that's what Elijah thinks either. You need to stay away from him and you need to stay away from the hall. Olivia warned you that she heard him and that publicist of his talking about getting rid of you."

She pointed at the screen of his phone, at the shadowy images of herself and Elijah as he gently lifted her up from the snow. "He wasn't the driver."

"No," Deacon conceded. "But that doesn't mean that he wasn't behind the attempt."

"I thought you two were starting to bond," she said. "You weren't as snarky with him earlier as you usually are."

"My mistake," Deacon said. "I hadn't seen the video yet."

"You wouldn't have seen it if he hadn't told you what happened," she reminded him. "He wouldn't have done that if he was behind it."

Deacon groaned with frustration that she was probably

right, but he was reluctant to admit it. "I don't know. He probably assumed you told me," he said. "Why didn't you?"

"Because it's not going to stop me," Edie said. "Nothing's going to stop me from getting to the truth."

God, she was stubborn—too stubborn to see what serious danger she was in. If that driver had just meant to scare her off the night before, it hadn't worked.

Deacon wasn't certain that anything would. But he was compelled to point out, "Something might."

"What?" she asked, as if she expected him to arrest her or something.

But he just succinctly replied, "Your death."

Chapter Eight

Elijah's head pounded and his eyes were gritty with fatigue. He should have slept well the night before because he'd been in his own bed instead of on a couch and there had been no one waking him every hour to shine a bright light in his eyes to check his pupils. But he'd lain awake, listening to all the creaks and groans of the old building. David had renovated it, but so much of the original structure had remained, maybe including the ghosts the old woman professed she could hear.

Morgana Drake had been staying at the hall on and off since it had opened, but she wasn't looking to improve her physical or mental health. She was looking for ghosts, and she claimed that she'd connected with them here at the hall.

A few times over the years since he'd moved into his suite in the main structure, Elijah had been worried that he had heard them, too. But when he'd investigated, he'd found a real person weeping—either a guest or, more recently, the sheriff's daughter. He released a shaky breath of relief that Holly Howell had quit; the hall had caused enough issues between her and her father. Hopefully now, knowing what—or actually *who*—had really killed her mother, she and her dad could heal.

That was all he wanted for them, and for any guest of the hall.

Throats cleared, drawing Elijah's attention back to the conference room and the people sitting around the long table. Employees, partner, publicist—he'd called them all to this meeting, one he probably should have held yesterday. But he'd been busy trying to chase down Edie Stone, only to realize, after he had, that she had no inclination to help him prove his brother's innocence, probably only his guilt.

Bode stared at him with an expression of concern, probably worried that Elijah was losing it because he'd called this meeting and had yet to address any of them.

But he wasn't the one who asked, "Are you okay, Elijah?" Amanda Plasky was the one who posed the question to him, and she reached across the table to lay her hand over his, her long nails scraping across his skin.

He jerked his hand from beneath hers and curled it into a fist on his thigh. "Yes, I'm fine. I should have called this meeting yesterday to discuss everything that happened the other night."

"You have a serious concussion," Amanda said. "You should be resting and not worrying about the hall." She gestured her manicured hands at everyone gathered around the table. "We can all handle everything for you."

Dr. Gordon Chase chuckled, drawing everyone's attention to where he sat farther down the table next to Rosemary Tulle. He'd once been her professor, just as he'd once been Elijah's. While the psychiatrist had retired from academia, he hadn't been ready to give up helping people, so Elijah had been able to convince him to join the staff at the spa. "I don't think you need to worry about Elijah," he told Amanda. "From what I hear, he was driving all around town yesterday, even met with a certain reporter at the diner."

Elijah hadn't seen the man in the diner, so someone must have told him about it. Maybe Rosemary.

"You met with that reporter?" Bode asked as if he was appalled. "You really did take a hard blow to the head."

He gave his younger brother a pointed look. "I thought she could help you."

Bode grimaced. "I don't need that kind of help."

She hadn't been willing to help, so it was a moot point anyway. But Elijah wasn't about to admit to that in front of everyone, that the reporter suspected Bode was as guilty as the rest of the island probably did.

So he focused on his reason for this meeting: protecting the hall. "We need to put out a preemptive statement," he said. "The more we say about the recent, uh . . ."

"The murders," Dr. Chase finished for him when Elijah couldn't bring himself to complete his sentence. Amanda apparently didn't consider him that helpful; the publicist must have glowered at the older man, who held up his hands and said, "That's what they were."

There was no denying that. No denying that employees and contractors at the hall had been responsible either because Teddy and David had worked there.

"Well, the more information we put out about them," Elijah continued, "the less it'll look like we're concealing." There had been enough hidden over the years at Bainesworth Manor, and now at the hall.

"That's brilliant, Elijah," Amanda praised him. "We'll put out a statement that a former contractor at the hall is the one responsible for the previous misfortunes here, and now that he's dead, there is no further threat to any of our guests, or to any of the public as well."

Rosemary glanced from the publicist back to Elijah. Then she cleared her throat and said, "But that's not been proven.

In fact, there are several people who don't believe that David Cooke was responsible for Erika Korlinsky's murder."

Amanda gave a dismissive sniff. "Who? The sheriff? That annoying state trooper? They just want to make trouble for Elijah."

"Elijah isn't the one in danger of going to prison," Bode muttered as his usually tanned skin lost its color except for the dark circles beneath his eyes. He didn't look as if he'd gotten any more sleep than Elijah, and he hadn't had to get up every hour last night to check on him. Maybe Adelaide had had him up, though, or maybe the fear of losing her and his freedom had kept him awake.

Elijah had to find a way to help his brother and his niece, to clear Bode of any suspicion. And the only way to do that was to find Erika's real killer, something he was apparently going to have to figure out on his own because Edie wouldn't help him and everyone else seemed to have settled on Bode as the only suspect.

Amanda continued on in her dismissive tone. "I'll send out some press releases, and I'll make it clear that the cases are closed—"

"But they're not," Rosemary persisted, and she must have earned her own glare from the publicist. She didn't hold up her hands in surrender like their mentor had, though; she just shook her head with disgust before turning toward Elijah. "I agree with you that we should not be concealing anything else."

"Of course you would," Amanda said, and now she was the one muttering.

Rosemary had been furious with them when they wouldn't tell her that Genevieve had gone missing from the spa. But at the time they hadn't been authorized to release any information to her; she hadn't been listed as the teenager's mother.

"But if you put out incorrect information that can be easily disproved, you're going to look even more like you're hiding something," Rosemary explained.

"I agree," Elijah said.

"That's why we shouldn't say anything," Bode said. "Hell, I'm not even sure if we can, since Erika's death is still an open investigation."

Elijah sucked in a breath and nodded. "You're right. We need to check with a lawyer first. And we need to find a good one." That had been another reason he'd called the meeting: to discuss hiring a criminal lawyer. The attorney the hall had on retainer was only versed in real estate and corporate law.

"I know a real good criminal attorney. I can refer you to him," Dr. Chase offered. They all turned toward him, and Elijah wondered if everybody else was wondering what he was: Why had Dr. Chase needed a criminal lawyer? As if he'd sensed their curiosity, the former professor added, "Mitchell Cummings is the son of a friend of mine. He's very well respected in Portland."

And Elijah felt a flash of guilt that he'd done what so many people had of him . . . thought the worst.

"Thank you, Gordon," he said. "I really appreciate the referral."

Dr. Chase nodded his head with its thick, gray hair. He had to be pushing seventy, but he didn't look much older than Elijah. No wonder he'd chosen to continue working. But Elijah was always careful not to overbook him. He didn't want to lose him.

Now Amanda . . .

Bode had spoken so highly of the publicist, and she had run a successful publicity campaign to promote the exclusive spa as a wellness center. But she seemed reluctant now to tell the truth. Edie wasn't going to accept Amanda's press release as fact and few other reporters would either.

Bode's opinion of her seemed to have slipped as well because he said, "Why don't we talk to this lawyer first—before we release anything?"

Elijah couldn't argue with his brother's logic and neither could anyone else.

"I'll get ahold of Mitchell and see when he can make the trip to the island," Dr. Chase said as he headed toward the door to the hall.

Elijah pressed the button on his desk, which unlocked and opened the door. As it swung in, a couple of people nearly fell inside with it . . . the woman who called herself a medium, Morgana Drake, and a much younger, very blond woman named Heather Smallegan. She was the personal trainer who worked for Bode, but Elijah suspected she wanted to do more than just work with the sexiest man alive. Color flushed her face. "I'm sorry," she said. Probably at getting caught trying to eavesdrop. "I have a client who's specifically requesting you, Bode."

He nodded and jumped up from the conference table, probably grateful to be able to focus on anything else but the murder . . . of the mother of his child. "No need to apologize, Heather. We just finished up our meeting," he said. "I'll walk to the gym with you."

She smiled brightly at him when he approached her, and Elijah swallowed a groan of frustration. The last thing his brother needed to do was get involved with another member of their staff, especially when the last one had wound up dead. But before he could warn either of them, they were gone—leaving just Morgana, who shied back against the wall when Dr. Chase walked past her. But she didn't rush off like she usually did when either Elijah or Dr. Chase approached her.

The woman needed help, but so far she had refused to talk to him or his mentor. Amanda flounced out past her, sparing the older woman no attention. And for once she'd spared Elijah none either after he'd pulled his hand from hers. Maybe she was finally beginning to understand that he was not interested in a relationship. He would have said he wasn't interested in getting involved with anyone right now, but an image of Edie, with her sparkling green eyes and tousled blond hair, popped into his mind. And as he always did when he was with her, he smiled.

Rosemary headed toward the door, and the older woman who was probably waiting for her. But he called her back. "Miss Tulle—"

"Rosemary," she interjected. "Call me Rosemary, Elijah."

He smiled again. "Rosemary . . ." Maybe if she considered them friends, she would grant his request . . . although he wasn't sure why he was asking; he already had his answer.

But before he could ask Rosemary anything, she arched her head toward the older woman, who still stood in the doorway. "Morgana," she said. "Have you been looking for me?" And there was a hopeful note in the psychologist's voice; obviously, she wanted to help her. Rosemary seemed to want to help everyone. She'd definitely been a wonderful addition to their staff.

But the older woman shook her head, tousling brassy red curls around her wrinkled face. "No, not you. You don't hear the voices."

Elijah had worried before that the woman could hear voices due to schizophrenia, but she exhibited no other signs of that condition. So then he'd figured she was eccentric . . . and truly believed she was what she said she was: a medium.

"No," Rosemary agreed. "I don't, Morgana. Are you hearing them now?" She apparently shared the same concerns Elijah had had about the older woman.

Morgana ignored the question and focused on Elijah. "You . . . you can hear them."

Goose bumps raised on the skin beneath his shirt and suit jacket as a shiver threatened to pass over him. He shook his head. "No. Remember, Morgana, I can't hear anything." That was what he'd told her when she'd asked him before.

"Not right now," she said, but her brightly painted lips curved into a smile. "But you do."

Rosemary's brow furrowed beneath a lock of her black hair. "Have you changed your mind about Dr. Cooke?"

"What—what do you mean?" he asked although he could guess what Morgana thought of him—what everyone else thought of him.

Morgana nodded. "I can see now that he's different."

"Different from what?" Elijah asked. Or from whom? She knew about the manor; that was why she'd come here. Had she only heard about it from people talking about it, or had she personally experienced it? She was old enough that she could have stayed here . . . many decades before the hall opened.

"I think he might be the one who can help them . . ." she murmured, without addressing his question. "The only one. . ."

Before either of them could ask what she meant, she whirled around on her heel and hurried off—almost as if someone had called out to her that only she could hear.

Elijah couldn't suppress the shiver now that slithered down between his shoulder blades.

"Well, I guess it's all up to you now," Rosemary told him with a teasing smile.

While she was joking, his shoulders sagged slightly with the burden of it—because that was how he felt—like it was all up to him. And while he agreed with his brother that they needed to consult with a lawyer before releasing any statements, he wanted to talk to Edie again. Maybe he could convince her to help him find more suspects for Erika's murder, at least one that she could get to confess.

"Do you have Edie's cell number?" he asked.

Rosemary's dark blue eyes widened with surprise. "Edie Stone?" she asked, as if there was another Edie on the island.

A smile twitched up his lips, and he nodded.

"But I thought you were going to wait to release a statement. . . ."

"I'm not going to give her a statement," he said. Then he snorted. "Like she would even take a prepared press release . . ."

Rosemary smiled now, but she pulled her cell phone from the front pocket of her bag. "True. She's not that kind of reporter."

He'd gleaned that from what he'd found out when he'd googled her. She didn't go for the easy or superficial stories. She always had to dig deeper . . . deeper than most people wanted her to dig, probably. She hadn't tried too hard with him at the diner, though; maybe she'd known he didn't have the answers she wanted.

Only his grandfather did . . .

And Elijah wanted her nowhere near him. So, just as he'd told her, he couldn't let her onto the grounds.

Rosemary finished scrolling through her phone, and then, in his pocket, his cell vibrated with an incoming text.

"I forwarded her contact to you." Her smile widened. "It's up to you what you do with it. . . ." She turned then and walked away.

Even though everyone else had gone, he hesitated in the doorway of the empty conference room. If he headed back to his office, there would be something waiting for him—messages, or maybe Dr. Chase with that lawyer information. So instead of walking out, he leaned against the wall and pulled his cell from his pocket. He didn't just open the contact information for Edie Stone; he called it.

"Stone," she answered it shortly and succinctly. "What do you want?" She sounded impatient, as if she was in a rush to do something . . . like she'd seemed when she'd arrived back at the boardinghouse the afternoon before.

"You know it's me?" Elijah asked.

And her throaty chuckle emanated from the phone pressed to his ear, sending a tingling sensation down his body. Maybe that wasn't in reaction to her, though, but to the shadow he noticed in the hall. He'd thought everyone had left. He was about to peer out into the hall, but Edie's voice drew his attention back to the phone, back to her.

"Dr. Cooke . . ." she murmured. "No. I wasn't sure who you were, but I can't afford to miss any calls in case someone's offering me a scoop. You offering me one, Dr. Cooke?"

Testing his theory about how she might receive it, he said, "The hall will be sending out a press release soon. . . ." As soon as they ran it past an attorney . . .

"I'm not the fucking AP," she replied.

And he laughed now, with delight at her response. "I thought you might respond that way," he admitted, and he was happy that he was right about it. Maybe he was right about her.

"But . . ." she murmured. "Just out of curiosity, what will this press release say?"

"It will basically say something along the lines that despite recent events at the hall, there is no risk to our guests' privacy or to their safety."

She snorted. "So it's all bullshit."

"I hope it's true," he said. He hoped that nobody else would be hurt.

"And you called me about this?" she asked. "About an upcoming press release?"

"No."

"Then why did you call me, Elijah?"

The way she said his name, in that husky voice of hers, sent another tingling sensation through him. He couldn't remember the last time anyone had affected him like this. He'd always been so serious, so focused, even as a kid. Then he'd been focused on getting off the island and never coming back. But here he was . . .

"Elijah?" she prodded. And now she sounded impatient again.

"Did I catch you in the middle of something?" he wondered. Despite what he'd learned online about her, or maybe because of it, he wanted to know everything about her. She was a fascinating woman.

"More like at the start of it," she said.

He had that odd chill pass through him again. "I hope it's nothing dangerous."

She laughed, but it almost sounded more like a nervous twitter than the sexy, husky chuckle he'd heard from her before. "Depends. . . . What did you want, Elijah?"

"I don't know . . ." he admitted.

And she chuckled again, that deep-throated one that had parts of his body tightening that he barely acknowledged lately. He'd been so damn consumed with the hall and the guests and the horrible things that had been happening recently.

But letting her—of all people—affect him like this was dangerous. He still wasn't sure he could trust her. But he wanted to find out. "I want to talk to you," he said.

"You're not doing too much of it right now," she pointed out.

"In person," he said. He'd seen her for too short a time the day before.

"You'll let me into the hall?" she asked.

He groaned. "I can't." She was too recognizable, and if one of his guests saw her, they might think he'd violated that privacy claim. And right now he had a couple of guests who were too well-known to want their reasons for being there to get out. One was on a mission to lose weight she'd gained before taking on her next movie role and red carpet. That was probably the one who'd wanted only Bode to work with her. The other was a politician with a vice he needed some help to overcome. He was Elijah's client. And Elijah had sworn to him that he wouldn't have to worry about anyone finding out he was at the hall. If he saw Edie, he would immediately recognize her. She'd taken down too many politicians for him to not know who she was.

That was why she'd come to Bane Island in the first place. She'd been trying to reveal all the deep, dark secrets of the man with whom Rosemary was involved, a judge who was rumored to be looking at a higher office. Like governor.

"Well, you can't come to the boardinghouse," Edie said. "I can't put them through that again. And I'm not sure you want to risk a repeat of yesterday at the diner . . ."

"Are you sure you want to risk it?" he asked. From what

the waitress had said, Edie might have lost an interview because of being seen with him.

She snorted. "You think I care what people think?"

"I'm not sure. Do you want to meet for drinks at the bar in town, the one on Main Street?" he challenged her. Not that he ever had much—if anything—to drink; he didn't want to risk any of the vices the rest of his family had, like his father had alcohol and Bode had women and Grandfather . . .

He shuddered, not wanting to think what he had.

Her sigh rattled his cell. "They play the jukebox a little loud. It will be hard to talk there. Why don't you just let me come to the hall?"

"I can't," he said.

"Then I guess we can't really talk, Elijah." And she clicked off her cell.

He ignored the twinge of disappointment he felt. Really, this was for the best. Her only interest in him was to get access to the hall and Grandfather. She didn't want to help him; in fact, she would probably only wind up hurting him.

After disconnecting her call with Elijah, Edie held on to her cell for a long moment with regret weighing heavily on her. Maybe she should have agreed to meet him . . . instead of pushing him to let her into the hall. But if he'd let her inside, she wouldn't have to do what she was about to do. . . .

She slid the cell into a pocket of her backpack and pushed open the door of her Jeep. Gravel crunched beneath her heavy boots as she stepped out onto the shoulder of the road where she'd parked. She was glad now that she'd waited for daytime, such as it was with the clouds hanging low and dark over the island. She'd never been out to this point on the island before, past the stone walls and tall gates of the hall, to the very end of Bane Island, which extended into the sea. To that lighthouse . . .

It stood at the top of a steep hill above a rusted old pier that she doubted ships even used anymore. The steel supports of the pier creaked and groaned like the bridge did whenever she drove across it, but this structure looked even flimsier and more rusted. The lighthouse didn't look as if it was used anymore either. Nearly all the glass was broken out of the windows in the lantern room and its cupola roof was rusted, like the metal bridge around that room. Good thing she wasn't going up there.

While the weather had seemed calmer when she'd gotten into the Jeep back at the boardinghouse, the wind howled now and swirled snow around her, and despite being above the sea, the spray of it shot up . . . stinging with its salty tang and icy cold. She shivered and pulled her hood tighter around her face. Then she slammed the Jeep door shut and locked it. Maybe it was just habit from living in cities and not wanting someone waiting for her in her back seat.

Or maybe it was the same odd sensation she'd had last night: that she was being watched again. She glanced around her, at the rocks and ledges on the seaside, and the pine trees and stones bordering the road on the interior side of the island. And she shivered as something moved among those pines, sending a clump of snow to drop from the branches onto the ground. She shivered.

And another howl echoed around her.

It wasn't the wind this time, but an animal.

A coyote, or maybe even a wolf. She had no idea what kind of creatures were on the island, but she remembered that when the sheriff had found that body a few weeks ago, those creatures had found it first. He'd had to shoot his gun in the air to scare them away from the remains.

She shuddered now . . . at the thought of those animals getting to her. She hadn't packed a gun in her backpack. Just the heavy-duty flashlight she'd bought at the hardware store last night, along with some extra batteries, a pair of mittens, a scarf, and some snacks and her cell.

But who would she call for help? Who would be close enough?

Elijah.

How had he gotten her number? And why hadn't he blocked his? Because now she had his number.

She'd thought she'd already had it in the proverbial sense, that she'd known what he was all about, but he was surprising her. With his wit and his sincerity.

And she felt a twinge of guilt that she was going to do what she was about to do . . . trespass to get onto the estate. First she had to find that tunnel, though.

Maybe the former sheriff had just been messing with her. And even if he'd told her the truth, there was no guarantee that the tunnels still existed. When Elijah and Bode had renovated the hall, the contractors might have stumbled across them and closed them down.

There was only one way she was going to find out. . . .

So, ignoring the howls of the wind and of those creatures, she started toward the hill. It was just a jumble of big boulders, slick from the snow and the mist from the sea. Some rotted boards lay near them, perhaps an old staircase up the steep slope that had deteriorated with age and neglect. She wished it was there now as she reached out toward the first boulder, trying to grasp it in her gloved hands to pull herself up. And as she did, she pushed her boots against the ground, sinking deeper into the snow. She made it onto the first one, on her knees. The snow melted through the denim, chilling her. She climbed the next the same way . . . with her hands and on her knees, and the snow and sea spray soaked through her gloves and her jeans, chilling her skin.

But it was better than trying to stand and falling . . . and maybe leaving herself either knocked out or incapacitated and at the mercy of the animals that had begun to howl louder . . . as if they sensed her vulnerability.

She shivered with fear and with cold. The higher up she got on the hill, the stronger the wind whipped around, almost as if it was trying to push her down. She felt like she was playing king of the hill with Mother Nature and, of course, Edie was losing.

Or so she'd thought . . . until the ground leveled off . . . and she realized she'd made it to the top. She rose from her knees and nearly stumbled back a step as the wind struck her hard, slapping her across the face, freezing her damp clothes against her body. She shivered and rushed forward, toward the lighthouse, stepping into the protection of its long shadow. The limestone tower was tall. Taller than she'd even realized, and she shivered again as she considered having to climb to the top of that. The staircase must have been inside, though, which was where she also wanted to be.

Fortunately, the door was on this side, facing the street. She suspected the other side just dropped off into the sea, and she worried for a moment that if she stepped inside, the whole thing might drop off into the ocean, with her trapped in it. She sucked in a breath as she neared the door.

She'd been concerned that it might be locked or boarded shut. But maybe the lighthouse wasn't as deserted as it looked . . . because the door opened easily, on hinges that creaked more softly than that metal bridge encircling the lantern room was creaking all those feet over her head.

She felt almost as if she needed to duck down, as if the thing was about to drop on her at any moment. So she quickly crossed the threshold into the relative shelter of that limestone structure.

Once she stepped inside, the door slammed shut behind her. It must have been from a gust of wind, but she felt for a moment like someone had purposely closed her inside. She even listened for the sound of a lock, for the telltale sign that she was trapped, but she heard only the wind and those other howls.

The animals. They hadn't given up on her yet. They would be out there, waiting. . . .

Or maybe they would be on the other end of the tunnel, wherever it ended on the grounds of Halcyon Hall. Sam Howell had told her how to get into the tunnel, but he hadn't told her how to get out . . . how to find the way onto the property. Or did it open into a building?

She should have asked him more questions, but she'd been surprised that he'd given her this much. A way inside . . .

Or so she hoped.

Maybe it was a setup, though, some sick joke. Maybe there was no tunnel at all. She pulled the big flashlight from her backpack and bounced its beam around the inside of the limestone tower. A spiral stairwell hugged the inside of the stone walls, leading up, while from those broken windows up above snow fluttered down onto the drifts that had already accumulated on the floor. Where were the stairs leading down . . . if there were any?

Because the lighthouse was already high on this hill, it would have to be a steep staircase down to be beneath the grounds of the hall, beneath the wall that encircled it.

She bounced that beam of light around the area again. Where the hell was it? She trudged around the floor, kicking through the drift, and was surprised that it was wood beneath the snow and not stone. So maybe the floor was suspended over something.

She shined the light across the floor then, and noticed a depression in the snow, as if it was melting away in just one area, or perhaps filtering through something. She kicked her boot back and forth until she cleared that small, depressed area, and the flashlight glinted off the hinges of a trap-door. She drew in a deep breath of salty, moldy air before she crouched down and looked for the handle to pull open the door. It was just a small, rusted ring, but like the outside door, when she pulled on it, it opened easily.

The lighthouse, and this trapdoor to whatever was below it, hadn't been here unused all the years since the manor shut down. Someone had been using them.

She doubted it had been the former sheriff; he looked so frail, it was doubtful he could even get out of his hospital bed without help. So who?

And would they be using them anytime soon . . . like while she was using them? She shivered again and nibbled at her lip for a moment before finally peering inside that trap-door. Her light bounced off a long ladder . . . one that seemingly dropped down into a black hole so deep that she couldn't see the bottom. But surely it had to end in the tunnel . . . or in the sea?

"Only one way to find out . . ." she murmured. And because she knew she was going to need two hands on that rickety ladder, she put the flashlight back into her pack. Then she stepped onto the first rung and started down . . . into what felt like oblivion. There was no light, nothing to guide her way. She had to feel for each rung with her boot . . . taking one at a time until finally her feet struck something harder than those spongy wooden boards.

Her heart racing, she reached for the flashlight again, pulling it out and flipping it on to send the beam bouncing around the rock walls that the tunnel must have been blasted through a long time ago.

The air was even thicker with mold and saltwater smell down here, and something worse . . . like something dead. Maybe those animals she'd heard brought their kills inside here . . . using it like a refrigerator or a lair. Her breath formed white clouds in the light bouncing off the walls from her flashlight. The tunnel only led one way . . . in the direction that the manor had to be.

If Sam Howell hadn't lied to her . . .

So she started off, ignoring the scurrying sounds of critters concealed in the shadows. She willed them to stay there, to let her pass. And she hurried down that tunnel, feeling claustrophobic at the closeness of the stone walls on either side of her. It seemed to stretch forever until it finally opened to a larger area. Old crates were piled inside the space, but when she shone her flashlight on them, she noticed only shards of glass from bottles broken long ago. This must have been the shipments during Prohibition.

And those deliveries might have been made to other parts of the island, because more tunnels opened off this room. She had no clue where they led, but if she wanted out—and she sure as hell wanted out—she had to go back up . . . so she looked for the one with an incline. And she chose that one.

As she walked along it, light crept in from somewhere, and snow swirled into it. She was nearing the end, and then, finally, she was stepping out into the relative light of a steep ravine. The tunnel had emptied out into it. While it was strewn with boulders, there was also dirt beneath the snow and trees that she could wrap her arms around, that she

could use to pull herself up, out of the snow, so it was easier
to climb to the top than it had been to get to the lighthouse.
And as she reached the level ground above the ravine, she
could see beyond those trees to the building in the distance.
It looked big and made of stone, reminding her of a castle.
Or a prison. Or the hall . . .

She had found her way inside the grounds. Now how
would she get inside that building?

And was that where the old man was? Or was James
Bainesworth in one of the other structures? She saw them
in the distance, too, smoke rising from chimneys of small
stone cottages. The hall was more of a compound than one
building. So where was James Bainesworth? And, more im-
portantly, where were the records she sought?

She started toward the hall, figuring that was where she
would find the others, even if she wasn't certain she wanted
to be found yet. And as she walked, she realized the size of
the building had fooled her into thinking it was closer than
it was.

Her skin chilled even more beneath her damp clothes
until she felt numb but for the pounding of her heart and the
strain of her lungs trying to breathe in the frigid air. The snow
was deep, sucking her boots down, so that she struggled to
lift them again, to walk forward.

Maybe she needed the services of the spa herself—of
the fitness part—because she felt grossly out of shape all of
a sudden. And exhausted . . .

So that when big arms closed around her, she didn't have
the strength to fight. And when she opened her mouth to
scream, a big, gloved hand closed over it and her nose,
cutting off her breath.

Had this been a trap?

Had the former sheriff led her to her death?

Chapter Nine

"I'm sorry to disturb you, Dr. Cooke, but you'd instructed us to be extra-vigilant," the security guard said as Elijah joined him in the small room that was crowded with the monitors for all the cameras set up at the gates, around the hall, and on the grounds. "I noticed something on those new cameras that were installed recently near the ravine."

Where the sheriff had found that body when searching the grounds for Genevieve. And because of the condition of the young woman, they'd had to wait for DNA confirmation before they'd known whether or not it was Rosemary's missing daughter. So Elijah had wished that he'd had more cameras on the grounds then and had forced his former head of security to install some additional ones. His cousin Warren hadn't wanted to have that extra surveillance and hadn't been good at making sure the guards regularly checked the footage from those cameras.

"Thanks, Bruce," Elijah told him. "I appreciate your diligence." And he would probably be promoting him to the position of head of Halcyon Hall security because Warren had vacated that position when his brother, David, had murdered him.

He swallowed a sigh at all the losses the hall had suffered. They could not lose anyone else.

"See," Bruce said as he pointed to the screen. "A person climbs up and out of the ravine, but I don't know where they came from. . . ." He gestured toward the other monitors. "I rolled all the footage back at the gates and at the back of this building . . . and nothing . . . so who is it?"

Bundled up in a parka, with the hood tight around her face, it should have been impossible to identify her, but somehow Elijah just knew . . .

It had to be Edie.

"Then, whoever they are, they just disappear behind these trees. . . ." Bruce motioned toward where the shadow fell behind some snow-laden pines, but then another, bigger shadow loomed over that one, merging the two shadows into one.

"Someone grabbed her!"

"I can't tell for sure what happened," Bruce said. "No other cameras picked up any motion after that."

So whoever had grabbed Edie knew where the other cameras were and how to avoid them. Panic gripped him, squeezing the breath from his lungs so that his chest ached. "We've got to find her!"

And not like Deacon had found Erika in that very same ravine Edie had climbed up from. Had that person been chasing her? The same person who might have chased Erika?

"We will," Bruce said.

But he hadn't been at the hall yet when Erika disappeared, when she'd been found. He was one of the additional guards Elijah had hired after he'd found out Olivia had had a stalker, so Bruce didn't know how long Erika had been missing before her body had turned up. And, like Elijah, he couldn't know what had been happening to her when she'd been gone.

Bruce gestured toward the monitors as all the cameras now displayed live footage. "I have guards out there, searching, so I'll let you know if anyone finds them."

"I'm going to stay here," Elijah said, "until we do." But already he could feel the walls of the small room closing in on him as fear made him edgy. "Or I'll go out searching myself . . ."

"I would advise against that, Dr. Cooke. It's getting really cold out there," the security guard said. "I hated to send my team out, but I think—whoever it is—must be an intruder since there's no footage of them coming out of the hall or any of the other buildings. They might be a reporter."

"I'm pretty sure it's a reporter," Elijah said.

"I expect there will be more of them showing up on the island once the weather clears a bit. Perhaps we should put out a statement that the pop singer is no longer staying at the hall."

A photo of Olivia on the grounds had been published—thanks to the former head of security, Elijah's cousin Warren. So Bruce was right that more reporters would be flocking to the island soon. But right now . . .

"If that's the reporter I think it is, she isn't interested in any of our guests," Elijah said. And for that reason, he should have agreed to let her come to the hall for their meeting.

Because now that she'd snuck onto the property, he had no idea where she was and if she was safe . . .

Edie was not okay. She was terrified. Pinned with her back against the giant of a man who half carried, half dragged her through the snow, she couldn't reach into her backpack and pull out anything to defend herself. Like the heavy flashlight. Or her cell phone . . .

If she was going to grab anything out of her pack, she had to get away from him, and right now she could barely move. He'd pinned her arms against her sides, locked under his, and he had one hand clamped across her mouth, so she couldn't scream. She could barely breathe.

He carried her along with him, her feet dragging through the snow for what seemed like a long distance to her. He wasn't heading toward the hall but away from it.

This wasn't a security guard. Who the hell had grabbed her? And what did he want with her?

She wriggled and kicked out with her heavy boots, but if the rubber soles connected with his legs, he betrayed no pain, no discomfort. He was barely breathing hard as he trudged through the snow with her. He kept close to the trees, in the shelter of the pine boughs. Probably so nobody would see them.

So nobody could help her.

She had to get away before he dragged her any farther from the hall. At least he hadn't brought her back into the tunnels.

She would have had no escape down there, no way to get away from him quickly. If she could . . .

She kicked out again and struggled, jabbing out with her elbows. And finally he grunted as she connected an elbow with his ribs. But instead of releasing her, his arms tightened, making it even harder for her to breathe with the pressure on her lungs.

The fear gripping her.

Then he stepped out from beneath the pine boughs into the dark shadow of a garage, or maybe it was a house. What might have once been garage doors were now double doors, and the man pushed through them into an open living space. But he didn't stop there; he headed toward the stairwell that led up to the second floor.

And finally his hand slipped from her mouth. She drew in a deep breath and then she screamed as loud as she could. The sound hurt her own ears, had her flinching at the volume of it, had her throat burning from the strain of it. But the man just kept striding up those steps, lifting her in front of him until he deposited her on the second floor and into a room. There was a bed in it and a couple of chairs. One of them had wheels on it and was turned toward the window.

Then it spun back and she stared into a face that was eerily familiar and yet very strange at the same time. His eyes were that arresting pale blue and shone with intelligence like Elijah's, but they were so much colder, like the wind that had sliced through her back at the lighthouse.

And whereas Elijah had a few silver strands in his hair, this man's was all silver and still thick for his age. His body was thick, too, not heavy, but almost as if it was still muscular . . . despite how old he had to be.

"Dr. James Bainesworth," she murmured.

This was where she'd wanted to be, whom she'd wanted to meet, but now that she was here, she felt no victory . . . only the fear that had been coursing through her veins since the other man had grabbed her. He finally released her, shoving her farther into that room . . . with Bainesworth.

She hadn't seen her abductor yet, and maybe she shouldn't. Maybe it was smarter not to look directly at him. Wasn't a kidnapper more willing to let his hostage live if she couldn't identify him?

But yet, because of her instinctively inquisitive nature, she couldn't *not* look at him. The guy was a giant, well over six feet tall and very muscular. His hair was clipped short, and while it was more gray than brown, from the lack of wrinkles in his face, she doubted that he was much older than she was. While she was in her early thirties, he was probably early to late forties. He wore a big coat that he shrugged off his broad shoulders now, revealing a set of dark blue scrubs beneath it.

And her skin chilled with dread. "Who are you? Why did you bring me here?" And the most important question, "What the hell do you intend to do with me?"

Some sick experiment? Was that how that woman had died, the personal trainer? Erika Korlinsky? Had this weirdo in the scrubs tried something on her? She turned back toward the wheelchair. Probably on the orders of this man?

The burly man confirmed as much when he said, "Dr. Bainesworth ordered me to get you and bring you here."

She glanced uneasily at the older man in the wheelchair. "Why?"

"You're a trespasser," Bainesworth replied matter-of-factly.

"What—what makes you think that?" she asked. How the hell could he know? "I could be a guest."

Bainesworth snorted. "Maybe, but you're not. I saw where you came from . . ." He gestured toward the window behind him.

Over his shoulder, she peered through the glass, and she could clearly see the direction from which she'd come . . . the ravine. The tunnel . . .

He knew. That knowledge glittered like the intelligence in his pale blue eyes. And it was almost as if he'd been expecting her. Had the former sheriff warned him?

"So, who are you?" he asked.

But just as she'd seen the knowledge in his eyes of where she'd come from, she could also see that he knew who and what she was. He could have recognized her from the news specials she'd done, or . . .

"You know," she challenged him. But she wasn't about to reveal the identity of who she suspected of being his source any more than she had ever revealed hers. Just in case she was wrong, and he didn't know that Sam Howell had talked to her.

"You're a reporter," he said with another disparaging snort. "If you're here about that pop singer, she's already checked out."

"I know," Edie said. "She's staying where I am."

"The Pierce sisters boardinghouse," he said.

And she shivered. He not only knew who she was but where she was living. Had he had his goon following her around town? Was that who'd stalked her on the street the night before, who'd tried to run her down in the parking lot the night before that?

"So, if you're not here to harass the singer, why are you here, Ms. Stone?" Bainesworth asked.

"To harass you . . ."

The old man grinned as if delighted. "But if that's the case, why were you fighting my nurse?"

She hadn't been able to fight the man; he was too big. Too strong. And she wasn't entirely convinced he was just James Bainesworth's nurse.

"Because people have been dying around here," Edie said. "And he grabbed me without saying a word to me about where he was taking me and why. And with the way he had my mouth covered, I could barely breathe." She turned back to the guy and glared at him.

"Were you rude to our trespasser, Theo?" James asked. "That's so not like you." He made a tsking noise with his tongue before turning his head toward Edie again. "And you,

Ms. Stone—I heard you scream, so you had enough breath and strength to do that. He must not have been too rough with you."

Edie shivered at his tone; he almost sounded as if he was disappointed. Or maybe he was worried that someone had heard her. She hoped like hell that someone had—someone not as creepy as these guys.

"Please, Theo, get Ms. Stone something to drink to warm her up," he said. "What would you like, Ms. Stone? Coffee? Tea? Hot cocoa?"

"I'm fine," she said. And inside now, out of the wind and in the warmth of his home, she actually was getting too hot in her big down parka, so much so that perspiration was beginning to bead on her upper lip.

He noticed, as he seemed to notice everything, and said, "Take off your jacket. I have to keep it warm in here . . . for my old bones, you know."

His bones might have been old, but everything else about him seemed young and sharp and somehow still very intimidating.

"Maybe bring her a cool beverage," James suggested to his nurse, who finally turned and walked out of the room, having to duck to pass beneath the doorframe.

"Is he really human or a robot you've programmed?" she asked the old man.

Bainesworth chuckled. "Jamie calls him Igor."

"Jamie?"

"My grandson," he said, then a grimace of disapproval wrinkled his old face even more than it was. "You probably know him as Bode James. He legally changed his name for some gimmicky, branding thing: Bodies by Bode . . ." He snorted.

She wondered if that was the only reason that Bode had

changed his name, or if he'd gotten sick of being associated with his grandfather. She'd seen firsthand at the diner yesterday with Elijah how hard it was to be a descendant of James Bainesworth.

She replied, "Good gimmick and smart brand. He's built quite a career. Books. DVDs. Streaming channel. Famous clients." She gestured toward the window. "This . . ."

"*This* was already here."

"In ruins," she reminded him. "Shut down for years."

He narrowed those pale eyes as he studied her face. "That's why you're here." It wasn't a question; he definitely knew. From Sam Howell?

"Yes." And she couldn't believe that she'd actually found him. No. He'd found her. From his perch. She could tell the carpet was worn in front of that window. He must have been parked there all the time, watching. . . .

Or orchestrating?

Had he had his nurse following her this entire time? Was that how he'd known exactly when she was going to come up from the tunnel? Because he'd known when she'd gone into it?

Theo might also have been the one who'd tried running her over, so should she stay and talk with Bainesworth? Or should she take this opportunity to try to escape? Of course that giant nurse was downstairs somewhere, and she would have to get past him to get outside. She doubted he would let that happen . . . unless Bainesworth told him it was okay for her to leave.

Would he let her leave?

She studied the old man's wrinkled face. He was old, but she suspected that didn't make him any less formidable than he'd ever been. "Since Theo is Igor, does that make you Dr. Frankenstein?"

Bainesworth chuckled but didn't deny it . . . or anything else.

Yet. But she hadn't asked him any real questions. So that she didn't overheat, she finally loosened the strings of her hood and pushed it back, and she lowered the zipper of her parka a bit.

"Your hair is such a beautiful color," Bainesworth remarked. "You should grow it out. Make the most of it."

He might have just been an old chauvinist who believed that women were more feminine-looking with long hair. But she suspected there might be more to his comment, and despite the warmth of the room and her heavy jacket, she shivered. "If I did that, I'd look like those other women whose bodies turned up here." She shook her head. "No, thanks."

"Other women?" he queried, as if he didn't know . . . as if he didn't know everything.

"The personal trainer," she said. "The sheriff's wife, and that other woman . . . the one the sheriff found here when he was just a boy."

James shook his head. "I don't know what happened then. I'd been pretty much banished from the island at that time, after the manor had shut down. While my wife—my *ex*-wife—stayed in the village to raise our daughters, I rarely returned. She would send the girls to me in Portland when I had visitation."

He should have been in prison for what he'd done, for what he'd continued doing after the illegal lobotomies had been stopped. And the babies . . .

Bonita claimed she hadn't willingly given up her child. Had any of the women?

"You know everything that's been happening around here now," she surmised.

He nodded. "Of course, since my grandsons sought me out and brought me back to the island, I've kept myself apprised of what happens here. But the Cooke boys were responsible for all those bad things."

"Elijah and Bode are Cookes."

He shook his head. "They're Bainesworths—through and through, no matter that they might want to believe otherwise."

"How does that make them any better than Cookes?" she wondered.

"It makes them smarter," he said with a wicked grin.

"And you think you're smarter than all of them," she surmised.

"I am," he said matter-of-factly.

She would have called him arrogant if she didn't believe that it was probably true. He had escaped the prison time he'd deserved. So, she asked him the question she really wanted answered. "Why did you do it?"

He arched a silver brow. "Why did I do what?" he asked. "Try to help people?"

She snorted. "Those young women were abused, and their babies were stolen."

He shook his head. "We were having such success with treating the prisoners we housed here that other people with problems were brought here to be helped as well. Those young women were *treated*, and if they were pregnant and didn't want to keep their babies, we did help find homes for them."

"Where?" she asked. "Where are your records?" She especially wanted to find Bonita's child for her, so the woman would stop searching, so she wouldn't be so lost.

Cutlery clattered, drawing her attention back to the doorway. The nurse ducked down again and stepped inside with them. He carried a tray that he placed on the table in the corner of the room. Then Theo spoke, first clearing his throat before saying, "I brought up coffee and tea and some of those pastries you enjoy, sir."

"Thank you," Bainesworth said. Then he gestured toward the table. "Please, have something, Ms. Stone. You must be thirsty and hungry after your adventure."

He definitely knew exactly where she'd been and how she'd gotten onto the property. That was why he'd been at the window, watching for her even before she'd come up from the ravine. *Had* Sam Howell called to warn him? Maybe the two men had ties yet that even age and poor health hadn't severed.

Or . . .

James Bainesworth might have been keeping tabs on her before that, before she'd visited Sam Howell. He could have had Theo following her for a while. Why? To make sure she didn't find out what he was clearly trying to hide?

His pale eyes twinkled as if he was enjoying this . . . enjoying being one step ahead of her and probably everyone else. That was how he'd escaped punishment all those years ago, while the women who'd stayed at the manor were never able to escape from their trauma.

"What about the records from the manor?" Edie persisted. "Where are they now?"

The tray clattered again as Theo fussed with the cups and plates, laying them out on the tabletop. Was he distracted or trying to distract her?

"Coffee or tea, miss?" he asked.

She shook her head. "Nothing, thank you . . ." She was not about to eat or drink anything these two ghouls served her; she was afraid that she would wind up like that personal trainer had.

Dead in the ravine.

"You don't know what you're missing," James said with another tsking noise with his tongue. He rolled his chair past her to the table, where he picked up one of the pastries. "Theo is a master baker, you know. He makes these cream cheese Danishes himself."

Her stomach betrayed her with a slight rumble. She was hungry, but she wasn't stupid. Careless sometimes . . . but never stupid. "I'm not interested in food," she said. "I'm looking for answers."

He sighed wearily, as if she'd bored or disappointed him. "The manor shut down nearly fifty years ago, Ms. Stone. What the authorities did with those records after that I couldn't tell you. . . ."

She narrowed her eyes. "If the authorities actually had those records, wouldn't charges have been brought against you?"

"For what?" he asked. "For legal private adoptions? The mothers all signed off on them. And as for the treatments, those were at the request of the courts for the prisoners who'd been committed here instead of prison due to their mental incapacities. And as for the girls who were sent here, either their parents or the patients themselves requested their treatments. People want to get well, Ms. Stone. That's why there is a market for this business my grandsons started. People want to look good and they want to feel good."

"Many of those girls weren't here willingly," she reminded him. "They were committed here."

"As I said, their parents signed off on treatment."

"What about the girls who were never seen again?" she asked. "The ones who disappeared?"

He shrugged. "Back then security was focused on keeping the prisoners locked up. Not the patients whose families had brought them here. Some of them, unfortunately, ran away."

"What about the ones who committed suicide?"

He sighed again, a heavy, regretful-sounding sigh. "We can't save everyone, Ms. Stone. Surely you know that?"

Her skin chilled even beneath her heavy coat. He knew *everything* about her. Not that her past was some big secret . . . *anymore* . . . just for those first ten years of her life, and it had been more of a secret kept from her than from anyone else during that time. She hadn't realized until after her mother was arrested that she hadn't been her mother. And Edie hadn't been able to keep her from being sent to prison for kidnapping or from taking her own life over losing the child she'd considered hers after carrying her for nine months and caring for her for ten years.

Elijah had found out the truth about her. Had he shared that information with his grandfather? Or had James Bainesworth done his own research? She glanced around the room but didn't see a computer. That didn't mean that he didn't have one somewhere else in the house.

When she turned toward the doorway, she tensed and sucked in a breath of surprise at the sight of the man standing there. It wasn't the nurse; he stood by the table in the corner of the room.

"Elijah can tell you that you can't save everyone," James said. He was already focused on the doorway where his grandson was standing; he had probably known the minute that Elijah had stepped into the house . . . the way he seemed to know everything. "He couldn't save everyone either."

A muscle twitched along Elijah's obviously tightly clenched jaw. He shook his head and murmured, "If you're talking about the sheriff's wife, Shannon Howell didn't kill herself. David Cooke did."

But Edie realized he'd blamed himself, blamed his inability to save her from her death. And even though she hadn't committed suicide, he acted as if he still blamed himself, his broad shoulders sagging slightly with the burden of the responsibility he seemed to carry.

"Are *you* all right?" he asked her, his voice gruff with concern. Had she become an additional burden to him?

She nodded.

"One of the security guards reported hearing a scream out this way . . ." he murmured.

She could imagine what Elijah must have thought, how he must have worried . . . that someone else was being hurt like so many other women had been hurt here.

"I'm fine," she assured him. But she wondered if she would have stayed that way if Elijah hadn't shown up when he had. What was his grandfather still capable of doing?

Because she knew what he'd done in his past . . .

And no matter how he'd tried to justify it, she thought he'd enjoyed mistreating those young women, and the prisoners, too.

And would he have mistreated her . . . if his grandson hadn't arrived?

Elijah crossed the room to grasp her arm and tug her toward the doorway. "You need to get out of here," he said, as if warning her. It was clear that he didn't trust his grandfather either. He glanced at the nurse, too, as if assessing the threat the man posed.

From how easily he'd overpowered and carried her, Edie considered Theo a big threat. And not just to her . . .

Would he let them leave?

He shouldn't have let them leave—not so soon. Not before James had had a chance to talk to her more, to find out how determined she was to learn the truth, to assess just how big a threat she was.

Once he heard the door close downstairs, he turned back to Theo. "Follow them. Find out what she already knows."

"Mr. Bainesworth . . ."

Despite his size, Theo wasn't very brave. But then, he wasn't scared of a physical threat. He was afraid of himself . . . of what he might be forced to do to protect the secrets. . . .

Chapter Ten

Elijah wanted to be furious with Edie . . . for so many reasons. But she looked so shaken and, once they stepped outside the carriage house, so very cold.

He was, too, with the wind whipping snow against his suit jacket and wool pants. He hadn't bothered to grab a coat, not when the security guard had gotten the call with the report of a scream being heard on this part of the property while they'd been searching for the intruder. Just as he'd known she was that intruder, he'd known she was the one who'd screamed, and he'd known exactly where she was. "Are you really all right?"

She nodded, and her teeth chattered a bit.

He opened the passenger door of his SUV for her. "Get in before you freeze."

He'd left it running when he'd pulled into the driveway and rushed inside the carriage house. He could have sent one of the security guards to investigate, but the man who'd heard the scream had returned to the hall when he hadn't been able to pinpoint where it had come from.

Elijah had had no doubt about where she was and with whom, so he'd taken off before anyone could join him. Or stop him . . .

Not that they would have tried. His new team seemed to respect him more than his cousin had. If only his grandfather would respect him as much . . .

He suspected that to James Bainesworth, he would always be the small boy who'd cried and cowered from *Grandfather* when his mother had forced Elijah to come along to Portland on a visit to her father.

Theo didn't seem to respect Elijah any more than James did. The man acted like his grandfather's guard dog, or perhaps his henchman. Elijah suspected the burly nurse would do whatever his employer told him to do. Like stop them . . .

Elijah hurried around the front of the SUV, jerked open the driver's side door, and slid onto the seat. Then he closed the door, shutting out the cold and, with the automatic lock when he shifted the SUV into reverse, shutting out any threat.

Or so he thought, until Edie reached across the console and pressed her warm fingers against his cheek. His pulse quickened as his skin began to tingle. Though maybe that was just because he was so cold.

"You're freezing," she said. "You're not even wearing a jacket. But then, it seems you rarely do. . . ."

"I rarely leave the hall," he admitted with a heavy sigh. And when he had to, he did it in a hurry, like the night David took Olivia and Holly. And now . . . after hearing about the scream . . .

"Are you taking me there now?" she asked, her lips curving into a hopeful smile.

He shook his head.

"So what? You're going to dump me off at the gates?" she asked. "Leave me to walk back to town in the snow?"

He glanced through the windshield, but he could barely see beyond the hood of the SUV with how heavily the snow had begun to fall. "Aren't you parked on the street outside the gates?" he asked. "What did you do? Scale the wall or use Holly's employee badge to get inside the back gate?"

Her eyes widened with surprise, and he chuckled. "You didn't think of that, huh?"

She shrugged. "Deacon's probably burned it by now so that she can never return."

"I don't blame him if he has," Elijah admitted. "She should never come back here."

"Would your guests understand your saying that?"

"After what happened to her mother here, after what nearly happened to her, yeah, I think they would understand."

"Is that going in your press release?" she asked, her green eyes bright with her teasing.

She was so beautiful . . . and so aggravating.

"I thought you weren't the fucking AP," he reminded her.

And she laughed. "You seem so prim and proper, Dr. Cooke, but there are hidden depths to you."

He sighed. "God, I hope not."

She laughed again. As much as he wouldn't have minded getting trapped inside the SUV with her, he didn't want to be right outside his grandfather's house. So he put the vehicle into Drive and, with the wipers fighting the falling snow, he drove to the hall.

"So, you're not dumping me at the gates," she mused as he stopped in the employee parking lot.

If he escorted her through the back way, hopefully none of the guests would see and recognize her. "I'm bringing you inside to warm up," he said. "No pestering the guests for interviews."

"I don't want to interview your guests," she said.

He heard the sincerity and believed her. "No, you just

interviewed the man you wanted to," he surmised. "Was he everything you'd thought he would be?"

She shivered and he hadn't even opened the doors yet. "He was . . ."

He nodded and acknowledged, "He has that effect on people."

"Even you?"

"Maybe most especially me," Elijah admitted.

"But you and your brother went into business with him," she said.

He tensed. "How do you know that?"

"You don't think I checked out the ownership of the hall, the tax filings? The names on the corporation paperwork?"

He sighed. "Of course you did." But instead of answering her question, he pushed open the driver's side door of the SUV. The snow was falling hard, so hard that the streetlamps in the parking lot barely illuminated the area darkened by the thickness of the clouds and the sheets of snow. He rushed around the front to her side, but she'd already opened the door.

"It's really bad," she murmured.

So bad that he put his arm around her and steered her toward that back entrance. The door opened as if the guard had been watching for his return. But it wasn't one of the guards who stepped out; it was the psychiatrist, Dr. Gordon Chase.

"Elijah, what are you doing out in this?" he asked. "Without a jacket . . ." He turned his attention to Edie then and arched a bushy gray brow. "I'm sorry. I don't think we've met."

She gave Elijah the side-eye, which he found entirely too sexy. "May I speak to him?" she asked.

"Dr. Chase isn't a guest," he said, and a smile twitched up his lips with amusement that she'd actually heeded his warning about that. "So yes, you may speak to him. Dr. Chase, this is Edie Stone."

Dr. Chase let out a chuckle of delight. "Oh, that's wonderful. You're the reporter who has everyone on edge around here."

She arched a blond brow. "And why would that be . . . unless people have something to hide?"

He laughed again. "Everybody has something to hide, Ms. Stone. I'm certain even you."

She hadn't tried to hide it; Elijah had easily found out things about her past, things she'd revealed in interviews. Maybe she'd only made the admissions in order to gain the trust of the subject she was interviewing, but she'd made herself as vulnerable as the people she'd interviewed. And today, sneaking onto the grounds, she'd made herself even more vulnerable.

Chase turned to Elijah. "I'm surprised you're letting her into the hall. Ms. Plasky is not going to like this at all. . . ."

"Ms. Stone somehow got herself onto the grounds and into the carriage house with Grandfather," he shared.

"Ohhh . . . you are resourceful," the psychiatrist praised her.

She smiled and nodded. "Yes, and now I'm freezing." She moved to step around the man and into the hall.

Dr. Chase chuckled again and met Elijah's gaze. "And now I understand why you're not as cold as you should be."

Elijah furrowed his brow at the psychiatrist's cryptic remark. Did he think Edie Stone had Elijah hot and bothered? He wasn't some hormonal teenager struck dumb over the pretty girl. Hell, he'd never been that hormonal teenager; he'd thought Deacon and David had been idiots for not seeing how Shannon had manipulated them into fighting over her.

He'd never understood that kind of emotion . . . that kind

of passion. But Edie Stone did bring out feelings in him he'd not experienced before . . . infuriation . . .

And intrigue . . .

And that made her very dangerous to him, especially now, when he had to focus on saving the hall and his brother. "Did you get ahold of that lawyer you mentioned?" Elijah asked.

Chase nodded. "Yes. Mitchell is going to check his schedule, and this weather . . ." The guy hunched his shoulders and shivered. "And he'll let me know when he can get out here."

"I'm glad you realized that he needs to come here," Elijah said.

"I know you won't leave this place," Chase said. "Not now . . . not with everything that's happened around here."

That feeling he'd had while waiting in that tiny security room came over him again, that sensation of being trapped. He was stuck here at the hall. Even just the two hours he'd been away yesterday, when he'd talked to the trooper and Edie, had had things piled up on his desk.

He couldn't deal with Edie now.

"Did Rosemary leave yet?" he asked Gordon. If she hadn't, she could take Edie back to the boardinghouse with her.

Gordon nodded. "Yes, she heard the weather was getting bad and wanted to leave before the roads got any worse. Fortunately, I don't have as far to go." Like Bode, the psychiatrist lived in one of the stone cottages on the property.

"But still . . ." Elijah said as he stepped around the older man, ". . . drive safely."

"You stay safe, too," Gordon advised with a pointed glance in the direction Edie had gone. The man was perceptive; he had obviously discerned that Elijah was in over his head with the reporter. Then the psychiatrist turned away, ducked his head into the collar of his jacket, and faced the snow the wind hurled at him as he headed out to the parking lot.

Elijah had to use his body to help close the door against the force of that wind. Then he turned around to find Edie already walking down the corridor, as if she knew where she was going or maybe she was just trying to get away from him.

Before she got too far away, the security guard who had brought her intrusion to Elijah's attention stepped outside his office and blocked her way. "You found her," he spoke over her head to Elijah. "She was the one Mike heard screaming?"

"*She* is right here," Edie pointed out. "And I was fine."

Elijah narrowed his eyes and stared at her skeptically. "I found her in the carriage house," he told the guard. "With my grandfather."

Despite how new a hire the man was, he must have heard about James Bainesworth because he shuddered.

"I was fine," she repeated. "And I can speak."

Even when she wasn't around, she still held a piece of his attention, but now he turned all of it on her. "So then, tell us how you got on the grounds," he challenged her. And with his hand on the small of her back, he guided her into the security room with all the monitors. "Bruce, pull up that footage you showed me."

The security guard grinned as he joined them in the small space. He had to step around them to get to the controls, which had Edie moving back . . . against Elijah. He felt trapped again . . . but under the weight of the attraction he felt for her as much as the close confines of the room.

Bruce pressed some buttons and played back the video of her climbing out of the ravine. "Here it is. . . ."

"That's the first time the cameras picked you up," Elijah said. "So, how did you get into the ravine? Did you climb over the wall somewhere? Did you come up one of the cliffs from the ocean?"

She shrugged. "I don't know. I was just out for a walk and somehow stumbled onto the property."

Elijah snorted. "A walk? In the middle of a blizzard?"

"It wasn't that bad when I started out," she said.

He sighed. "That's about the only thing I believe that you've told me."

"Do you want me to call the sheriff, Dr. Cooke?" Bruce asked.

"Please, call Deacon," she challenged the security guard. "He can give me a ride back to my Jeep or home since we live together now."

Bruce was so professional that his eyes barely widened in surprise before he turned to Elijah, who was already addressing Edie's bold claim. "You were trespassing," he reminded her. "Deacon will have to arrest you if we choose to press charges."

She shrugged as if she was unconcerned, but there was a stiffness to her body that betrayed her nerves. She probably wasn't as worried about Deacon arresting her as she was about him lecturing her for risking her life coming to the hall and talking to his grandfather.

And until Erika's killer was found, it was a risk. The only thing Elijah believed for certain was that his brother was innocent. Now, after David's duplicity, he had no idea who was guilty.

"I could call the state police instead," Bruce said. And he pulled a card from his pocket. "I have Sergeant Montgomery's direct line."

Elijah tensed now, and he wanted to ask how Bruce had obtained that card. When had the trooper given it to him? And what was he supposed to report to her about?

Bruce hadn't been hired until after Erika's body had already been found, so he had no information to give her. And because the sergeant's mind was so made up that Bode was guilty, Elijah did not want her any more apprised of what happened at the hall than she already was.

"I'll deal with Ms. Stone personally," Elijah said, and he took her by the elbow and escorted her out of the security room, closing the door behind him so that they were alone in the hallway.

"Am I supposed to be afraid now?" she asked him with a slight smile curving up the corners of her sexy mouth.

His stomach muscles tightened with dread that someone might fear him for any reason. "I hope you're not."

Her smile widened, and she assured him, "You don't scare me, Dr. Cooke."

"You scare me," he admitted.

She arched her blond brows over the green eyes that glittered with mischief as she teased him. "Why? Are you afraid I'm going to learn all your secrets?"

He shook his head. "I'm afraid that you're going to learn that I have none."

"You heard Dr. Chase . . . everybody has something to hide," she reminded him.

"Even you?"

She shrugged. "I'm not hiding anything. I just don't always choose to bring it up."

"Exactly," he said.

"So you're saying you and I have something in common?"

He studied her face for a moment before nodding in acknowledgment. "Yes, I think we do." And maybe because of that, he could trust that she wouldn't harass his guests if he allowed her into the hall. After all, none of them could help her find out more about Bainesworth Manor; few of them were from the area and had even heard of its history . . . except for Morgana.

So maybe he could trust Edie to be inside the hall. But he wasn't going to trust her with anything else, anything like his heart, though that was something most people probably doubted he possessed. Just like they doubted his grandfather had one, or a soul.

Even though Elijah just stood silently in front of the door to the security room, Edie braced herself for him to whisk her back out the employee entrance to his SUV. So she zipped up her jacket and reached for her hood, knowing that he'd probably only brought her inside to show her the security footage and get her to explain how she'd gained access to the property.

A twinge of guilt struck her that she hadn't told him about the tunnel. But if she did, she was certain he would block it off and she wouldn't be able to use it again. She wanted to go back down there, wanted to explore the other tunnels off that main room, and wanted to see if she'd missed anything, like those records that James Bainesworth had claimed the state confiscated. She doubted that any authority had had access to those records or Bainesworth would have probably been in prison if he'd done even half the things he was rumored to have done. No, more than likely he'd hidden those records somewhere nobody would think to look . . . like those tunnels.

She wanted to go explore them more, but she was as reluctant to leave Elijah as he seemed to be to let her go. She couldn't imagine that he had any intention of letting her any farther inside the hall, not after telling her so many times that it wasn't possible because he couldn't risk the privacy of his guests. But he just stared at her with those pale blue eyes, as if he was considering asking her something, and her pulse quickened in anticipation and excitement.

As eager as she was to explore the tunnels some more, she didn't want to leave yet. She didn't want to leave *him* yet. "Not sure what to do with me?" she teased. "Are you reconsidering reporting me for trespassing?"

"I'm reconsidering something," he murmured. But before he had the chance to say any more, the door behind him opened and the burly security guard nearly collided with him.

"Dr. Cooke," he said, "I was just going to see if I could catch you. . . ."

"Why, Bruce?" Elijah asked.

"I just saw something else on the cameras," he replied.

"Near the ravine?"

The man shook his head. "No. I detected movement on the cameras close to the hall. And with the weather as nasty as it is, I can't believe a guest would be out walking around in this. There are weather advisories against going outside at all right now in these conditions."

Maybe that was why Elijah hadn't pushed her out the door already.

Elijah glanced at her. "Were you alone, or did you bring anyone trespassing with you?"

"I wished I had when Igor grabbed me," she said. "But I always work alone." Which was why she freelanced. She could always find someone to buy her stories when she had them ready. But she preferred to cover what she wanted to cover—not what someone wanted her to, from the perspective they wanted to show.

"I don't believe it's an intruder like Ms. Stone," Bruce persisted. "I went over all the footage too many times to have missed anyone else coming onto the property. It has to be a guest or an employee, and I'm worried they could freeze to death. I'm going to send out some guards to find them."

Elijah began, "I could—"

"No," Edie protested, reaching out to grab his arm. "You can't go out looking for them like you did me. You're still cold from being out earlier with no jacket."

His eyes widened as if her concern had surprised him, and then he smiled. "I'm not going out there. I'm going to do an informal roll call—make sure we know where everyone is. Dr. Chase just left, and he said Rosemary left earlier."

The guard nodded. "I saw her drive out the gates. I can tell you who's left and . . ." He glanced at Edie. "Should we discuss this in front of a reporter?"

"You think I'm going to report that you have people coming and going freely on the property?" she asked. "And that you're concerned about the welfare and the privacy of your guests?" She nodded. "Yes, I can see where that might be quite damaging. . . ."

Elijah chuckled. "And we all know you wouldn't report anything as boring as that," he said. Then his smile slid away. "But I need to make sure that no guests or employees are in danger. . . ."

"Then don't let me stop you," she said, and motioned for him to step back into the security room.

He hesitated for a moment.

"You don't want me in there again with all those cameras," she surmised. "It's okay. I can wait for you. . . ." But she wasn't sure what she was waiting for . . . for him to bring her back to the boardinghouse or . . .

He was pulling his cell phone from his pocket. "I'm going to check on Bode," he said with obvious concern for his brother. "If anyone's out running around the property in this weather, it would more than likely be him. Bruce, would you please bring Ms. Stone to the conservatory, where she can wait comfortably while I handle this?"

The guard nodded. "Of course, and fortunately it is currently unoccupied."

Elijah seemed less concerned about that than his employee was. Maybe he was beginning to believe that she posed no threat to the privacy of his guests. "Thanks, Bruce," he told him, "And please send in a server to bring her something to drink."

Bruce nodded again.

"What about you?" Edie asked Elijah. "You must be freezing."

"Please order a cup of coffee for me," he said. "Hopefully I'll be there soon." He headed back into the security room with the cell phone pressed against his ear.

And Edie dutifully followed the guard.

"There are cameras in the public rooms," the guard said. "So if you harass any of the guests—"

"You'll what? Call Sergeant Montgomery?" she asked. "Why do you have her direct line?" She'd noticed how Elijah's lean body had tensed when the guy had admitted to having her card.

The guard's big body tensed now. "I'm not going to answer any of your questions, Ms. Stone." He turned his back on her then and continued down the hall from the back until it widened into what must have been the areas open to the public because the walls here were covered with polished mahogany wainscotting, and an Oriental runner covered the marble-tiled floor. He stopped in the hall and gestured toward a doorway, ushering her inside a big room made entirely of glass.

She chuckled. "I'd better not throw any stones in here,

huh?" she murmured, but when she turned around, the guard was already gone. For a big man, he moved quietly . . . like James Bainesworth's muscular nurse. Did Halcyon Hall only employ physically fit people?

Obviously they hadn't done as well checking their mental fitness for the jobs. Not after the groundskeeper had abducted Rosemary's daughter . . .

Which gave the security guard more reason to be vigilant about his job, but Edie really posed no threat to anyone but perhaps James Bainesworth, and that was only if she could find those records and any evidence of his crimes.

She doubted they were anywhere inside the hall; it had been deserted for so long before its extensive renovations. Either the weather would have ruined them or the construction. She uttered a heavy sigh and walked farther into the room.

With all the glass and the snow falling so heavily outside that glass, it should have been cold and dark inside the space, but it had a warmth and a glow to it . . . maybe because of all the plants. Some were as tall as trees, and vibrant greens with bright blossoms. From behind one of them stepped out a woman.

And Edie emitted a small gasp of surprise. "I didn't realize anyone was in here," she said.

And neither had Bruce, because he'd said the room was unoccupied. Maybe he wasn't as good at watching those monitors as he seemed to be.

"We're all here . . ." the older woman murmured, and she gazed around her with brown eyes that had that blur to them that Bonita's had, as if they weren't entirely focused on anything.

Was she talking about the plants? Because Edie looked around again and saw nothing but them and some tables and chairs. Her gaze kept returning to the woman, though, who was much more colorful than anything else in the room. She had bright red hair and rouge nearly the same color, smeared across her cheeks. The rest of her face looked red, too, as if she'd been outside, or maybe she was flushed with excitement. Her body, slightly bowed with age, was also trembling. With cold or that excitement?

"Who else is here?" Edie asked, and she looked beyond the woman to the windows, but all she could see was the snow, falling so heavily that nothing beyond it was visible.

"You can't see them?" the woman asked.

Edie shook her head. "No . . ."

"Can you hear them?" she asked.

Edie cocked her head and made a show of listening. All she heard was the howl of the wind hurling the snow against all the glass. The room seemed to shudder with the force of the storm. She shook her head. "No . . ."

The older woman sighed with disappointment before murmuring, "I think Dr. Cooke can hear them."

"Who?" Edie asked again. "Who does he hear?"

"The girls . . ." the woman murmured. "He hears the girls. They're crying. Sometimes they're screaming. . . ."

Edie shuddered now, like the walls of glass.

"Dr. Cooke rushed out of the little office when the last one was screaming. . . ."

Edie nodded with sudden understanding. "Oh . . ." This woman might have been standing outside the security room when the guards reported hearing her scream. "I think that was me. . . ."

The woman approached Edie until she stood just a foot away. Her dark eyes were very direct now and intensely focused on Edie's face. Then she reached out and touched her hair and nodded.

And Edie suppressed the urge to shudder again because it reminded her so much of how James Bainesworth had treated her.

"Did he hurt you?" the woman asked. "Like he hurt the others?"

Despite the warmth of her parka and the room, a chill raced down Edie's spine, and she couldn't suppress the shiver that raised goose bumps on her skin that had moments before been clammy with perspiration. "Who?" she asked. "Who hurt them?"

The woman shook her head, as if reluctant or afraid to answer.

"Did he hurt you?" Edie asked, and she intently studied the woman now. There were many wrinkles in her face; she was probably even older than Bonita Pierce. So she definitely could have been here when it was Bainesworth Manor. Or maybe she'd been hurt more recently, like Erika Korlinsky had been.

The woman shook her head. "No. I was a good girl."

And Edie nearly shivered again . . . this time with excitement. Here was a source—one she suspected would be honest with her, unlike James Bainesworth, who was too smart to be honest.

But before Edie could ask her anything, the woman nearly shoved her aside before rushing to the doorway. "What—where are you . . ."

The woman stopped in front of a man. It wasn't the guard returning with a server. Elijah was the one standing in the doorway. Maybe he'd learned it was his brother running around outside. Or maybe he'd rethought leaving her alone, especially if he and the guard had noticed, on one of those many monitors, that she wasn't alone; she was with a guest.

Who was this guest?

"Did you find her?" she asked Elijah.

He just stared blankly at the woman, so Edie answered for him, reminding her, "It was me. I was the one he heard screaming. . . ."

The woman glanced back at her with a dismissive shake of her head. "Not you. You're alive." She turned back to Elijah then and stared as intently at him as she had Edie a short while ago. "Dr. Cooke hears the dead, like I hear do. . . ." She reached out then and clasped his hands in hers. "We have to help them, Dr. Cooke. We have to help them cross to the other side. . . ."

Elijah was tense, his face tight with concern . . . for this woman. He nodded. "Yes, Morgana . . ."

She released a shaky little sigh then. "I'm glad. I didn't know . . . I thought you might be like *him* . . . that you might not care. But you care . . ."

"Yes," Elijah assured her. "I care."

"That's why you came back to Bane Island," the older woman said. "That's why you brought back the manor. You knew there was too much left undone. . . ."

Elijah shivered. But then, he'd probably never warmed up since he'd gone out without a coat, when he'd learned about Edie's scream. He would have been too far away to hear it. But did he hear the things that Morgana claimed he did?

Did he hear the dead?

Chapter Eleven

Elijah never knew how to answer Morgana when she made her claims of being a medium. He didn't want to dismiss her beliefs, but he didn't want to encourage her delusions either. But with Edie watching them, he was even more at a loss for how to deal with the older woman. And maybe she was getting to him with all her talk of ghosts. . . .

Because that must have been what Bruce had seen on the monitor.

Elijah had looked at the footage, too, but he wasn't sure what the man had seen had been human. So he wasn't concerned that a guest or an employee had been foolish enough to venture out into the storm.

The one he would have been most concerned about stood in front of him now, staring up at him with an expectant look on her face. Morgana's skin was so red; he couldn't tell if it was chafed from the cold. Had she been outside? Was it her image that had been so blurred with the snow falling heavily across the camera lens that Bruce had glimpsed on the monitor?

"Were you outside?" he asked her.

She shook her head. "No . . . they're here . . . they're with us now. Can't you see them?" And her grasp on his hands tightened. Her skin was cold, so very cold.

"Morgana . . ." he began.

Before he could finish, she must have discerned what he was going to say because disappointment flashed in her eyes. Then she released her grasp on his hands and rushed around him, out into the hall. Edie moved to follow her, but Elijah stepped into her path. She'd been so intent on pursuing the older woman that she slammed against him, her body flush against his.

And his breath escaped his lips in a gasp that stirred her hair, making it brush against his neck.

Instead of stepping back, she tipped up her chin and met his gaze. "I want to talk to her," she said.

"You promised not to harass the guests," he reminded her.

And she groaned.

He nearly groaned, too, at the tension gripping his body as attraction to her overwhelmed him. She wasn't like other women, like Morgana, who made an effort to look beautiful. If she wore any makeup, it was probably just mascara, and maybe not even that. Maybe her lashes were just that long, that dark a fringe around her vivid green eyes. Her features were so delicately honed that they didn't need any accentuating like Morgana with her rouge. Maybe that was all it had been; maybe the older woman hadn't been outside.

But he wondered, and he worried about her.

"Morgana is a guest?" she asked.

"She's definitely not an employee," he said. Then he felt compelled to add, "She has become more than a guest, though. She's kind of a resident since she stays for months at a time."

"That must be expensive," Edie mused. "How does she afford it? Who is she?"

He shook his head. "I really don't know. . . ."

"Was she here before?"

He nodded. "Yes, she's come and gone since we opened."

"I mean before that . . . when it was Bainesworth Manor?"

Until this morning, when Morgana had been waiting with the personal trainer, Heather Smallegan, in the hall outside his office, Elijah hadn't considered that. But now he wondered, too. "I don't know . . ."

"If only you knew where those old records were. . ." she mused, and she studied his face as intently as Morgana had when she'd talked to him about hearing and seeing the ghosts. And just as Morgana had, Edie uttered a sigh of disappointment over what she'd read on his face.

The truth. "I have no idea," he told her.

"That's why I need to talk to her, then," Edie said.

"About what?" he asked. "All Morgana wants to talk about are ghosts." He groaned and continued, "But I guess that's all you care about, too. The long-ago past."

"Someone needs to care about that," she said. "Someone needs to get the answers for those women. For the children who were born here and taken from those women . . . to the families of the women who were never found. . . ."

Her passion stirred his, and he nearly lowered his head to hers, nearly brushed his mouth across hers. But even as his neck began to bend, he pulled away and stepped back. "What about my family?" he asked.

"How can you protect your grandfather after everything he's done?" she asked, her face flushed with outrage.

"I'm talking about my niece," he said. "About her losing her mom and maybe her father, too, if Sergeant Montgomery has her way. What about Adelaide's answers about her mother's murder?"

Edie tilted her head as she studied his face. Then she nodded. "All right . . ." she murmured. "I'll help you. . . ."

"You will? I thought you didn't make a habit of finding killers?"

"I don't," she said. "But I do make a habit of finding out the truth. I'm just curious if you really want it. . . ."

He clenched his jaw. "My brother is not a killer."

"You were wrong before . . . about your cousin," she reminded him.

And he flinched at the jab, albeit not unwarranted. He had been wrong. And that would haunt him forever . . . just as Morgana claimed those ghosts haunted her.

"I'm sorry," Edie said. "But you can't be certain that you're right about Bode. Just like Sergeant Montgomery doesn't have enough proof to press charges, you don't have enough to prove him innocent."

"I thought it was presumed innocent until proven guilty . . ." he murmured. Then he sighed. "But it's not. In fact, it seems to be the reverse—that everyone presumes your guilt unless you prove your innocence."

"Are you talking about your brother or yourself now?" she asked.

His shoulders sagged slightly then, with the heavy weight of the burden he carried just because of his Bainesworth blood. "We've both been accused of things we didn't do," he said. "I'm sure your friend the sheriff has shared plenty of theories with you about things I've supposedly done, like try to run him down or . . . kill his wife. . . ."

"He was wrong," she said. She reached up and trailed her fingers along his jaw as she had so many times before. And as she had so many times before, she left his skin tingling and his pulse racing with awareness. "You are not a bad man, Elijah Cooke."

His heart lifted at the opinion that so few people on this damn island had ever shared. "You obviously didn't hear everything those people were saying in the diner yesterday. . . ."

She sighed now. "They were wrong. And I admire that you wanted to meet in town again, but since I'm here, let's talk about Erika Korlinsky."

He glanced around the conservatory. He didn't want to talk here, where the cameras were. While the camera didn't record audio, he still felt uncomfortable that Bruce, or another guard, could be watching them.

Especially when he wanted to do more than just talk to Edie. Maybe that was a good reason to stay here, though, instead of bringing her to his suite. But . . .

For once Elijah wasn't worried about doing the smart thing. Because trusting Edie was not smart. Trusting anyone was not smart.

Edie must have misinterpreted his hesitation for his wanting her to leave because she said, "Remember—there are weather advisories out. We're not supposed to even go outside right now."

"We're not going outside," he assured her. "Come with me." He led her down the hall, and instead of passing through the dining room, where there might have been guests, he walked through the kitchen.

"Chef!" the French chef called out to him. "You are going to love tonight's special."

"He called you chef." Edie's eyes widened with surprise. "You cook?"

He shook his head. "No. 'Chef' is French for boss." He turned back toward the tall, skinny man he'd hired away from a premier restaurant in New York City. "Chef Rene Rigaud," he said. "This is Edie Stone."

The chef nodded. "You look familiar. The reporter . . . something Stone . . ."

She nodded back at him. "Edie Stone. Nice to meet you."

"Do you eat?" he asked, his brow furrowed beneath the band of his pristine white chef's hat.

"Of course," Edie replied.

"No. I mean, do you really eat, or are you like other television personalities I know who starve themselves or, worse yet, purge my meals from their bodies?"

"No, I eat," she assured him. "I prefer to do my reporting in print, but if I have to go on camera, it's going to add pounds anyway, so I might as well enjoy them."

The chef grinned. "You, I like. You will have to wait a bit yet for the food. An hour or so . . ." Then he turned to Elijah. "What table, Chef?"

Elijah's stomach tightened, but he really had no choice. He couldn't let the politician or that movie star see the infamous Edie Stone at the hall. "In my suite," he replied.

And Edie tensed.

"Rene recognized you. I am sure some of our guests would as well," he said. "I have assured them that their privacy is safe at the hall."

"But am I safe with you?" she asked.

"No," the chef answered before he could. "Dr. Cooke is a dangerous man. He will make you see yourself how you really are, not just who you think you are."

"Sorry," Elijah murmured with a smile. The chef had been his client for years at his practice in New York City.

Rene continued as if he hadn't spoken. ". . . and he'll help you figure out how to be happy."

"And that's a bad thing?" Edie asked.

The chef grinned. "Of course, because then you have no excuse for bad behavior."

She chuckled. "Oh, now I understand."

Elijah sighed. "I don't think either of you need an excuse for bad behavior."

The chef grinned. "No. Just bad meals."

"You don't make any of those," Elijah assured him.

"I'll send the serving bowls to your suite, along with a bottle of the wine I recommend pairing with your meals."

"That won't be necessary," Elijah said. He wasn't sure he trusted himself to drink with Edie Stone.

As if the chef had read his mind, he told Elijah, "You don't have a problem with alcohol. You don't have a problem with anything."

Elijah stared at Edie and shook his head. "I wish I could say that was true. . . ."

"'Physician, heal thyself'?" Rene teased.

Elijah chuckled. "Hard to heal myself when other people are the problem." And how they perceived him and his brother just because of who their grandfather was—James Bainesworth.

Then Chef Rigaud repeated back to him what Elijah had told him so many times. "You cannot change other people; you can only change yourself and how you react to them."

Elijah nodded in agreement as he wished that was completely true. But he felt as if he had no control over how he reacted to Edie, over the way his pulse quickened, his breathing got shallower and his heart beat so hard and fast. While he acknowledged that it was probably a bad idea, he led her through the kitchen, down a short hallway, to his suite. He had one of the few on the first floor, behind the reception area, so that if a situation arose in the middle of the night, he would be available.

Unfortunately, he'd had to be available quite a bit over the past few weeks. For the sheriff's visits, for the things Deacon had found . . .

Or lost . . .

He punched in the code for the lock on the door and pushed it open, so Edie could enter first. She stood in the doorway without stepping over the threshold. For once she was quiet, her body seemingly tense beneath the jacket she must have unzipped in the kitchen.

"I thought you weren't afraid of me," he reminded her of what she'd claimed earlier.

She shook her head. "No, it's not you. It's . . ." And she pointed inside his suite.

Elijah stepped around her then, so he could see what had her frozen in his doorway. Wind and snow blasted him in the face, and he understood why she was cold. The French doors that opened from his sitting area onto the patio flapped back and forth as the wind blew through them, swirling snow around the hardwood floor, atop the puddles that must have been from snow that had already melted. He sure as hell hadn't left the doors open; someone must have either forced them open to break into his room . . . or had fled out them when he'd opened the door. Maybe that was the phantom who had appeared on the camera behind all the snow. The intruder.

But who the hell would break into his space?

And why?

When Elijah rushed inside his suite, Edie probably should have turned around and run . . . for help. But she couldn't leave him alone to battle either the elements or whoever might have let those elements inside his suite.

Because she doubted he'd left his patio doors open in the middle of December.

But she teased, "Glad I'm not paying your heating bill." Before stepping inside to join him, she scanned the shadows of the sitting room, making sure that nobody lurked within them, ready to attack.

Elijah shut and locked the patio doors and turned back to her. "I don't know how those got opened."

"You're not going to say that it must have been an accident, that they weren't latched?"

He glanced back at the doors, and a muscle twitched along his tightly clenched jaw. "They don't look like they were forced open from the outside." Nothing was broken, not the glass or the jambs. But that didn't mean that someone hadn't broken into them . . . with a less-damaging kind of tool.

Or a key.

"You should call security," she suggested. "Have them search the rest of the suite." In case the intruder was still here and armed.

But she and Elijah were already inside, and she saw and heard nothing now but the muted howl of the wind that he'd shut outside the doors.

He rushed past her then and pushed open a couple of other doors, interior doors to what must have been his bedroom and a bathroom. He shook his head. "If anyone was in here, they're gone now."

"You should still call security," she insisted. "Maybe your intruder was who Bruce saw on that monitor. Maybe he can identify them."

"I'm not even sure that was a person he saw. With the

snow falling so hard in front of the camera, it could have been anything."

"At least have him check the cameras outside here," she urged. For some reason it really bothered her that someone had broken in here and invaded his privacy, which was ironic because she'd pretty much done the same thing. But she didn't mean him any harm.

But would it harm him . . . when her big story broke about Bainesworth Manor? Would it affect the spa like he and his publicist seemed to think it would?

Elijah shook his head. "I don't have cameras near my suite," he said. "Either in the hall or outside."

"So you like to poke around in other people's lives but don't want anybody poking in yours?" she asked, and she was only partially teasing him. She wasn't the only one who probed for people's deep, dark secrets. As a psychiatrist, Dr. Cooke could probe even deeper into the dark than she could.

"I don't poke," he said. "I help, or at least I try to help." He uttered a weary sigh, and his shoulders slumped, as if he carried a load of guilt.

And she felt a twinge of guilt for maybe—albeit inadvertently—reminding him of what he considered past failures. Maybe his cousin . . .

She doubted that man had ever officially sought Elijah's counseling or been honest with him, not like the chef obviously had. "Rene Rigaud gave you a glowing recommendation," she reminded him. "For how you've helped him."

Elijah nodded, but he was clearly distracted as he kept looking back at the patio doors. The snow that had blown in melted now on the hardwood floor into the puddles that had already been there. How long had the doors been open?

"You still should call security," she persisted, and she stepped closer to him to get her message across and because she was worried about him. "Or at least check to see if anything's missing."

He patted his shirt pocket. "My wallet and phone are on me. I don't have anything else of value in my room."

"No laptop? No patient records?" she asked because that would have been the only reason she would have broken into his suite.

"Those are kept in my office," he said. Then he pointedly added, as if warning her, "And there are cameras around it."

Because it was against her nature not to push, she stepped even closer to him and asked, "What about the records from when the hall was the manor? You really don't have any idea where those could be?"

His lips curved into a slight smile. "You never let up. . . ."

His smile compelled her to smile, too. She liked getting him to lighten up—in general, but most especially on himself. She reached up and trailed her fingertips along the edge of that granite jaw of his. His skin was cold but warmed quickly under her touch. "I wouldn't get anywhere if I let up. . . ."

"How did you get here?" he asked, and he stared down at her as if bemused.

"In your suite?" she asked, and she arched a brow. "You're the one who lured me in here under the pretense of protecting your guests' privacy or some such nonsense. . . ."

His smile widened and his pale blue eyes warmed with amusement. "Some such nonsense . . ."

She nodded. "Yes, I think you just want to have your way with me, Dr. Cooke . . ." She trailed her fingers, then, from his face, down the side of his neck where his pulse leaped under her touch to the tie fastened tightly around his throat. ". . . after you ply me with food and wine."

He shook his head. "I think you manipulated your way in here, Ms. Stone. I think you're the one trying to seduce me."

She arched her brow again and smoothed her hand down the length of his tie, over his chest, which was surprisingly muscular and hard beneath the silky material of his dress shirt. "Really?"

"You're the one who's always touching me," he pointed out.

And she pulled her hand away from his chest and stepped back. "Well, if you don't like it . . ."

"I like it when *you* touch me . . ." he murmured.

"Whose touch don't you like?" she wondered. But then she thought of the publicist, who was as protective of him as she was of the spa. Maybe she was possessive as well.

He grimaced instead of answering her. Then he reached for her hand and put it back on his chest. "I shouldn't like it . . ." he murmured. "I shouldn't like you. . . ."

Instead of being offended, she chuckled and toyed with the buttons of his shirt. "Why shouldn't you like me?"

"Because what you want to do might risk everything my brother and I have built here . . ."

"Going to prison for murder might risk that, too," she remarked.

"That's what we're supposed to be talking about," he said, as if reminding her, but she wondered if he was really reminding himself. "You're supposed to be helping me find Erika's real killer."

"And I warned you that you might not like what we learn."

He stepped back then, and her hand dropped from his chest. He hadn't been offended by her teasing him about him, but when she'd said something about his brother, he was clearly upset. Because he wasn't as convinced of his brother's innocence as he wanted to be?

"I don't know what it's like to have a sibling," she admitted. "I was an only child." Her parents had literally put all their eggs in one basket . . . or surrogate's womb. Edie was the only one who'd survived.

"David was more a sibling to me than Bode was," Elijah admitted. "Jamie . . . *Bode*, was so much younger than us." He straightened his shoulders and lifted his chin, his resolve clearly restored. "But I know how much he loves his daughter. He would never take her mother away from her . . . not after we lost our own."

She stilled. "I'm sorry. I didn't know your mother was dead."

He shrugged. "I don't know if she is or she isn't. She left Bane Island when Bode wasn't much older than his daughter is now."

"How old were you?" she asked.

"Eight . . ." He shrugged again, as if it didn't matter . . . as if he didn't matter. He cared so much about everyone else's well-being. Who—besides that publicist—cared about him?

And Edie realized that as the urge to reach out to him came over her again, she cared. Maybe too much . . .

"That's a tough age," she said. "I was just a couple of years older than you when I found out the truth, that the woman I thought was my mom was actually my abductor."

Elijah tilted his head and studied her face, his pale blue eyes so intense that Edie shivered despite the warmth of her coat. The chill in the room from the doors being open was fully dissipated now. "That must have been devastating."

She shrugged off his sympathy like he'd shrugged off hers. Perhaps they did have things in common. "It was better to know the truth," she said. "Then I understood why we kept moving, why she kept changing our names, our appearances, and I had imagined all kinds of scenarios . . . but nothing like the truth."

"That's why the truth is so important to you."

She nodded. "Yes, it is."

"So then you'll help me find out who killed Erika Korlinsky?"

She nodded again. "I'll need to learn more about her. We should talk about her."

Still staring intently at her, he stepped closer. "For some reason I would rather talk about you."

"I don't like to talk about myself," she admitted.

"You're a psychiatrist's nightmare . . ." he murmured.

"Am I yours?" she asked with a smile.

He shook his head. "Not now . . . not anymore . . . you're my one bright spot right now." And he leaned closer, as if he intended to kiss her. But then he stopped, frozen in place, just inches from her mouth.

Close enough that she could reach up, that she could tug his head down to hers. That she could slide her mouth across his . . .

If she wanted, and she wanted—really badly—to kiss him, but before she could give in to temptation and grab him, he stepped around her, heading toward the door to the hallway. Then she heard it, the rattle . . . something or someone was coming down the hall. Then a waiter was there, rolling a room service cart into his suite. The young man's brow furrowed as he noticed the water pooled on the floor.

"Sir, is everything all right? Do you need me to get housekeeping to clean that up?"

Elijah stared at the puddles for a moment, as if he'd forgotten they were there. Then he shook his head. "No. I can take care of that. . . ." And he stepped into the bathroom, pulled out some towels, and dropped them onto the puddles, while the waiter rolled the cart over to the table and transferred the covered chafing bowls onto it. The table had already been set . . . for one . . . but Elijah pulled out another plate and wine goblet and set of cutleries.

Edie's stomach had been rumbling back at the carriage house, but she wasn't as hungry now as she'd been then. Now she was more interested in Elijah, in talking to him, in flirting with him. . . .

And that was so not like her. She should leave now, before the temptation to do more than flirt got too strong for her to resist. But with a snowstorm raging outside, there was a very good chance she was going to be stranded at the hall.

"I—I should call the boardinghouse," she said. "Make sure they don't worry . . ." And she was already pulling out her cell. Evelyn had a pretty good idea of what she was up to, so she unsurprisingly sounded anxious when she answered halfway through the first ring.

"Edie!"

"So you have caller ID," she said.

"Just for you," Evelyn said. "It comes up as trouble."

Edie smiled. "I'm sure it does."

"How much are you in?"

"That depends. Has anyone called the sheriff on me yet?" Because she wasn't entirely certain that the hall security guard hadn't; he'd seemed really intent on getting trespassing charges pressed against her.

"What have you done?" Evelyn asked.

"I think you can guess."

"You got into that place!"

"Yes, and I'm not sure I'm going to be able to get away. . . ."

"You want me to call the sheriff for you? That's what you're really saying," Evelyn surmised.

Edie laughed. "No. I'm telling you not to worry about me. The weather's terrible and I might be forced to stay here."

"The weather is terrible," Evelyn agreed. "But staying there will be more dangerous than driving home in this snow."

From how James Bainesworth's nurse had grabbed her the minute she'd climbed out of the ravine, and then the way she and Elijah had found the patio doors open in his suite, Edie wasn't entirely sure that Evelyn was overreacting. But Edie reassured her nevertheless. "I'm sure I'll be safe here. So you'll have to save my poison for tomorrow."

"Edie—"

"Don't worry," she said, even as she felt a little flood of warmth that the woman cared about her. She clicked off the cell before Evelyn could argue with her anymore.

And she turned to find Elijah escorting the waiter out of the suite. He closed the door then, shutting her inside . . . alone . . . with him. "That was a bit presumptuous," he said, "assuming that you're welcome to spend the night with me."

Her pulse quickened, and she, who was usually so quick-witted, stuttered back, "I—I wasn't . . ."

And he chuckled as he walked up to her like he had before . . . until he stood directly in front of her, staring at her so intently . . . and so closely . . . that she could feel the heat of his body, the heat that burned between them. Damn it. She was attracted to him.

And he was obviously attracted to her, too, as his eyes grew darker, the pupils enlarging to cover that pale blue. He really was a beautiful man, with features so chiseled and hair so black but for those few silver strands at his temples.

He leaned down . . . until his mouth was close to hers and he murmured, "Hungry . . . ?"

Her heart slammed against her ribs and her mouth dropped open. Then his fingers touched her chin, and he closed her mouth for her again, chuckling as he did. "For food," he said. "What did you think I was talking about?" And he led the way to the table the waiter had laden with food and wine.

"You surprise me, Dr. Cooke . . ." she murmured.

"That's better than boring you," he said.

She nodded. "Very true."

"Let me take your coat," he said. "Now that it's warmed up in here . . ."

She was definitely warm, but that had nothing to do with the temperature in the room and everything to do with him, especially when his hands cupped her shoulders and then skimmed down her arms as he shucked the coat from her. Trying to focus on anything but his surprisingly big hands and the fact that he was standing so close to her, she asked, "You're really not worried about finding those doors open?"

He shrugged. "Nothing's been taken or damaged. So I have no idea. Maybe I did just leave them unlatched."

"You don't believe that," she said.

He sighed. "No. I remember locking them." He held out her chair until she took the seat, then moved around the table to take his. And he stared across at her, his eyes narrowed. "Did you have time before the ravine and the carriage house to sneak in here?" he wondered aloud.

She smiled. "Sounds like something I would do. But I didn't get the chance to do anything before Igor grabbed me."

He chuckled as he poured wine in her glass. "Now you sound like Bode."

"That's what your grandfather said."

"What else did my grandfather tell you?" he asked as he held the wine bottle over his glass, though he had yet to pour any of the deep purple liquid into it.

She shivered and murmured, "To grow out my hair . . ."

Elijah groaned and then poured a generous amount of the wine into his glass.

And she chuckled. "He really gets to you."

"He really gets to everyone," he said.

"Then why go into business with him?"

He gestured around him. "For this . . . for what Bode and I want it to be, a place for people to feel good—physically and emotionally . . ." He sighed and took a big sip of the wine.

"What about you?" she asked. "Do you feel good?"

He stared at her for a long moment before chuckling again. "Which of us is the shrink . . . as Deacon calls me?"

"Reporters and shrinks are a lot alike," she said. "We both ask a lot of questions and want to know what makes people tick."

"But I do it to help them," he said. "You do it to expose their dirty secrets. To sell stories . . ."

She flinched and finally took a sip of the wine . . . a big sip. The pinot noir was rich and dark, with a silky elegance . . . so much like the man who sat across the table from her. But while he might want to feel superior, he wasn't . . . for so many reasons. "I help, too, or at least I'm hoping to help. . . ."

"How?" he asked.

"I want to reunite those women with the babies they were forced to give up," she said. "Like Bonita . . ."

"Bonita?"

"The Pierce sister who screamed at you the other night," she said. "She's the one who was here. . . ." She peered around the room, with its coffered ceiling and gleaming hardwood floors. It was elegant now; it might have even been then. But it hadn't been a good place. "She was damaged, her adolescence and her child stolen from her."

"Grandfather claims the women willingly gave up their children," Elijah said. "That that's why their families probably sent them here in the first place . . . to avoid scandal."

"Then why won't he show me the paperwork?" she asked. "The records that prove these were legal adoptions."

Elijah shrugged. "I don't know."

"He claims that the authorities took the paperwork from back then," she said. "But it was never returned?"

"I never saw any of it," he said. "There wasn't much left here when Bode and I started working on the place."

"So only your grandfather probably really knows where the documents are." She took another big gulp of the wine.

And Elijah chuckled. "Obviously, you know that getting the truth out of him won't be easy."

"You'll let me talk to him again?" she asked. "You'll let me back onto the property?"

"If you tell me how you got onto it in the first place . . ."

She narrowed her eyes and studied his face as the wine began to warm her inside; she didn't know if it was him or the wine, but she was beginning to feel a little light-headed. "I'm not sure I trust you," she murmured.

"I'm beginning to think it's a mistake to trust anyone," Elijah admitted.

"What about your brother?" she asked. "Do you trust that he really had nothing to do with the death of that woman?"

Elijah nodded and then pressed a hand to his head.

"Are you still suffering aftereffects from your concussion?" she asked with concern.

He shrugged. "Or maybe from this glass of wine on an

empty stomach. We should eat before this gets cold or Rene will never forgive me." He lifted the lids from the dishes, filling the room with the scents of beef Wellington and mushroom risotto and grilled asparagus.

"Wow," she murmured in appreciation. "Evelyn is a good cook and all, even with the arsenic, but this smells wonderful."

"It'll taste even better," he promised.

"How'd you get a chef like that to come out to this god-forsaken island?" she asked. But from what she'd discerned of their conversation in the kitchen, she suspected the chef felt as though he owed Elijah if not his life, at least his happiness.

Elijah shrugged off whatever credit he could have taken. "Some people like the solitude of such a place, especially after so many years of living in the chaos of a big city."

She tilted her head and considered it. "Maybe." She could see its appeal. "It feels very Armageddon when the bridge closes down."

"It is very Armageddon then," Elijah mused, his words slurring a bit. "I'd better eat." He picked up a fork and cut it through the flaky pastry wrapped around the beef. Steam escaped, carrying the scent of spiced meat.

Edie picked up her fork, too, and even though she felt a bit as if she was cheating on Evelyn, she dug into the Wellington and the risotto and the asparagus. "This is amazing."

"Rene is a genius," Elijah agreed, but he wasn't eating like she was. In fact, he didn't look well, his face suddenly losing all its color. And his eyes began to roll back in his head.

She jumped up from her chair to help him, but the sudden

movement brought a wave of dizziness over her. And she realized something was wrong—very wrong. . . .

Elijah toppled over then, sliding out of his chair onto the floor.

She opened her mouth to cry out to him, but she could only gasp for air. Then she grasped the edge of the table to steady herself, but it was too late. Her legs gave out and she dropped to the floor near where Elijah lay, his eyes closed.

He was either already unconscious or . . .

Dead.

Had someone poisoned them?

She fought to retain consciousness so that she could cry out for help, but when she opened her mouth, no words came out. And no words formed in her mind as it began to go completely blank and the world went completely black as oblivion claimed her, too.

Chapter Twelve

The ringing cell jerked Bode awake just an hour or so after he had fallen into a deep sleep—the first he'd had since finding out that body was Erika's, that the mother of his child was dead.

Every time he'd closed his eyes, he'd reread the letter she'd written him. Or at the least the one he'd thought she'd written when she'd disappeared nearly three months before her death.

And now he was haunted by wondering where she'd been when she'd been missing and what had been happening to her . . . and who had been responsible. It had to be that Teddy kid, the groundskeeper who'd held Rosemary's daughter, Genevieve, for weeks.

Genevieve had managed to escape.

Erika had not.

Hearing a cry through the baby monitor, Bode grabbed for the phone—too late, though, because its ringing had already awakened Adelaide. "Yes!" he nearly shouted into the cell as he rolled out of his bed and headed toward the nursery next door. It wasn't even ten o'clock yet, but Bode and especially Adelaide went to bed early.

"Mr. James, this is Bruce with security," a man greeted him. "There's a problem up at the hall."

He rubbed his hand over his face, trying to clear the sleep from his eyes to focus on the conversation and the shadows of the nursery as he approached the crib.

"Elijah handles that kind of stuff . . ." he murmured with a twinge of guilt. His brother handled far more of the day-to-day operations than Bode did. Their partnership was not the equal one Bode had proposed when he'd pitched the spa to his older brother. But then, that hadn't been entirely his fault; it wasn't until they'd gone into business together that he'd learned what a control freak his older brother was. It wasn't until they'd gone into business together that he'd gotten to really know Elijah at all.

"Dr. Cooke is the problem," Bruce said. "He's not answering his door to Ms. Plasky, and she is demanding that we open it up."

"Ms. Plasky is still at the hall?" Bode asked. He would have thought she'd left shortly after that morning meeting.

"She couldn't get across the bridge, so she turned around and came back to use a room."

And she'd undoubtedly hoped to share his brother's, but Elijah had been adamant that they were not to date any employees. If only Bode had listened . . .

He wouldn't have his daughter. He leaned over the railing of her crib to find her smiling up at him. Love flooded his heart, and he couldn't imagine a world without this sweet baby in it. It was just too damn tragic that her mother wasn't in it as well.

And what had happened to her . . .

Bode shuddered. No. Elijah was smart not to let Amanda Plasky in his room. While Bode teased Elijah about the publicist's obvious interest in him, he was dealing with an awkward problem of his own . . . with Heather.

"Ms. Plasky is not the only one who's demanding to see your brother," the guard continued. "Sheriff Howell is also demanding to get onto the property."

"To see Elijah?"

"To see Edie Stone."

Bode snorted, and the sound made Adelaide's eyes widen with surprise. Then she kicked her feet and opened her mouth with a little bubble—probably of gas, but he preferred to think she considered him funny. Just as he thought the sheriff's presumption was funny. "The sheriff is way off base. There's no way my brother would let Edie Stone onto the estate, let alone into his room." But even as he said it, doubts began to niggle at him. Elijah had allowed her into his hospital room the other night.

But that had been at the hospital, not at the hall, where other people might see her or, worse yet, that she would see them and report about them. "He wouldn't have . . ." he murmured.

The guard cleared his throat and then said, "He did. She somehow got onto the property—"

"How?" Bode bellowed, and Adelaide's face scrunched up as she started to cry. He put the cell on speaker, set it on the changing table, and lifted her out of her crib. Rocking her in his arms, he asked in a softer tone, "How did she get past your security?"

"I don't know, sir," the guard admitted. "She turned up on one of the cameras and then disappeared, but your brother found her."

"And instead of escorting her off the grounds, he brought her back to his room?" he asked dubiously.

"The weather is terrible, sir, and yes, the chef confirmed

that Dr. Cooke had a meal for two delivered to his suite . . . and he didn't open the door when the waiter went back to retrieve the serving bowls earlier this evening."

A knot tightened in Bode's stomach. If it was anyone else but Elijah, he would have considered that he'd gotten intimate with the reporter and hadn't wanted to be interrupted. But with everyone coming to his door . . .

"Open it!" Bode said. "And I'm on my way . . ." Because somehow he knew he was going to be needed.

One minute he'd been feeling all warm inside from the wine and the company . . . and the next his head had gone fuzzy . . . and he was unconscious. It had been a less painful way to be knocked out than the blow his cousin had given him days ago, but . . .

Elijah awoke with that same pounding headache. Maybe he'd cracked his skull when he'd fallen. Had he fallen?

He must have because he was lying down now. But the headache and the dryness of his throat . . .

He hadn't felt like this since college . . . when he'd learned that he couldn't drink much without getting hungover and sick. But he hadn't had that much to drink.

Just the one glass. But God . . .

He felt sick, his stomach churning with it. And when he opened his eyes, the room churned, too, like a boat riding high waves. He groaned and flinched at the sound of it.

"You're alive," a deep voice murmured, followed with a heavy sigh of relief.

"I must be," Elijah said, his own voice just a rasp because of the dryness of his throat. "Or I wouldn't feel this bad." Then he remembered that he hadn't been alone, and he jerked upright on his bed and peered around the spinning room. "Where is she? Where's Edie?"

And was she okay . . . ?

Had whatever caused him to black out just affected him?

Maybe she'd drugged him so that she could search his suite. Because he saw only Bode in his bedroom with him.

Was she gone?

"She's out in the sitting area with the sheriff," Bode said. "She came around faster than you did."

"So she was affected, too?" he asked. He'd definitely gone down first, his suddenly boneless body sliding out of his chair. He remembered that . . . and their conversation over wine and the meal.

Wine.

"She's fine now, but I treated you both with a shot of naloxone. I don't think she had as much in her system. What the hell did you take?"

"You think I took anything?" Elijah asked. "We were just drinking the wine and eating."

Bode shook his head. "That damn Rene. I knew it was a mistake, your hiring him."

"Rene did not poison us," Elijah insisted.

"I saw the meal on the table. The risotto had mushrooms in it," Bode said. "Maybe they were bad."

Panic gripped Elijah. "Did anyone else have this reaction?"

Bode shook his head. "No. There were no reports of any of the guests having reactions, and Rene is fine, too," he admitted. "So what the hell happened? Did she slip something into your glass?"

"You said that she was affected, too," Elijah reminded his suspicious brother.

"Yeah . . . but not as badly as you were. . . ."

"I drank more of the wine," Elijah admitted. They'd been talking about Grandfather, and everything had just kind of overwhelmed him . . . like his attraction to Edie Stone. He'd wanted so badly to kiss her earlier, but then he'd heard the tray rattling down the hallway toward his suite. Now he wished he'd ignored the waiter's arrival.

That he'd kissed her when he'd had the chance.

"So the wine must have been bad." Bode nodded. "That makes sense."

"No. Rene would never have ordered something that wasn't good." That wasn't exquisite, which the wine had seemed. No. It had to be something else. And he remembered those open patio doors . . .

"Someone was in here," he said. "Someone was in my suite. . . ."

"Yeah, Edie Stone."

"No. Someone else."

Someone who must have come in and put something in those glasses before the wine was poured into them.

For what end?

To make them sick?

Or to kill them?

No. Not *them* . . .

No one could have known that he would bring Edie into his suite. The poison—or whatever had been put in those glasses—must have been meant for him alone.

Everything felt so surreal to Edie, as if she was wandering through a dream that wasn't necessarily hers. But then, she'd often felt like the life she was living wasn't her own . . . that she was someone else. Maybe that was because she'd grown up feeling that way.

"What the hell were you thinking, to trespass onto the manor?" Deacon asked her as he leaned over the couch on which she was lying. It was surreal to her that the sheriff was here, and what was even more surreal was that he held a baby in his arms.

Bode's baby.

She remembered waking up, or partially regaining consciousness, to find the fitness guru leaning over her. Deacon had been standing behind him then, as if he hadn't entirely trusted that Bode was treating her and not killing her. But Bode had given her a shot of something that had brought her back around, that had had her heart pumping normally, had had her breathing normally again even though she still felt so odd, so disassociated.

"Elijah . . ." she'd rasped his name then. And Bode had just shaken his head before he'd picked up his brother from the floor and carried Elijah's tall body almost as easily as the sheriff held the man's child.

"Jamie . . ." the sheriff had murmured as if in protest. But he held the baby with the ease of a man who'd had a child of his own. An ease that Edie had never felt around children herself.

Even now she stared at the child with apprehension. But the baby had fallen asleep in Deacon's arms, oblivious of everything that had nearly happened here tonight. Of how her uncle could have died . . .

"Elijah," she murmured again. She could hear the deep rumble of voices coming from his bedroom. Bode's and his.

Elijah had regained consciousness as well. A slight breath of relief shuddered out of her.

"What the hell were you thinking?" Deacon prodded her. "Why were you trespassing?"

She glared at him. "Because there was no other way for

me to get inside." She'd tried, but Elijah had refused to let her through those gates.

"Yes, because you're not a guest," Deacon said. "So you have no business being here."

"I need to find out the truth."

"At the expense of your life?" Deacon asked. "Of your freedom?"

She snorted at his hypocrisy. Like he hadn't been determined himself to go after the manor, after the Cookes. . . .

"Is Elijah pressing charges against me?" she asked. She would have stood up, but her legs felt a little shaky still. *She* felt a little shaky still. Shaky was better than how helpless she'd felt . . . when she'd watched Elijah pass out, when she'd known she was about to pass out herself.

Deacon snorted. "He needs to worry about the charges that can be pressed against him."

Her brow furrowed with confusion, and she shook her head, trying to clear that surreal, dreamy feeling from it. "I—I don't understand. What charges?"

"Holding you here against your will," he said, and he must have tensed because the baby in his arms tensed, too. He lowered his voice and continued, "Which is kidnapping and then drugging you."

She shook her head again, even though it was beginning to clear quickly now. "No. He didn't do any of those things," she said. "He would much rather have gotten rid of me than let me stay."

"Exactly," Deacon said. "He tried to get rid of you just like Olivia overheard him and that publicist saying they were going to do. He intended to get rid of you—permanently— by poisoning you."

Olivia had warned her, but Edie hadn't taken the threat seriously then. And she didn't now. So she just chuckled and said, "Evelyn is going to be so jealous that someone else poisoned me."

"You owe Evelyn," he said. "She sent me here to bring you home. She was worried sick that something terrible was going to happen to you here. And she was right."

Tears stung Edie's eyes; maybe it was the aftereffects of being drugged and nearly dying, or maybe it was the feeling that flooded her heart, the surge of warmth that Evelyn Pierce actually seemed to care about her. That anyone really cared about her.

"Are you okay?" a deep voice rasped as Elijah stumbled through his bedroom doorway.

"You need to lie back down," his brother said as he followed him. "You're not all right yet. The doctor I called, who guided me through administering the naxolone, said that you need to take it easy for an hour or so to make sure that one shot was enough to counter the overdose. You still have a few more minutes to go."

Elijah's pupils were still enlarged, his skin still deathly pale. Maybe she looked the same because she felt so odd yet, but it wasn't just the aftereffects of the drugs. She had a strange surge of tingling and awareness and so damn much attraction for this man. "Are you okay?" she asked.

He nodded. "Are you?"

She nodded.

The sheriff passed off the baby to Bode. Then he said, "*I'm* not okay. I need to know what the hell happened here tonight."

"They must have been drugged," Bode answered. "The doctor I called said that if the naloxone brought them around, it must have been some kind of opioid. Maybe morphine or fentanyl."

"Don't they need to go to the hospital?" Deacon asked.

"No," Edie answered. "I am fine. I am not going back to that hospital." Not after nearly getting run down in the lot.

"Me neither," Elijah said. "We can monitor vitals here."

"The doctor said that as long as they were breathing normally and their blood pressure was fine, there was no need, especially given the weather, for them to go in," Bode said. "They just need to be watched to make sure that they're fully recovered from whatever it was. . . ."

The sheriff gestured at the table. "Probably something was slipped into their food or wine. I'll have the state police crime techs collect and send all of this to their lab for processing."

Bode groaned. "So Sergeant Montgomery will be back around." He glanced toward the open door to the hall, as if he was tempted to rush out of it now, to get away before the trooper could show up here. But then he turned back to his brother and, with his free arm, he reached out, wrapping his arm around his shoulders. "Elijah, you need to take it easy."

"Of course he can't take it easy," Edie said defensively. "Someone just tried to kill us."

"Someone?" Bode asked, suspicion sharpening his tone. "You were in here with him. Just the two of you."

"And both of us were poisoned," Edie pointed out.

"How?" he asked. "It couldn't have been in the food. Other people ate it with no issues. Someone had to put it in the wine."

"Elijah poured the wine," she said. "I didn't even touch his glass."

"So you poisoned her," Deacon accused his old nemesis. The history of animosity between the two of them went back years . . . to their childhood, Edie knew that.

"And myself?" Elijah asked. "Don't be an idiot."

"Don't make this idiot arrest you," Deacon challenged him.

"He didn't do it," Edie said. "I would have noticed. He didn't have the chance to slip anything into the bottle after opening it, and . . ." Her brow furrowed. And she peered up at Elijah, who leaned heavily against his brother. "The glasses . . ."

"You saw him put it into the glass?" Deacon asked.

She shook her head. "No, but someone could have before he poured the wine into it." She pointed toward the French doors. "Those were open when we came in."

Bode's brow furrowed as he stared at his brother. "You said something about someone being in here, but I thought you were talking about the waiter or . . . I didn't realize your room was broken into."

"Nothing was broken . . ." Elijah murmured. "But the doors were open."

"You wouldn't have left them open in this weather, or even unlocked. You're too careful," Bode said. "So someone must have had the code to the door to your suite to get in here. Then maybe they slipped out the French doors when they heard you coming." He seemed to clasp his daughter a little closer to his chest. "You're coming back to the cottage with us."

Elijah shook his head. "No, I have to stay in the hall," he insisted.

"Not here, not in this suite," Deacon said. "This is a crime scene." He gestured then, as if to shove them all out into the corridor. "We need to get out of here and let the techs from the state lab process the scene, if they can make it here from the mainland. I barely got out here from the boarding-house. The roads are bad." He glanced at Bode then. "Which is the only reason I trusted you to treat them."

Bode snorted. "You didn't trust me. They were barely breathing, so you had no other choice."

A muscle twitched along Deacon's tightly clenched jaw. He begrudgingly conceded, "No, I didn't."

"Thank you for helping me," Edie said as she realized she hadn't expressed her appreciation to Bode yet, but there'd been no time before he'd focused on his brother. He'd even helped her first, but maybe Deacon had forced him to. No matter what, he had saved her life.

Bode's face flushed slightly, and he nodded. "I'm just grateful that we have some medications and supplies and equipment here at the spa," he said.

"In case some of your guests OD?" the question just slipped out; asking questions was second nature to her.

Bode narrowed his eyes. "I'm not going to give you an interview, Ms. Stone. And even though my brother doesn't seem to want to press charges against you for trespassing, I am co-owner of the spa, and I would like to press charges—"

Elijah gripped his arm and shook his head. "No."

"But Elijah, you could have been killed toni—"

"She didn't put anything in the wine," Elijah said. "And if you press charges against her for trespassing, she could press charges against Grandfather for kidnapping—"

"What did that old bastard do?" Deacon asked the question now, in such a bellow that the baby awoke with a fearful cry.

"Nothing," Edie said. And technically James Bainesworth hadn't hurt her. But he had scared the hell out of her, and he'd enjoyed every minute that she'd been afraid of him. He really was an old bastard.

Deacon's dark eyes narrowed as he studied her face with obvious skepticism. He wasn't the only one. Bode looked skeptical as well, and his arm around his daughter seemed to gently—protectively—tighten.

"What did Grandfather do?" Bode asked the question of Elijah.

"He saw her first on the property and had Theo bring her straight to him."

"Why? What did he want with you?" Deacon asked her.

She shrugged. "Entertainment."

"People have died over his entertainment," Deacon murmured. "Let's get you the hell out of here. Right now." And as Bode had his arm around Elijah, Deacon slid his arm around Edie and guided her toward the doorway. As he walked forward, he nudged the Cooke brothers. "You need to vacate this room, too, until Sergeant Montgomery can get some techs out to the island to process it."

Bode groaned a protest. "At least let me call her," he said. "So she doesn't think I'm trying to hide anything."

"Anything else?" Deacon taunted him.

As if they'd choreographed the move, Edie pulled away from Deacon and Elijah pulled away from his brother when they stepped into the hall. Elijah clasped her arm and tugged her farther away from the others.

"Are you really okay?" he asked, his pale eyes intently studying her face with such concern in them.

Her heart warmed. She nodded. "I'm fine."

"Good," he said. "Because I'm not . . ."

She reached out for him then, wrapping her arms loosely around his waist as he staggered a bit. "You need to go to the hospital."

"No," he said. "I'm not going to die. I'm wishing I was, though." He pressed his hand against his forehead. "This is why I don't drink."

She had a hell of a headache and a dry throat, but it wasn't worse than any other hangover she'd had over the years. Fortunately, those had been few and far between and reserved just for events involving her family . . . like Elijah drinking that wine seemed to have to do with his frustration with his grandfather and his concern for his brother.

If he wasn't a regular drinker, maybe nobody thought he would consume anything out of the wineglasses. Maybe whatever they'd been drugged with hadn't been meant for him but just for her.

She glanced back down the hall, toward where Bode and Deacon continued to bicker. Could Bode . . .

But she wasn't even sure he'd known she was on the property, let alone going into Elijah's suite. Who had heard?

Morgana.

The chef.

The security guard.

And maybe his grandfather. It didn't seem that a whole hell of a lot escaped the attention of James Bainesworth. She sure hadn't.

She shivered.

"Don't go . . ." Elijah murmured.

"You want me to stay?" she asked.

"I want you . . ."

Her pulse quickened with excitement, with attraction . . . with all the feelings Elijah Cooke brought out in her that she couldn't remember feeling in a very long time . . . if ever. . . .

"Edie, we need to get going," Deacon said. "I have to swing by my dad's to check on him."

Edie glanced down the hall at the sheriff. And Elijah finished what he'd been about to say, "Don't go out without your jacket."

All her feelings turned to disappointment. But when she turned back toward him, she caught the glint in his eyes . . . the amusement and the attraction. He knew what she'd thought he was going to say, and he'd seen her disappointment that he hadn't . . . that he didn't really just want her—want her.

And she wondered if they hadn't been poisoned, if she would have spent the night with him, doing more than talking about his brother and Bainesworth Manor.

If they would have done any talking at all . . .

Because this attraction she felt for him wasn't one-sided. He clearly felt it, too.

The snow had begun to let up enough that it was easy to see Edie Stone walking out of the front doors of the hall. The sheriff had a hand on her elbow, but she walked steadily and easily and didn't need his support. She wasn't suffering any long-term effects from her overdose.

How the hell had Edie Stone made it onto the estate? And how had she once again survived unscathed from an attempt on her life? What was it going to take to kill that damn reporter?

Chapter Thirteen

"What the hell is wrong with you?" Bode asked Elijah the minute Edie and Deacon walked out the lobby doors.

Elijah rubbed his aching head at the volume and indignation of his brother's voice. He glanced down at his niece, who had somehow managed to fall back asleep in her father's arms. "What do you mean—what's wrong with me? You know I've been drugged."

"What about before that?" Bode asked. "Why didn't you call the police the minute you caught Edie Stone trespassing on the property?"

"Because I didn't catch her first, Grandfather did," he reminded his brother.

"And what was she going to press charges about over that? She was the one trespassing, and hell, he was probably who she wanted to talk to anyway. Not that it did her a damn bit of good, I bet. I can't imagine she got any more answers out of him than we ever do."

"Grandfather was the person she wanted to talk to," Elijah admitted.

Bode chuckled then. "Hurt your ego that the girl you like is more interested in your grandpa?"

"What—what do you mean . . . girl I like?" he asked.

"We're not in high school." And even in high school, Edie would have been more than a girl—after the life experiences she'd had. She would have always had more wisdom than her age.

"It's obvious," Bode said. "The romantic dinner . . . the way you look at her . . . I've never seen you like this. . . ."

Elijah touched his head again. "What? Hungover?"

"Interested in someone," Bode said. "Really interested . . ." He groaned. "Why her? Why a reporter, Elijah? You think going out with an employee or a colleague could compromise the hall. What about dating the reporter who wants to destroy it?"

"She doesn't want to destroy the hall," Elijah said. He doubted she had any interest in it or their privacy-seeking guests at all.

Bode's eyes narrowed. "Really? Then what the hell is she doing sneaking onto the property, talking to Grandfather?"

"She wants to find out the truth about Bainesworth Manor," he admitted. "She wants to find out what happened to the babies who were born there, to the girls who disappeared—"

"And you don't think a huge scandal about the history of the hall will destroy it?" Bode asked. "God, maybe you still need more naloxone. Obviously, whatever drug you took hasn't worn off."

Elijah's head wasn't just pounding; it felt unfocused, fuzzy. He shook it to try to clear it. "I need a shower. Some clothes."

Bode pointed toward the doorway to his suite. A piece of yellow tape stretched across it. Deacon must have strewn it there when Elijah had been talking to Edie, making sure she was all right.

He shuddered at the thought of what could have happened

had Bode not come to their rescue. He really looked at his brother now and noticed that he wore pajamas. He must have already been in bed.

How long had he and Edie been passed out?

How much longer could they have survived?

He reached for the tape and jerked it free.

And Bode gasped. "We're not supposed to go in there. Sergeant Montgomery told Deacon to put that tape there and make sure nobody went into your suite."

"I need some clothes and my toiletries," Elijah said. And he also needed to look around to see what had happened and how.

He'd poured that wine, but wouldn't he have noticed if something had been put into the glasses? He stepped around his brother and walked back into the suite. The food had congealed on the plates, cold for a long time. Not much of it had been eaten.

He'd had more of the wine than she had. His glass was nearly empty, while hers was half full. He glanced at the wine bottle then and realized he hadn't opened it. It had already been opened, maybe left out for a while to breathe.

Where had it been sitting? And who could have tampered with it? Anyone inside the hall . . .

Any guest or employee . . .

Why?

To make them sick or to kill them?

The cold blast of wind in her face had chased away the last of Edie's grogginess from being drugged. Maybe getting away from Elijah had helped clear her mind as well.

What the hell was it about him that affected her so much?

That made her want to tease him and flirt with him instead of doing her job?

Not that she believed he had any idea where the old records were, or even what his grandfather had really done so long ago, before he'd even been born. As she could attest, James Bainesworth was clever—too clever to ever admit to anything incriminating . . . probably even to his family. Maybe most especially to his family.

The thought of family reminded her of Deacon's reason for leaving the hall so abruptly . . . that and the turn that he took when he pulled through the gates that had been left standing open for them. Instead of turning toward town, he turned toward the pier . . . where she'd left her Jeep next to the lighthouse.

But surely he wouldn't drive that far, just to his father's cabin. "Why do you have to check on your dad?" she asked. "Is everything all right?" She glanced across the console at him.

Deacon gripped the wheel in tight fists, maybe because the roads were so bad, or maybe because he was worried. "Helen called me earlier. Said she had to come into town to pick up a prescription for my dad, but the roads got so bad that she couldn't make it back. She had to stay at her house in town. And she's worried that he won't be strong enough to stock the woodstove once it burns through what she put in it."

Having been in that probably uninsulated cabin, Edie shivered at the thought of it being without heat. If the wood-stove went out, it wouldn't take that long for his frail father to freeze.

"I'm sorry," she said. "You should have gone directly to your dad's and not worried about me."

"Evelyn was frantic," he said, and a muscle twitched along his tightly clenched jaw.

"Just Evelyn?" she asked.

"Olivia, too," he said. "She's still unnerved by the conversation she overheard between Elijah and his publicist talking about getting rid of you."

She chuckled. "I'm sure Amanda Plasky would love to get rid of me." So that she would have no competition for Elijah.

Not that Edie intended to compete for him. But . . . she couldn't deny that she was attracted, incredibly attracted, to him.

"I sent away Ms. Plasky and that security guard, Bruce, before you regained consciousness," he said. "I didn't want them contaminating the scene."

"She's at the hall? I didn't know she lives there."

"She doesn't. The state police closed the bridge earlier this evening before she could make it off the island. So she came back to the hall to stay in a room for the night."

She'd probably intended to stay in Elijah's.

"You actually owe her for saving your life," Deacon remarked. "She was the one who got frantic when Elijah wouldn't open his door."

She chuckled again. "I'm sure she did. . . ."

"You think something's going on between her and Elijah?"

"No," she said. And she was absolutely certain of that; she'd heard how formally he'd greeted Ms. Plasky at the hospital a couple of nights before. "He's not like his brother."

"Let's hope not," Deacon said. "The last person who got involved with his brother wound up dead."

"Do you really think Bode is responsible for her death?" she asked. Because she had promised to help Elijah investigate . . .

Deacon sighed, and despite the defroster fan blasting on

high, the windows steamed up. It was that cold outside, but at least the snow wasn't falling as heavily as it had been earlier. The wipers just brushed away a few flakes instead of the sheets of it that had been falling earlier.

"I think Bode is somehow involved," Deacon said carefully—a little too carefully. "But I shouldn't be speculating. It's not my case anymore. Sergeant Montgomery didn't even want me investigating what happened tonight at the hall to you and Elijah."

She sighed now, and the passenger window steamed up so completely she couldn't see out, couldn't see how close they were getting to the former sheriff's cabin or the lighthouse. "I don't know what happened tonight."

"Somebody doesn't want you exposing any of their secrets."

Elijah had claimed not to have any, but even if he did, she doubted he would have poisoned himself . . . or her. "But how would someone have known I was going to his suite with him, that I would be eating and drinking with him?"

Deacon shrugged. "I don't know. How long were you in there before the meal came?"

"An hour," she said. "But we found the patio doors open when we entered."

"And you said Elijah poured the wine in the glasses."

She nodded. "Yes."

"You didn't say he opened it," Deacon pointed out.

She let out a soft whistle. "Damn, now I realize why you have the reputation you do."

"For killing my wife even though I didn't?"

She shook her head. "Not your reputation on Bane Island. Your reputation as a detective in Portland."

He chuckled. "You checked me out?"

"Don't take it personally," she said. "I check out everyone."

And so far she'd found no skeletons in Elijah's and Bode's closets but for the ones their grandfather had stashed there years before they were even born.

"So, what did you find out?" he asked.

"You're a damn good detective," she said.

But he shook his head now. "If I was good, I would have proved my wife was murdered two years ago. Hell, if I was good, I would have already solved Erika Korlinsky's murder."

"Cut yourself some slack," Edie said. He reminded her very much of Elijah now, beating himself up over something that wasn't his fault. She didn't think he would appreciate her pointing out any commonalities between the two of them, though, so she just said, "You didn't get back the DNA results that identified her until just a week ago."

Deacon, who had slowed the SUV to a crawl through the deep snow on the road, murmured, "Now I have to try to identify my dad's driveway. . . ." He lowered his window to peer out.

Having only been there once, Edie wouldn't be much help, but she leaned over the console and peered out, too. "There," she said, pointing to a mailbox. The driveway itself was blown shut.

Deacon cursed. "The plow service I hired for him needs to get out here so Helen can get back to the house."

"Helen?" she asked. "What about us? Are you going to be able to make it through that?"

Deacon nodded. Then he put the SUV in reverse and backed up before switching to Drive and stomping on the accelerator to plow through the drift and on down the driveway.

As it slammed through the drifts, Edie braced her hands against the dash. Fortunately, the driveway wasn't very long, and the cabin soon appeared, aglow with lights, before them. The window must have been repaired since Edie's visit.

At the sight of the lights, Deacon emitted a little sigh of relief, even as tension gripped his body. Clearly he wasn't thrilled at the thought of checking on his father. He had yet to shut off the SUV or reach for his door.

"Do you want me to stay in here?" she asked.

"No," Deacon said.

"You really aren't comfortable with your father?" she murmured.

"No. I want him to tell me what he told you when you met with him earlier this week," he said. "I want to know what information he gave you that enabled you to get onto the property and into an interview with old man Bainesworth."

"It wasn't an interview," she assured him. "At least not from my end. He asked more questions than I did."

"Like how the hell you got past security?"

No. Bainesworth had already known that, but she wasn't about to admit it to Deacon, who was clearly already pissed that she'd talked to his father. But not so much that he wasn't going to let her talk to him again . . .

He would have been more pissed to realize that his father must have talked to James Bainesworth after her visit, that he'd tipped him off that she now was aware of the tunnels.

Because Bainesworth had been expecting her, had he already had his "nurse" go through the tunnels and dispose of whatever he might have hidden down there?

Like old records?

And bodies?

She shivered despite the warm air blasting out of the vents. "We should go inside and make sure the woodstove's stocked," she reminded him.

He glared at her before he turned off the ignition. "Okay . . ." Finally, he pushed open his door.

And Edie did the same, the bottom of it pushing through a drift. When she stepped down from the SUV, she sank into that snow above her knees, and it went over the top of her boots, trickling down between the thick, lined rubber and her heavy wool socks. She grimaced as she fought to close the door again before heading around the front of the SUV toward the cabin.

Deacon's legs were longer, so he'd already made it to the door. The snow wasn't quite as deep there, but deep enough that he had to kick it aside to lift the welcome mat. He cursed.

"What?" Edie asked.

"The key's gone . . ." he murmured.

"Somebody probably forgot to put it back," she said because that was what she did every time she used her hide-a-key at her town house in DC. She reached for the doorknob then, suggesting, "Maybe it's not locked."

"He would have told Helen to lock up behind herself."

"On Bane Island?" she asked. "Don't people leave their doors unlocked in small towns?"

"Not on Bane Island," Deacon said. "And not my father. He knows better than most how damn dangerous this place can be."

But the knob turned easily beneath Edie's hand, and she pushed it open with a chuckle of triumph. "See . . ."

Deacon shook his head and reached beneath his jacket. "No, this isn't right. . . ."

"Maybe Helen left in a hurry," she suggested. "Trying to get to town before the blizzard got too bad."

He released a shaky breath that formed a thick white cloud in front of his face, and then he nodded. "Yeah, I guess I'm just a little on edge after the way we found you and Elijah just a little while ago."

She shivered then. "It could have been worse," she said. "We're both okay."

Deacon shook his head. "I doubt that. I think something's going on between the two of you."

She shrugged. "So what if it is?" And she wondered about that. What would it affect? Her objectivity? Her journalistic integrity? "Never mind," she said, hoping he wouldn't answer her now.

"You could have died tonight," he said. "I don't want anything to happen to you."

"Don't want to deal with the paperwork?" she teased.

He chuckled. "You make me realize how it must feel to have a younger sister. . . ."

"How's that?" she asked.

"Like a pain in the ass," he said.

She laughed and reminded him, "We'd better check on *Dad* now. Why don't you grab some wood if you can find it beneath that snow?" She pushed open the door and stepped inside and shivered. It was even cooler in the cabin than it had been on her first visit. "Bring an armload," she told him as he pushed snow off the woodpile and gathered up some chunks of it.

Leaving the door ajar, she stomped the snow from her boots and continued on down the hall. Maybe she shouldn't have been so loud, in case Sam Howell was sleeping. But if he was, she must not have awakened him because he hadn't called out like he had the first time she'd come to his door. He hadn't asked who was there.

And when she stepped into the open living area, she saw why. Sam Howell wasn't sleeping. He was dead . . . and not from the cancer that had already ravaged his body.

No. A big gash had opened his throat, spraying blood

across the wall, the woodstove, and even the ceiling, as well as his blankets and his bed.

A straight razor lay on the floor beneath his hand, which dangled over it, a pool of blood beneath them both.

She'd been frozen there, just staring . . . but a sudden succession of heavy thuds behind her made her jump. And a scream tore from her throat . . .

"I love you. . . ."

His father had never said those words to Deacon. And now he would never have the chance.

Deacon wasn't sure if Sam Howell would ever have professed his feelings if he'd lived, though. He'd certainly had opportunities over Deacon's entire life to praise him or express his affection for him. And he hadn't . . .

Because maybe he hadn't loved him.

Olivia did. The minute he and Edie had shown back up at the boardinghouse, she'd wrapped her arms around him and hugged him. "I love you," she repeated after leading him into the parlor and the warmth of the fire that burned brightly in the hearth.

"I love you," he said.

"Are you all right?" she asked, and she pulled back and peered up into his face.

He nodded. "Just numb . . ."

The shock hadn't worn off yet. He couldn't stop reliving the minute he'd stepped out of the hall and seen what Edie had. His father lying there in the middle of a crime scene, blood sprayed all around the room like water from a pulsating lawn sprinkler.

In that moment of shock, Deacon had gone so numb that the wood had dropped from his arms onto the floor, startling a scream from Edie, who'd likewise been frozen in place with shock until that moment . . . until he'd dropped the wood.

"Can I get you anything?" Edie asked, and he glanced over his shoulder to find her hovering in the doorway.

God, she was tough. Despite her scream, she'd pulled it together immediately after. And she'd been the one to comfort him, to get him out of the house, away from that sight. . . .

She'd shoved him into the passenger's side of the SUV and used the police radio to call in the death.

Suicide?

Murder?

What the hell had it been?

Deacon still didn't know.

And he wouldn't be the one investigating it . . .

Sergeant Montgomery had taken that away from him, just as she had the incident at the hall. Clearly, if either he or the Cookes were involved in any way, she wanted to handle it herself. Hell, maybe she considered him a suspect in both things that had happened that evening.

But he'd gotten over his past resentment of Elijah . . . for the most part. And what he'd told Edie earlier was true; he thought of her as a younger sister, and he didn't want anything to happen to her.

"You should go upstairs," Olivia told the reporter. "You must be exhausted after everything you've been through."

While he and Edie had waited for the state police to arrive, he'd called Olivia and told her everything that had happened that night. How he'd found Edie . . .

And how he'd found his father.

It could have been the same way.

"You can get me something," Deacon told Edie.

She nodded. "What? Tea? Some of Evelyn's cookies?"

Fortunately, Olivia had reassured the Pierce sisters enough about Edie and him that they'd gone back to sleep, just like all the other boarders. Holly had obviously tried waiting up for him with Olivia, but his daughter was curled into a ball on one of the antique couches, drool trailing out of the corner of her slightly open mouth. Even as a gangly teenager, she was still his little girl. Just like that baby was Bode Cooke's.

Maybe he hadn't killed her mother.

But then who had?

And was that the person who'd tried to kill Edie and Elijah tonight and may have successfully killed his father?

"What do you want?" Edie asked when he hadn't answered her yet.

He turned away from Holly then to focus on her again. She'd pulled off her parka and had left it dangling from one of the hooks of the coat tree in the foyer. She'd left her boots there, too, so she stood before him in her wet socks and jeans with her face chafed from the cold. And even though she probably wasn't much younger than Deacon, at the moment she didn't look much older than his daughter.

"I want the truth," Deacon said.

She nodded. "Me, too. I'm sure Sergeant Montgomery will let you know what the techs believe happened tonight."

He shook his head. "I want the truth from you. What did my dad tell you about Bainesworth?"

She shook her head now. "Nothing . . . nothing that would incriminate either of them."

He narrowed his eyes at her careful phrasing. She was holding something back, something he needed to know. "Edie, I don't think my father committed suicide."

No matter that it might have been staged to look that way,

with the razor on the floor beneath his dangling hand. Deacon had no doubt that crime scene techs would find Sam Howell's prints on it as well.

But that didn't mean that he was the one who'd pulled that razor across his throat.

No. Deacon suspected someone else had done that.

"Your father was very sick," Edie reminded him. "Suffering . . ."

"He has been for years," he said. "But he didn't kill himself before. And he was stronger then. Hell, I don't think he even had the strength left to do that. . . ." He shuddered as he remembered the deep gash and all the blood.

Thank God Helen had gotten trapped in town. He was glad that she hadn't had to see that.

He was sorry that he had, that Edie had.

But maybe it was good that she had, that she knew exactly how much danger she was in. Not that it was likely to stop her investigation.

"But why would someone kill your father?" It was Olivia who asked this question, Olivia who didn't know how close Deacon's father had been to James Bainesworth.

He suspected Edie knew, that Sam Howell had admitted more to her than she was willing to admit to Deacon.

"To keep him from talking . . ." he murmured.

"To keep him from talking about what?" Olivia asked.

While Edie just stood there, silent and tense.

"Bainesworth Manor," he replied. "He was part of it back then, looking the other way and probably even covering up the crimes of James Bainesworth."

"But that was all decades ago," Olivia said. "Why would someone kill him *now* over that, especially when he was already dying?"

"Because he'd recently started talking to someone about it . . ."

Edie shuddered then. "He didn't tell me anything that would incriminate either of them," she repeated.

"Maybe somebody didn't believe that," Deacon said. "And if they killed him because they believed he talked, they probably tried to kill you tonight because you listened . . . because they think you know. . . ."

She wrapped her arms around herself then and shook her head. "But I don't . . ."

"You and Elijah could have died tonight," he reminded her. "You have to tell me everything you know so I can protect you."

She drew in a breath and lifted her chin. "I can protect myself," she said with pride.

And Deacon groaned with frustration. "Edie, you and Elijah were barely breathing when we found you. You had a hell of a close call tonight. If not for Bode having that overdose antidote . . ."

"I appreciate your concern," Edie said. "But I'm exhausted. I'm going up to bed now." She stepped back out into the foyer and headed toward the stairwell.

"You're worried about her," Olivia said.

He nodded. "I think whoever tried to kill her tonight is going to keep trying. . . ."

Until they succeeded . . . just as they had with his father.

Chapter Fourteen

"You must have heard them last night. . . ."

Elijah jerked his gaze up from his desk to the open doorway of his office and found Morgana Drake standing there like she'd been the day before. Had it just been a day ago. . . ?

He glanced at the faint light of dawn outside his office window. Not quite a day ago.

He'd been up all night, waiting for the state police to arrive. He'd thought the storm had been holding them up, but when Sergeant Montgomery had finally arrived a short while ago, she'd said they'd come from another crime scene. Then she'd refused to say anything else to him until she inspected *his* crime scene.

That was why he'd left his office door open, so that she could let herself in when she deigned to join him. He hadn't expected anyone else to be awake yet.

Even Bode had returned to his cottage with Adelaide hours ago.

He blinked his eyes, which were bleary with sleep deprivation and probably the aftereffects of his near-overdose and focused on the self-proclaimed medium. Morgana wore an oversize brightly colored robe, and her bright red hair was in even more disarray than usual, as if she'd just awakened. Hell, maybe she was even sleepwalking.

"What did you say?" he asked her.

"The girls . . ." she murmured. "You must have heard them last night. You were so close to them. . . ."

He tensed and rose stiffly from his chair to approach her. "What do you mean?"

"You nearly died," she said. "So you were close to them. What did they tell you?"

He pressed his hand to his pounding head. "I don't know, Morgana." He would have questioned how she knew how close to death he'd been, but with the way she was always lurking around, she undoubtedly heard about everything that happened in the hall.

While she'd denied knowing Erika or what had happened to her when the sheriff had questioned her a week or so ago, had she told Deacon the truth? Would she talk to Elijah now if he seemed sympathetic to her concern for the ghosts who seemed to be so very real to her?

"You couldn't understand them?" she asked.

Unwilling to lie to her, he just replied, "I'm not sure I heard anything. . . ." Except a buzzing in his ears before he'd slid off his chair, but that buzzing could have been the attraction that he felt for Edie Stone as much as any effect of the drug they must have been slipped. "But what do you think they'd tell me? Would they talk to me about how they died . . . here at the manor?"

Her head bobbed in a quick nod. "Yes, that's why they can't leave. They can't find peace yet."

"Were you here then?" he asked. "Did you stay here years ago?" Until Edie had suggested it, it hadn't occurred to Elijah that Morgana Drake could have been here when it was Bainesworth Manor. But maybe that was because he'd believed that whoever had been here when it was the manor would never return, no matter what it was called now.

After he and Deacon and David found that body all those years ago, it was a wonder that any of them had ever returned. Deacon certainly hadn't wanted to, and honestly, Elijah had never intended to return to the island, let alone the estate.

"I was a good girl. . . ." Morgana murmured.

What did that mean? That she wouldn't have been sent here? That only bad girls were sent here?

His stomach churned with frustration over how mental illness had been handled back then and even now, like it was a stigma, like it was a curse. . . .

"I'm sure you were," he assured her. "But what about the girls you hear, the ones who can't rest?"

She shuddered. "They were *bad* girls. . . ."

"Why, Morgana?" he asked. "What made them bad?"

Her dark eyes widened, and she stepped back into the hall.

"Wait," he said. "Don't go. . ."

But she was already rushing off. And seconds later, when Sergeant Montgomery stepped into his doorway, he understood why. "Did I interrupt something?" she asked.

He shrugged. "I really have no idea. . . ." Was Morgana talking about something that had actually happened, or was it all just in her imagination, like the ghosts she claimed to see and hear?

"Well, I hope you can answer the other questions I have for you," she said with a disapproving frown.

"If you're going to ask me if I have any idea what happened tonight, I won't be able to answer that," he said.

"You're going to claim ignorance?"

"I'm going to claim that I was drugged," he said, and

some of the attitude he used to have with Deacon crept into his voice, the patronization. He'd patronized Deacon just because he'd liked to aggravate his old school bully; maybe that was why he'd used the tone with the trooper because she seemed quite like a bully herself. "I don't know how, but I suspect it was slipped into the wine I shared with Edie Stone since we were both drugged."

The trooper shook her head like a mother disappointed in her child. "I can't believe you were having dinner with the reporter. I doubt your brother was very happy about that either."

Montgomery had been at the hospital when Bode had warned Edie to stay away from him. So Elijah couldn't deny that his brother disapproved of the relationship—or attraction at least—he had with Edie Stone. But he pointed out to the trooper, "Bode saved our lives."

"Funny how he knew exactly what to give you in order to reverse the overdose. . . ."

"He called the doctor on staff in the ER. And we've had training, as have many of our employees, in how to treat overdoses," Elijah explained. "The hall sometimes helps guests who struggle with addiction."

"But wouldn't he have had to know what you and Stone had taken to know what would work?"

"I think all patients are now administered the same emergency drug as we have here to reverse overdoses. But you must know that. You've probably been trained to administer it, just like we have," he said. Elijah was tired, and not just because he'd had no sleep; he was tired of having to defend his brother to this woman.

"I thought Bode James contributed to addiction issues—"

"My brother is totally against all drugs, even alcohol and red meat," Elijah said. "He's the healthiest person I know."

"He's like a cult leader. He's not genuine," the woman insisted. "And that fanatic fitness agenda of his causes eating disorders for his followers."

"What?" Elijah asked, and he furrowed his brow to try to figure out what she'd just revealed. Some kind of prejudice against his brother . . . because of his career? "Bode does not lead a cult. He has clients who seek him out to help them get healthier." And he was so damn good at it that the hall had a waiting list for guests.

Her skin flushed with embarrassment, or maybe with outrage, because she continued, "His books, his television appearances . . . they all promote an unrealistic ideal of fitness."

"Is that why you don't like my brother?" he asked. "Because he's fit?" He might have expected that from a man who was jealous of Bode's physique. Hell, he was sometimes jealous himself. But most women were obsessed with Bode, maybe too obsessed . . . like the adoring Heather Smallegan, who was probably only going to cause more problems for Bode.

She shook her head. "The only reason I don't like your brother is because he refuses to answer my questions. He's hiding what he knows about Erika Korlinsky."

"He doesn't know what happened to her," Elijah insisted. "And that's why I was talking to Edie Stone tonight." And not just because she'd trespassed on the property. "She was going to help me figure out who really killed Erika."

Sergeant Montgomery widened her dark blue eyes with feigned interest. "And did you two manage to solve that murder before nearly getting murdered yourselves?"

He glared at her. "Getting drugged kind of sidetracked us for a bit there. . . ." That and his attraction to Edie. He'd wanted to talk about her more than he had his niece's mother.

"You were lucky," she said.

He shuddered and nodded. "I know."

"Sam Howell wasn't as lucky tonight. . . ."

He tensed. "What?"

"That other crime scene," she said. "It was just down the street from here."

"Sam Howell was murdered?" His blood chilled when he remembered that Edie had just gone to see the man a couple of days ago.

"You tell me."

He shrugged. "How would I know anything about Sam Howell?"

"He was rumored to be on your grandfather's payroll."

"That would have been before either you or I was born," he pointed out. The trooper was probably quite a few years younger than he was. There were no lines on her face and what hair escaped her cap was pure blond with no gray in it . . . unlike his. "And the only thing I've heard about Sam Howell lately is that he has terminal cancer. That must be what finally took his life."

She shook her head. "Cancer didn't take a straight razor to his throat."

Elijah gasped at the brutal image that popped into his mind. "Oh my God . . . that's horrible."

She nodded. "It wasn't pretty. Too bad your girlfriend was the first to find him."

He pressed his hand to his head again, trying to ease the pain pounding inside it along with the confusion. "What are you talking about?"

"Edie Stone—she was the one who found him."

Then he remembered. "The sheriff was going to check on him. . . ."

"And Ms. Stone beat him inside. Apparently it wasn't her first visit with the sheriff's father. . . ."

Elijah's stomach did a sickening lurch even though he'd already suspected that was how she'd gotten onto the property, and probably why his grandfather had found her so quickly.

Sam Howell had set it up somehow. Had he set up Edie?

Had whoever killed the former sheriff poisoned them as well?

"Have you talked to Ms. Stone already?" he wondered.

She nodded. "Yes, she gave her statement at the scene. She believes, from how the razor was found beneath Mr. Howell's hand, that he might have killed himself. . . ." She narrowed her eyes on his face. "Sounds like the claims you made about the sheriff's wife, that she killed herself . . . when your cousin was actually responsible."

"I didn't know that at the time," he said. "I didn't know my cousin nearly as well as I thought I did."

"The same could be true of your brother," she suggested.

Elijah shook his head. "No, my brother wants to help people," he said. "That's why he promotes fitness, for health. The last thing he wants to do is hurt anyone, especially his own daughter. There's no way he killed her mother."

"What about Sam Howell? What is Bode's involvement with the former sheriff?"

"My brother doesn't even know Sam Howell."

"Did you?"

He shrugged. "I had a few brushes with him when I was a kid," he admitted.

"When?" she asked. "What kind of brushes? Did he arrest you?"

Arrest James Bainesworth's grandson? Hell, Elijah had had a free pass to do whatever he'd wanted on the island back then—even antagonize the sheriff's own son.

"No. Over twenty-five years ago, Deacon, David, and I found a body here . . . when the manor was in ruins."

"Whose body?"

He shrugged. "I don't know. The sheriff never followed up with us. I don't know if anyone ever found out her identity or how she wound up here."

"And you never followed up?"

"I was barely twelve years old," he said. And he hadn't wanted to think about her, about that corpse, when he was awake. It was bad enough that she'd kept coming back to him in his nightmares.

The sergeant had a small pad in her hand and she scribbled down a note on it. He suspected that she was going to follow up. She asked him some more questions about the dinner he'd shared with Edie Stone, but she didn't write down anything else. She'd probably heard it all from her already.

When she'd interviewed Edie after she'd found the sheriff's father . . .

Did Edie really think Sam Howell had killed himself? Maybe that was what she wanted to believe, so she didn't have to face how close she'd come to dying, too.

Because whoever had killed Sam Howell could have tried killing them . . .

Or just Edie?

Which of them had been the real target of that attempt to overdose them? Her? Or him? Or perhaps . . . both of them?

Maybe it was the aftereffect of that near drug overdose. Or maybe it was just prior lack of sleep, but Edie could have stayed in bed the entire day. Probably would have, had her cell phone not been constantly vibrating on the nightstand next to the bed.

She'd been so deeply asleep that she'd just subconsciously noted that vibrating of her cell. She hadn't bothered waking up enough to actually check it . . . till now.

She stretched out her arms and legs and pushed down the heavy comforter before she reached for it. As she did, it vibrated again. And she recognized the number, and a zing of excitement shot through her to her core. "Hello . . ." she murmured, her voice husky with sleep and desire. Some of her dreams returned to her now, dreams about him.

Thank God she'd dreamed of Elijah Cooke instead of Sam Howell.

"Are you okay?" Elijah asked, and his voice was husky, too, with concern, and then impatience. "I've been calling you for hours."

"I've been sleeping," she said. "Haven't you been?"

"No," he said, and his voice was gruff, as if that irritated him. "I've been worrying about you."

Warmth flooded her heart that he actually sounded sincere, like he really cared, even if he wasn't particularly happy about it. She was beginning to care that same way about him, more than she wanted to, more than she should when caring about anything but her investigation now could be a dangerous distraction.

"I was just about to come to the door and risk your landladies shooting me," he said.

She jumped up from the bed. "You're here?" And she ducked down to squeeze under the dormer to look out the attic window onto the street below. Sure enough, his charcoal-gray SUV was parked at the curb. She couldn't see him through the tinted windows, but her skin tingled with awareness that he was this close. "I'm surprised they haven't taken a shot at you already," she said.

"Looks like Deacon's here, or at least his sheriff's department SUV is," Elijah said. "So maybe they feel safe."

Knowing Deacon was still in the house made Edie feel trapped. The sheriff was treating her very much like an over-protective older brother would probably treat his little sister. She needed to get away from him, and she needed to get her Jeep back.

"Are the roads clear?" she asked. The one in front of the house appeared to be and no more snow was falling for once.

"Yes," he said.

"Will you give me a ride?" she asked.

He hesitated a long moment before replying, "Where?"

She hesitated before answering him now because she worried that he would figure out why she'd parked her Jeep at the lighthouse. Though with all the snow that must have blown through those broken windows and onto the trapdoor, she doubted he would notice it. But she wasn't going to give him that destination until she joined him.

"Down the block," she said. "Drive a little way down the block and I'll sneak out to meet you." Pretty confident that he would agree, she disconnected the call.

Then she dressed quickly and warmly before creeping quietly down the attic stairs to the second floor. She couldn't hear any voices behind the closed doors; either people were sleeping behind them or they were downstairs. She moved to the back stairwell and crept quietly down that to the kitchen. Fortunately, it was between lunch and dinner time, so nobody was inside it. But she'd left her boots and parka by the front door, so she had to borrow a jacket and a pair of boots that had been left at the back door. Probably Evelyn's because it was all just a little too big.

She quietly opened the back door and stepped out into the snow. Then she hurried away from the house before anyone could catch a glimpse of her sneaking off and try to stop her. Because if they saw her climbing into a Halcyon Hall vehicle, they would definitely try to stop her.

It idled at the end of the block, its exhaust rising like clouds into the already dark sky. It wasn't snowing yet, but it looked like it might at any moment. Of course, there was always a gloom over the island; maybe it was as cursed as the locals claimed it was.

Or was it just the hall that was cursed?

After what she'd seen last night, after finding Sam Howell like she had, she would sooner believe it was the entire island that bore a curse. Maybe from the sins of its past . . .

Was that what had happened to Sam Howell? Had he paid for the sins of his past with his life?

Or had his suffering, both physical as well as maybe from guilt, finally been too much for him to bear a moment longer?

He might have ended his own life. That was what she'd told the trooper when the sergeant had taken her statement. Even Helen had confirmed as much with a phone call from town . . .

That the pain had been so unbearable for him that she'd gone to the pharmacy for the stronger morphine patches that hospice had prescribed for him.

He wouldn't need those anymore.

The passenger window was rolled down as she approached the side, and Elijah called out a question: "Are you getting in?"

Her pace had slowed as she'd drawn closer to the SUV. Thoughts of last night had distracted her mind, but her heart rate quickened with the sound of his voice. And as anxious as a rebellious teenager to see her forbidden boyfriend, she jerked open the passenger door and jumped inside to join him.

"You're smiling," he remarked with surprise.

"I'm happy to see you," she admitted. And on impulse, she leaned across the console and brushed her lips across his.

He gasped with surprise. Maybe he'd felt the same jolt she had the minute her mouth had touched his. A jolt of desire so intense that she wanted to deepen the kiss. Hell, she suddenly wanted to do a lot more than kiss. Remembering where they were, how close to the boardinghouse, she pulled back and fought temptation.

But she couldn't stop smiling at the sight of his handsome face, and he was incredibly handsome even with the dark circles beneath his pale blue eyes. His black hair was mussed, too, as if he'd been running his hands through it. She wanted to run her hands through it, to see if the silver strands woven in with the black tresses felt as silky as they looked.

"I can't believe you even want to see me again after last night," he murmured.

She shrugged. "As first dates go, it wasn't my worst. . . ."

And he laughed, a deep chuckle that had her skin tingling despite the heaviness of Evelyn's jacket. Her toes even curled within Evelyn's boots. "I didn't realize that was a date. If I had, I would have pulled out all the stops. . . ."

"Poisoned champagne instead of pinot noir?"

"That's right," he said. "Only the best . . ."

She laughed, delighted with how he bantered so easily with her. From everything she'd heard about Dr. Elijah Cooke, she'd thought he was super straitlaced and serious.

The only thing her sources had really gotten right was that he was clever. So very clever, and that was irresistibly sexy to her.

"Fortunately for me, it sounds like your previous dates have set the bar pretty low," he said. "Drive-by shootings instead of poisonings?"

She shrugged. "You know . . . just coffee or a drink or a movie. Nothing exciting. Like a near-death experience."

He sighed. "It does tend to put things in perspective. . . ."

She shivered then. "I got a little more perspective right after that. . . ."

"When you found Sam Howell dead," he finished for her. "Sergeant Montgomery informed me and questioned me about it. She says you suspected it was suicide."

She shrugged. "I don't know for certain. But it would make sense that a man with terminal cancer and in incredible pain would take his own life."

"What did he tell you that day you visited him—besides how to trespass on my property?"

A smile tugged at her lips. He was smart, maybe too smart for her own good. Sam Howell was smart, too. "He figured out pretty quickly that I wasn't a priest, so he wasn't about to confess all to me. I think he'd already made peace with himself. It was Deacon who he still wanted to make peace with. I think that was why he hadn't died yet. . . ."

"Then why would he have committed suicide?" Elijah asked. "If he had business left unfinished with his son?"

She shrugged. "I don't know."

"Seems more likely that somebody might have helped him end his life . . ."

She shrugged again. "If it was actually a murder, at least you and I have an alibi for it."

"Yeah, we were passed out on the floor of my suite," he

murmured. "I don't think we're the ones whose alibies Sergeant Montgomery is concerned about, though."

She furrowed her brow. "Bode? She's blaming him for killing Sam Howell?"

"Probably for poisoning us, too," he said.

"Is that why you were trying to reach me?" she asked. "You need my help to prove his innocence?"

He leaned across the console then and pressed his mouth to hers, kissing her deeply . . . so deeply that she lost her breath and had to pull away and pant for air as her heart raced.

"That's why?" she asked. "You wanted to kiss me?"

"I wanted—no, I needed—to see you. To make sure you were all right . . ."

The intensity of his concern shook her. There were depths to this man that reminded her of the old adage of still waters running deep, and she suddenly felt herself being pulled along with them, under the current. She struggled to breathe, to slow her racing heart, as she felt herself drowning in all the emotions running through her.

What the hell was happening?

What the hell was Elijah Cooke doing to her?

Sergeant Beverly Mae Montgomery had told the crime techs to take their time processing the scene in Elijah Cooke's suite. And while they dusted every item in the room and bagged up the evidence from the meal the psychiatrist had been sharing with the reporter, Mae waited for them to finish . . . while interviewing everyone who'd been present at the hall the night before. Despite this being the holiday season, the spa hadn't closed, though with as few guests and the horrible weather they had, they probably should have.

Unfortunately—for her—the weather had finally broken enough for the bridge to reopen, which meant her prime suspect could flee from the island if he wanted. But while Bode James was the primary suspect in the murder of his former lover, even she doubted he would have tried to kill his brother. While they were nearly a decade apart in age, they seemed close.

Too close for Bode to risk killing him . . .

A preliminary test on the wine bottle had picked up the presence of a narcotic . . . one that would have killed them had they drunk any more than they had. So who wanted Elijah Cooke and Edie Stone dead?

Chapter Fifteen

Elijah stared through the windshield at the snow blowing around the old limestone lighthouse. The windows in the lantern room were broken out and the balcony around that room was so rusted that it looked as if the metal would break apart and drop onto the rocks below it at any moment.

"So, this is where you wanted me to bring you for our second date?" he asked Edie.

She chuckled. "I had to figure out some way to top that first one."

"Or was the diner our first date and the poisoning our second?" he mused.

"Maybe the hospital was our first," she said. "It was quite romantic when you rescued me from the snow."

He nodded. "True. I am at my most romantic when I am seriously concussed."

"Then you followed it up with that date at the diner, showing off the town's high opinion of you," she said.

"Well, I was still pretty concussed," he said in his own defense. "Or else I wouldn't have showed off like that."

"Yes, you are quite humble, Dr. Cooke," she said.

He chuckled. "I think Deacon might disagree with you." The sheriff had always thought him insufferably arrogant, and Elijah usually had been with Deacon. But he'd been humbled lately, when he'd realized how little he'd known about so much. . . .

"A humble man like yourself probably finds it easier to let others sing his praises for him," she continued. "It's clear how much respect you have in this town."

He snorted.

And she laughed at the sound. "Too bad you don't show this side of yourself more often."

"What?" he asked. "Stupid?"

She shook her head. "Human. Most people don't think you are."

He sighed. "I'm all too human." He tore his gaze from the lighthouse to turn toward her. He hadn't trusted himself to look at her again, not after that kiss, not after his body had reacted so primally to it that he'd been tempted to pull her across the console and onto his lap. He groaned now because just thinking about that had his body tightening up again, begging for release.

As if she knew what she was doing to him, she remarked, "So, the poison dinner in your suite was really our third date," she said. "And usually I put out on third dates."

He gasped.

"Not that I usually make it to a third date," she admitted. And she sighed now.

Hiding his shock, he teased her instead. "What? Men find you too boring to pursue?"

She gasped now and smacked his shoulder. "That's the utmost insult, you know."

He shrugged. "I'm often called boring."

She shook her head. "You're not boring to me."

"And you're not boring to me, Ms. Stone," he said. "So why so few third dates?"

She shrugged now. "I'm too busy with work to have a personal life. What about you? Any wives and kiddies?"

He shuddered now. "God no."

And she laughed again. "You're definitely not boring, Dr. Cooke. So tell me why you're not married or at least married and divorced?"

"Like you, I'm just too busy."

"Yeah, getting concussed and poisoned probably does take up a lot of your free time."

He nodded. "You know it." He turned fully toward her then. "So, what do you do on fourth dates? Besides bringing them to deserted lighthouses?"

"You don't find that romantic?" She gestured out the windshield, which was beginning to steam up from their breathing.

He tilted his head and studied the structure. "It does have a certain tragic beauty to it." But then he turned back toward her. She was the true beauty. As quickly as she'd rushed out to meet him, she hadn't bothered with any makeup, but she didn't need it.

She was tilting her head now as she studied the lighthouse. "It really does . . ." she murmured. "Like it's witnessed horrible things but was strong enough not to let them destroy it . . ."

"Are we still talking about the lighthouse?" he wondered.

She gave him the side-eye look that he found so damn sexy.

"Are you referring to me or to you?"

He shrugged. "I'm not beautiful."

She turned fully toward him then and reached across the console to skim her fingers along his jaw. "You are . . ."

He snorted.

And she laughed.

"This is crazy," he murmured.

"I didn't think shrinks liked that word," she remarked. "Rosemary sure doesn't."

"I wasn't referring to a person," he said, "although maybe I am crazy for being so damn attracted to you that I can't even think straight."

"That could be because of the concussion or the drugs, too," she said. "I might not be to blame."

He reached out now and slid his fingers along the delicate line of her jaw, over her silky skin, and his heart raced at just that slight contact. "No, it's definitely your fault."

Her lips curved into a smile. "And that's a bad thing?"

He nodded. "You are on this mission for truth and justice, which I respect," he said. "But I also know that bringing up the past like that . . . well, it could destroy everything Bode and I have sought to do here."

"How?" she asked. "How can the truth hurt you?"

He pulled his hand from her face and leaned back against the driver's door. "Right now the guests who come to the hall, except for Morgana, don't know that it was once Bainesworth Manor. And they only know my brother as the world-famous personal trainer Bode James, and me as Dr. Cooke. They don't realize we're Bainesworths."

"That's not your fault," she said. "You can't be held responsible for what your grandfather did before you were even born."

He shook his head. "You remember our diner date. You heard what everyone was saying. . . ."

And suddenly he needed to escape all of that, who he was and the close confines of the SUV. Because if he didn't get away from Edie, he was going to do something stupid, something like make love to her . . .

So he pushed open the driver's door and stepped out onto the shoulder of the road. And now he could see it . . .

Not just the lighthouse but the Jeep parked in front of his SUV.

The wind had picked up, knocking the accumulated snow from it so he could see the roof rack. This was where she'd parked her vehicle yesterday before trespassing onto the grounds.

She stepped out then and came around the front of the SUV.

"How?" he asked her. "How the hell did you get from here to the ravine without freezing to death in that blizzard yesterday? Or did somebody pick you up from here and smuggle you through the gates?" Maybe she'd gotten to Rosemary like she was beginning to get to him. Or Dr. Chase . . .

Elijah's former professor had always been drawn to pretty women; it was the reason Gordon had earned a reputation at the university. While he'd been investigated and cleared of any wrongdoing, it hadn't changed the fact that he'd favored the female students, especially beautiful ones like Edie.

She'd gotten to Elijah, too. But it wasn't just because of her beauty . . .

She challenged him in a way nobody else ever had. She matched wits with him. Or, as was probably really the case, outwitted him.

Edie knew she'd taken a risk in asking Elijah to bring her to her Jeep. She'd worried that he might figure out that the lighthouse had been her key to trespassing onto the estate, especially when he'd kept staring at it. Now he was staring at her that intently.

So intently that she shivered. Or maybe she was just cold.

The wind roared in off the ocean, bringing with it the sting of that salty spray. She would rather be back inside the SUV with Elijah, touching him and kissing him.

And more . . .

Edie hadn't lied to him about rarely making it to three dates. She hadn't met anyone in a long while who had held her interest the way Elijah Cooke did. And she had never met anyone who had attracted her as much.

The wind tousled his black-and-silver hair and chafed the skin stretched taut over his chiseled features. Despite his denials, he was beautiful. So very beautiful . . .

"Edie?" Her name was a question on his lips.

She wasn't sure what he was asking anymore. Maybe because she was staring at him like she was, like he was staring at her, so damn hungrily.

"You're not going to tell me, are you?" he asked.

"Tell you what?"

"Who got you onto the grounds?"

She shook her head. "A reporter needs to protect her sources." A twinge of guilt had her sucking in a breath as the image of Sam Howell, his throat slashed open, flashed through her mind. She closed her eyes on it, trying to block out that memory, trying to block out the regret that she hadn't protected him.

She should have, but she'd been too late.

Just as it might have been too late for her and Elijah if Bode James hadn't saved them both last night.

Just as she'd nearly missed the opportunity to kiss Elijah like she had when she'd first climbed into the SUV with him, she didn't want to miss the opportunity to experience more than that kiss.

"It's cold out here," she said. And she reached for his

hand. He wasn't wearing gloves. Of course. And while he had on a wool coat, it probably wasn't thick enough to protect him from the icy spray and the frigid wind. She tugged on his hand, pulling him back toward his vehicle, which idled still on the shoulder of the road.

Instead of opening the front door, she opened the back and jumped onto the seat while tugging him inside with her. She didn't scooch across the seat, though, so when he jumped inside with her, their legs tangled, his body pressing against hers as he pulled the door shut. "Edie . . ." he murmured.

She slid her fingers up, into his hair, and pulled his head down for her kiss. The passion between them ignited, burning her up. Even as their mouths devoured each other's, she reached between them, unzipped her borrowed jacket and wriggled out of it. But it wasn't enough. She was still too hot. He was too hot.

He stared down at her, and those pale eyes that she'd once thought such an icy blue burned with desire. He wanted her every bit as much as she wanted him.

And that inflamed her.

She pushed his coat from his shoulders and then attacked the buttons on his shirt, pulled them free until his chest was bare to her gaze and her touch. She skimmed her palms over the soft, black hair that covered muscles as sculpted as she'd imagined when she'd touched his chest the night before.

His heart thudded fast and hard beneath her palm. And he uttered a low, deep groan. "Edie, you're driving me crazy."

"You drove," she said. And she was right there with him, going out of her mind with the need for a release.

And he chuckled. "You are such a maddening woman."

She laughed. "I can't tell if that's a compliment or not."

"For you, it is," he said. Then he undressed her, as quickly and as impatiently as she was undressing him.

Skin slid over skin as their bodies got even more entangled on that bench seat in the back of the SUV. His mouth was everywhere.

On her neck.

On her breasts.

His lips tugged on her nipples, pulling them even tauter than they'd been.

A moan escaped her, long and full of the pleasure he was giving her with his touch. His hand moved between her legs, and another moan tore from her throat as he brought her to the first peak.

It was good.

But it wasn't enough.

She reached for him, sliding her hand around him, running it up and down the length of his erection. His cock pulsated in her grasp, and he panted for air.

"Edie . . ." he gritted out between his clenched teeth.

Then somehow he was sitting down, and she was astride him. Then he was inside her.

They thrashed around, fighting to find a release. And when it came, it had them both screaming with pleasure. For Edie, it was more intense than anything she'd felt before. With anyone. Ever.

Her body shuddered in the aftermath of it, and she went lax against him. He held her for a long while, almost protectively, and his lips skimmed along her cheek and then her neck.

And inside her still, his body began to stir again.

She opened one eye and peered into his face. "Dr. Cooke . . ."

He clasped her hips and began to move her as he thrust.

"Dr. Cooke, you are incredible." And he was the most incredible lover she'd ever had.

This time they took longer; they weren't as frantic, as frenzied. They moved slower, touched gentler, but the feelings were no less intense. And when she came, it was even more soul-shattering than the first time.

And she, who never cried, nearly sobbed his name with the intensity of the feelings rushing through her. And she, who was never afraid, was scared out of her mind that for the first time in her life she might be falling in love, or at least deep into infatuation.

Gloved hands gripped the steering wheel so tightly, it was a wonder it didn't snap into pieces. This vehicle was parked farther down the road from the SUV that had been idling for so very long.

The anger that had started as the driver had trailed Elijah to the boardinghouse bubbled over now into pure, blind rage.

It was clear what they were doing here once they'd gotten into the back seat. It was clear that they were taking a very long time with each other.

And it was clear that their time was up now.

They both had to die.

One of the gloved hands moved from the wheel to the shifter, moving it from Park to Drive. And then the right foot pressed hard on the accelerator, thrusting the vehicle forward, hurtling toward the back of that SUV and striking it with such force that the airbag exploded from the steering wheel, exploded into the face of the driver.

The gloved hands fought it down, pressing the deflating bag out of the way so that the driver could see.

The back of Elijah's SUV had crumpled, the glass of the lights all broken and strewn across the snow. Were they dead now?

Injured?

Or would they once again survive and catch the driver?

Instead of waiting to find out, the gloved hand reached for the shifter again, slamming it into Reverse, and the crumpled vehicle spun backward along the snow-covered road. Then it was shifted into Drive with the need to escape.

To find a place to ditch the vehicle, and to lay low until there was news . . . of Edie Stone's and Elijah's deaths.

Chapter Sixteen

Nearly twenty-four hours later, Elijah was still wondering what the hell had happened. And he was probably more shocked over having had sex with Edie Stone in the back seat of a vehicle like a randy teenager than over someone trying to kill him.

Again.

Them.

Someone had probably intended to kill them both, like the night they'd been poisoned. But in the crash they'd only sustained some strained muscles, and that might not have been from the vehicle slamming into the back of his SUV.

It might have been because of how frantic they'd been to make love, how greedy for pleasure they'd been.

Even now, thinking about it, about her . . .

His body tightened with desire. With need . . .

He pushed open the driver's door of his rental vehicle, welcoming the blast of cold air against his face. He needed to clear his head. To clear away the desire . . .

Before this meeting.

They'd put it off too long already.

Bode turned around from where he stood in front of the double doors to the carriage house. "I could have done this on my own," he said. "You didn't have to come here after what you've been through."

Elijah shrugged. "I'm fine." Frustrated, but fine.

"You were nearly killed three times over the past week," Bode reminded him. "What the hell were you doing out at the lighthouse yesterday anyway?"

"Shh . . ." Elijah murmured with a glance up to the second story. Was the window open? Was Grandfather eavesdropping on them?

"You don't think he already knows . . . everything?" Bode asked. "Hell, he probably knows more than we do."

Elijah nodded. "That's why we need to talk to him."

"We need to talk to that lawyer," Bode said.

"Tomorrow," Elijah reminded him. Gordon Chase had set up an appointment for the criminal attorney he knew to come out to the hall. And before they talked to him, they needed to gather as many facts as they could to help Bode, and maybe to save Elijah's life if the same person who was after him was the one who'd killed Adelaide's mother. The baby must be with her nanny because Bode stood with empty arms before those doors. He also must have run over to the carriage house because no other vehicle was parked outside it except for the one Elijah had rented after Sergeant Montgomery impounded his for evidence.

What had she found?

Had she figured out what he and Edie had been doing when the crash happened? They hadn't been exactly open with her when she'd taken their report, but from how wrinkled their clothes were and how tousled their hair, she'd probably drawn her own conclusion.

Like she had about Bode.

Of course, his whereabouts had been the first she'd wanted to know. Like Bode would hurt him . . .

The way his younger brother was looking at him now, with such worry, warmed Elijah's heart. Despite, or maybe because of, all the unfortunate events at the hall, they were closer than they'd ever been. Too bad it had taken tragedies to draw them together.

Bode shivered and glanced at the doors. "I rang the bell. . . ."

"It doesn't look like Theo is here," Elijah pointed out, and then he reached around his brother and turned the door handle. "It's unlocked. . . ." And when he stepped inside, it was eerily quiet.

Was this how it had been for Edie the other night, when she'd found Sam Howell's body?

His stomach muscles tightened with dread as he walked through the open living area toward the stairwell leading up to the second story, where James Bainesworth spent his days in front of that window, watching over the manor.

That was what it would always be to Grandfather. The manor. *His* manor . . .

Despite the warmth inside the carriage house, Bode shivered again and shook his head. But he said nothing to break that eerie silence, and Elijah was pretty sure the same thoughts had crossed his brother's mind that had crossed his.

Had someone finally taken their revenge against James Bainesworth?

Elijah ascended the stairs slowly, then crossed through the open doorway into the bedroom at the top of the stairs. The wheelchair was turned toward the window, revealing only the back of James's gray head and his broad shoulders. He looked a bit slumped over, instead of the way he usually sat ramrod straight, as if he could stand up at any time and walk around.

Maybe he could.

Maybe the chair was just for show. Elijah could never be certain of anything with his grandfather. He glanced back at Bode as his brother joined him inside the room. The same dread Elijah felt was twisting Bode's handsome face into a grimace.

"Grandfather . . ." he called out.

"About damn time . . ." the old man muttered before spinning the chair toward them. "Where the hell have you two been?"

"Have you been calling us?" Elijah asked, and he automatically reached for the pocket of his shirt. But his phone wasn't there. He hadn't been able to find it since the crash.

Edie had used hers to call in the "accident." They both knew it was no such thing, though. Whoever had hit them had meant to hurt them, probably worse.

His phone was, no doubt, somewhere inside that impounded vehicle. He needed to check with the trooper to see if it had been found.

"I shouldn't have to call my family," James grumpily replied. "They should want to come and check on me."

And Elijah wondered when was the last time James had heard from either of his daughters. He suspected they had run away to escape from their father as much as they had to flee the island.

"They've been a little busy," Bode answered for both of them. "Elijah has been going through hell. Someone's tried to kill him twice."

"I thought that idiot contractor was dead," James murmured.

"The last two tries weren't David," Elijah said.

James's eyes widened with alarm then. "What do you mean? Someone else is after you? But why?"

"You tell me," Elijah suggested. "Why would someone be trying to kill me?"

James shrugged. "Why would you think I would have any idea? You do not confide in me, Grandson."

"I wonder why . . ." Elijah murmured.

And his grandfather glared at him. "I have a say in this business, you know. I am a partner."

"You're supposed to be a silent partner," Bode reminded him, and for once he sounded impatient with the old man, too.

"Silent, not deaf and blind," James said. "I've heard the sirens, seen the lights, and I want to know what the hell's going on around here."

"That makes three of us, then," Elijah remarked. "I have no idea who's trying to kill me and Edie Stone."

"Edie Stone? The pretty reporter?" James asked, his pale eyes bright with amusement, and then maybe even a flicker of concern. "Is she all right?"

"She is," Elijah said, although he'd been so damn scared when the SUV was struck with such force that she'd flown into the back of the front seats.

"And what about you?" James asked with a sniff as his gaze ran up and down Elijah.

He ran a hand over his head. He'd had a dull ache there since the concussion. "I'll live."

"Not if this person finally succeeds in these attempts on your life," Bode murmured. "We need to figure out who's after you."

"And you think I know?" James asked.

"You make a point of wanting to know everything," Elijah said. "And you actually seem to. You were ready for Edie that day, had Theo waiting for her. How did you know she was coming? Did your buddy Sam Howell tell you?"

James shrugged. "I don't know what you're talking about."

"Sam Howell is dead," Elijah shared, and he watched his grandfather's face, tried to see if there was even a flicker of surprise. And there might actually have been.

"I thought he was too ornery for even the cancer to take him," James murmured now.

"The cancer didn't take him," Elijah said. "Someone cut his throat."

James snorted then. "Why would someone bother to murder a dying man?"

"Maybe to keep him from talking any more."

He shook his head. "Sam didn't have as much to say as you'd think."

"Well, he won't be able to say anything to anyone anymore."

"Maybe he did himself in," James said with a sigh. "Sam Howell was not a strong man. That's why he drank so damn much, same reason your father does."

Bode flinched, as if offended that Grandfather had called their dad weak, while the truth didn't offend Elijah.

"While you're telling the truth here," Elijah said, "tell us everything you know."

"I'm in my nineties now, that could take some time," he said with a heavy sigh, "time that neither of us might have."

Elijah glared at him now. "Just think about this, old man," he said as his patience wore out, "if something happens to me and Bode, you're going to be carted off to a home."

Grandfather tensed. "What are you saying? Someone's trying to kill Jamie, too?"

"No, he's probably going to go away for a murder he didn't commit, one you probably know something about, if you know as much as you act like you do," Elijah said. "It's time to start talking, Grandfather, while we're both still able to listen to you."

"And where the hell is Theo?" Bode asked with a glance around. "He's hardly ever here."

"Is he out doing your bidding again? Abducting another woman like he abducted Edie?" Elijah asked.

"I don't know what the hell he's doing right now," James admitted, and he sounded pissed about that. "I do know things about him that you don't. Teddy Bowers was his son."

"But Theo . . ." Bode began, then trailed off.

"Theodore, same first name," Elijah said. That had occurred to him already. "But they had different last names and looked nothing alike." Teddy Bowers had been a scrawny kid barely out of his teens, and Theo was a beast. A monster.

Igor . . .

Had he helped his son abduct Genevieve Walcott? God, she'd been lucky to escape them, then. But she'd always said that Teddy had seemed to be acting alone.

"Is Theo your son, like his son claimed?" Elijah wondered.

James shook his head. "I was a doctor, not a pedophile or a rapist. The only children I had are your mother and your aunt, wherever the hell they are. . . ." He sighed. "That's your problem, you know. Everybody always thinks that women are weaker, that they're not as strong, not as smart, not as capable of murder. . . ."

Elijah nearly laughed at the hypocrisy of such a misogynist making that statement.

"You think a woman murdered Erika?" Bode asked, and his muscular body tensed at the thought.

The old man shrugged. "I don't know who murdered that

woman. I never met her. The mother of your child and I never met. At least I've met Ms. Stone. . . ."

Elijah wasn't as happy about that as his grandfather was. "Who else have you met? What else do you know about our guests? Our employees?" Because it was clear he knew more than they did. He knew about Theo, and if the nurse was under the same delusion his son had been that he was a Bainesworth by blood, maybe he felt entitled to everything Elijah and Bode had.

Like Bode had had Erika . . .

And Elijah had Edie . . .

Edie felt like she'd been hit by a bus. And maybe it had been a bus that struck the SUV. With the windows all steamed up, she hadn't seen it coming, even though she'd been facing the rear window. And after it had struck them, she'd been too stunned to try to get a look at it as it sped away from the scene.

Hell, she'd been too stunned before that, from the intensity of passion and pleasure she'd experienced with Elijah Cooke, to be aware of anything but him. Of how he'd made her feel . . .

Sitting on one of the small antique settees in the front parlor, she pushed off the blanket that Evelyn kept putting over her. Even though the fire was dying down in the hearth, she was overheated just thinking about Elijah Cooke.

And worrying about him . . .

She was safe here at the boardinghouse, where Evelyn and Bonita would make sure nothing happened to her. But he was back at the manor, where she suspected the person who wanted them dead was as well. Who?

She'd once cared only about finding out about the past

of the manor, but now she was more concerned about the future—about making sure she had one. And while she didn't know if a future together was possible for them, she wanted to make sure that Elijah would have one, too.

She needed to check in with him. At the thought of talking to him again, her pulse quickened with excitement. With attraction . . .

She hadn't tried to contact him yet because she'd hoped he was resting, and she didn't want to disturb him. He hadn't slept at all the night they'd been poisoned, and he'd looked so tired when she'd dropped him at the hall once Sergeant Montgomery had let them leave the crash site. Fortunately, her Jeep had been parked far enough away that it hadn't been damaged. If only she and Elijah had escaped unscathed . . . It was afternoon now, so she pulled her cell from her pocket and pressed his contact.

"This is Dr. Cooke. I am currently unavailable to take your call—"

She clicked the disconnect with his voice mail and punched in the main number for Halcyon Hall. When the receptionist answered, she said, "I'd like to speak to Dr. Cooke. This is Edie Stone."

The line went quiet. Had the receptionist hung up on her?

It wouldn't be the first time she'd ever done that, but it would be the first time since Edie had gotten closer to Elijah. Though how close were they? Close enough that he'd told the receptionist he would take her calls?

"Ms. Stone," a female voice greeted her coolly. Then she unnecessarily added, "This is Amanda Plasky."

Edie had already recognized the publicist's voice. "I asked to speak to Elijah," she said.

"You don't have his cell number?" the woman asked, and there was the lilt of amusement in her voice.

"I do," Edie said. "My call went to voice mail. I just wanted to make sure he was all right."

"He slept in quite late today and has been busy catching up with his work as hall director," the woman replied.

Edie was surprised that the woman had actually deigned to give her any information. That was a new attitude from her.

But then she added, "Perhaps he isn't answering your calls because he decided it ultimately wasn't worth it."

"What?" Edie asked.

"Trying to charm you into giving up your investigation of Bainesworth Manor wasn't worth it, not with his proximity to you putting his life in danger . . ."

"'Charm' me?"

The woman laughed. "Surely you didn't think he was seriously interested in you?"

Her whole life Edie had dealt with mean girls. From moving around so much the first ten years of her life, she'd always been the new kid, threatening the already established friendships at school. And when her biological parents recovered her only to send her off to boarding school a few years later, she'd encountered the meanest girls there . . . the ones who'd picked on her for being the milk-carton kid.

She'd learned long ago not to let them get to her. When they'd been unable to get a reaction out of her, they'd given up. She suspected that Amanda Plasky wouldn't lose interest in her as quickly, though—because she obviously saw her as competition for Elijah. And she wouldn't feel that way if he had just been charming her into giving up her investigation.

Yet a niggling doubt crept into Edie's mind, and a twinge of pain struck her heart. He was a brilliant man, far smarter than she was, and maybe he'd inherited some of his grandfather's ability to manipulate people into doing what he wanted, like James Bainesworth must have Sam Howell. Had he been worried that he'd lost his ability to manipulate the dying man, though, and hadn't dared to wait until the cancer claimed him?

"I haven't given up the story," Edie said. "I've just been sidetracked with a new one, trying to figure out who's trying to kill me. Obviously, you've been hanging around the hall a lot. Where were you yesterday?"

The phone went quiet again . . . until the dial tone beeped. Amanda had hung up on her. Edie smiled.

"Did you find my baby?" a voice softly addressed her from the shadows of the hallway. While it was just early afternoon, the sky had gone dark, with thick clouds.

"Bonita?" Edie called out, and the woman shyly stepped into the parlor with her.

"Did you find him?" she asked.

"Not yet," Edie said.

Tears glistened in those bleary-looking blue eyes of Bonita's.

"I'm going to keep looking, though," she assured her. "Maybe you can help me. . . ." She patted the threadbare cushion of the settee. "Come, sit with me . . ."

Usually the woman kept her distance from Edie, but now she crept nearer until she finally settled onto the edge of the cushion close to her. "Do you want some cookies?" the woman asked.

Edie smiled. Evelyn had been trying to feed her since she'd arrived back at the boardinghouse yesterday. Apparently, Bonita was following suit. She shook her head. "I'm not hungry. I'm just lonely. . . ."

A pang struck her heart at the honesty of that. She stayed in a house with a lot of other people, yet she really was lonely. Rosemary had the judge and her daughter. Deacon had Olivia and his daughter. And Evelyn and Bonita had each other.

Edie was the odd one out, just as she'd been since she was ten years old. It had never bothered her, not really, not until now. . . .

Not until she'd finally not felt so alone . . . yesterday, in Elijah's arms. . . .

And now that he wasn't even talking to her . . .

She sucked in a shaky breath. And Bonita slid closer to her and pulled the blanket up again, over them both. "I've been lonely for a long time," the older woman remarked. "Since my baby was taken . . ."

"Who took your baby?" Edie asked. "Was it Dr. Bainesworth?"

Bonita shook her head. "No, he didn't like the babies."

"Who liked the babies?" she asked.

"The nurses," Bonita said, and she had that faraway look in her eyes again as she slipped into the past. "The nurses liked the babies. . . ."

Edie had tried finding the employment records from the manor, but just like with the adoption records, she'd come up empty-handed. "Do you remember any of their names?"

"Oldie . . ."

Undoubtedly a nickname, and from the sound of it, she probably wasn't around anymore. "Did the nurses help you deliver the babies?" she asked. Surely the doctor would have had to help.

"The intern did . . ."

"Intern?"

Despite the warmth of the room, Bonita shuddered. "Yes . . ."

"Did he like the babies?" she asked.

Bonita shook her head. "He liked the girls. . . ."

At the mention of the girls, Edie remembered Morgana. "Do you remember any of the other girls?"

Bonita's head bobbed in a nod, but she offered no names.

"Do you remember Morgana?"

Her slight shoulders shrugged.

"Morgana?" another woman asked.

Bonita must have thought, like Edie had, that they were alone because she jumped up from the couch and rushed off, pushing past Rosemary, who stood in the doorway.

"You're home early," Edie said, and she was happy. She could ask Rosemary about Elijah, make sure he was really all right.

Rosemary stepped closer to her. "Yes, there's another storm coming, and I didn't want to get stuck at the hall." She shuddered now, as if she'd developed a sudden revulsion to the place she'd started working at to find her daughter. But then she'd liked helping people so much that she'd stayed. "Why were you asking Bonita about Morgana Drake? Do you think Morgana once stayed at the manor?"

Edie nodded.

And Rosemary gasped and nodded. "That would make so much sense."

"As much sense as Morgana can make," Edie said. "I've been able to talk to so few people who stayed there. The librarian in town . . ." And while she'd wanted to help Edie expose the hall, she hadn't wanted to share her personal story with anyone, most especially not a reporter. "And now Bonita."

"I'm surprised she was talking to you about it," Rosemary said. "She usually runs away if anyone mentions the manor."

"She wants me to find her baby." And that burden bore down heavily on Edie's shoulders. She had to help the woman because no one else had when the young Bonita had needed help the most, when she'd been mistreated so horribly. Tears stung Edie's eyes, but she quickly blinked them away.

Not before the psychologist noticed, though. "This is more than a story to you," Rosemary surmised.

Edie sighed. "I don't know what it is anymore. . . ."

"The death of you," another voice remarked as Evelyn walked in carrying a tray with steaming mugs and a plate of cookies.

She set it on the coffee table in front of Edie, who pointed at it and said, "So that's what you're calling this afternoon tea here? 'The death of me'?"

Evelyn snorted. "You're a lot safer eating here than you are at that hall. You shouldn't go anywhere near that place anymore."

"I have to go back," Edie insisted. To see Elijah and to speak to Morgana . . .

Evelyn shook her head. "No, you don't."

"I promised Bonita," Edie said, "I would help her find her baby."

"Maybe it's better if you don't," Evelyn said. "If she doesn't find out whether or not that Teddy Bowers kid was actually her grandson."

Bonita had shot and killed him—to save herself and Genevieve and Evelyn and the judge—but it would undoubtedly still affect her. Because Edie knew her well enough to believe that on some level she would understand . . .

"I still think it's better to know the truth—whatever it is—than to always wonder. . . ."

And thinking of that reinforced her resolve. She reached for her cell. Instead of trying to call Elijah again, she sent him a text. I need to see you. She needed to know what the truth was . . . between them. *Had* he just been charming her to get her to abandon her story and focus instead on helping his brother? On helping him?

Evelyn sighed. "Maybe, that's true. Maybe then she would stop running off to look for her baby."

Rosemary nodded in agreement. "It's always better to know the truth, no matter how horrible it might be." Then she shuddered.

"Will you talk to Morgana for me?" Edie asked the psychologist. "Will you see what she remembers about the manor?"

"You're not sure she was even there," Rosemary said. "Bonita didn't remember her."

"I'm not sure what Bonita remembers," Evelyn murmured with a glance at the doorway to see if her sister had returned.

"She remembered that Dr. Bainesworth didn't like babies and that a nurse named Oldie did, and she mentioned an intern, too, one who liked the girls maybe a little too much."

Rosemary's brow furrowed. "I think Dr. Chase once worked there."

"Dr. Chase?" Edie had met him briefly that day at the hall. "He doesn't look old enough to have worked at the manor all those years ago."

"He was probably still in med school at the time," Rosemary said. "I can talk to him, too. We're very close. As well as being a friend of my father's, he was once my professor. Elijah's, too."

And maybe that was why Edie should talk to him herself. She wondered if Elijah would allow her inside the hall again. Or if she would have to get herself there . . . through those tunnels.

Her phone vibrated in her hand. She hadn't realized she

was still holding it until then, and she glanced down at the screen and the text she'd just received in reply to the one she'd sent Elijah: Meet me at the lighthouse in an hour.

It took Edie almost an hour to extricate herself from the women who kept hovering around her at the boardinghouse. She'd had to lie to them and claim that she was going up to bed. But instead, she'd headed out the back door, like when she'd met Elijah before.

He wasn't waiting for her down the block, though. He was probably already at the lighthouse. Her pulse quickened at the thought of him, of all they'd done there.

Her vehicle, fortunately, was parked on the street because the driveway had been full when she'd returned last night . . . after Sergeant Montgomery had finally let her and Elijah leave the scene. Would she even be able to get to the lighthouse now? Or would the troopers have it cordoned off like they had last night?

But when Edie drove out of town, past the hall, she saw no sign of Elijah's wrecked SUV. She saw no sign of a vehicle that hadn't been wrecked either. Maybe he wasn't there yet.

Then a light flashed . . . shining down onto her windshield. On and off, on and off, the beacon shone down from the lantern room. But the beacon had been broken long ago . . . and if it had been working still, it would have pointed out to sea. Not at her . . .

This was a signal, probably from a flashlight. Someone was waiting for her inside.

Had Elijah come through the tunnels? Did he know about them?

Edie stepped out of her Jeep and scrambled up that rocky hill to pull open the door to the lighthouse. Fortunately someone had already opened it, pulling the snow away from it, or it might not have budged for Edie because so much snow had fallen since the day she'd gone inside it. She could hear footsteps on the stairs, coming down from the lantern room.

Anxious to see Elijah, she hurried up. "Why did you want to meet here?" she asked as a shadowy figure approached, shining that light in her face. She flinched and raised her hand, and as she pulled it from the railing, the shadow pushed her.

And she tumbled back, falling down those creaky metal steps. She reached out, trying to grasp anything to break her fall. The shadowy figure stayed above her, just watching as she struck those steps and her head struck the limestone wall.

Pain reverberated through her skull until everything went—almost blessedly—black.

Chapter Seventeen

Elijah opened the bag of items Sergeant Montgomery had dropped off for him with the receptionist a short time ago. Hopefully, his cell phone was inside, but when he upended the yellow envelope only his key ring and packet of insurance and registration paperwork dropped onto his desk.

Where the hell was his phone?

He wouldn't have put it past the trooper to keep it and go through his texts and emails. After the concussion and his overdose, he hadn't been able to remember his passcode for it, so he'd had it reset and hadn't put in another one yet. It would have been unlocked and easily accessible for Sergeant Montgomery to go through.

He groaned at his slip and reached for his laptop. At least it was synched with his phone, and he should be able to find it. And if it was with the trooper, he'd have something else to address with that lawyer he and Bode were meeting tomorrow. Like how she shouldn't have looked at anything on it unless she had a warrant.

When he opened up the link between his laptop and cell, he noticed the texts first. **Meet me at the lighthouse in an hour.**

But it hadn't been sent to him; it looked, instead, as if he'd sent it to Edie in reply to her. I need to see you.

Who the hell had used his phone to send her that message?

He clicked on the Find My Phone link, and the location came up not far from where he was at the hall. But it was outside the hall property, just down the road, at the lighthouse.

Whoever had lured Edie out there was already there, with his phone. Was Edie already there as well?

Panic pressing hard on his chest, Elijah grabbed the keys for his rental vehicle, opened his office door, and ran out into the hall, through the lobby, and out those doors to the parking lot. Snow blasted his face, biting into his skin, stinging his eyes.

Or maybe it was fear taunting him that had his eyes stinging. The fear that he was probably already too late.

Somebody had used him to lure Edie out there, and they would have only one reason to do that: to try to kill her again. Had they known that he would follow?

Was this a trap for him, too?

He didn't care. He wasn't going to wait for the sheriff or the trooper to rush to Edie's rescue. He was going to save her himself.

If he wasn't already too late . . .

Edie couldn't get warm. She reached out for the blanket she'd kept pushing off earlier, but her hand sank deep into icy snow instead. And she pried open her eyes to peer around her.

Where was she? What the hell had happened?

And then she remembered . . .

The light. The shadow . . .

The shove . . .

And she'd tumbled down the stairs. Faint light filtered through the windows high above where she lay on the floor. Snow filtered in along with that light, falling onto her face and into her hair. She reached up to find her cheek already cold, her hair nearly frozen with that snow.

She had to get up, had to get the hell out of here, or she was going to freeze to death. Or maybe worse yet, the person who'd shoved her down those stairs was going to come back to make sure she was dead.

Then she heard it, carried in on the wind like the snow, the sound of a car engine. It was already too late.

She'd been unconscious too long to get away now. She couldn't go out there, but maybe she should go down . . . into the tunnels.

Or was that what her attacker wanted her to do . . . ?

She wasn't sure she could even find the trapdoor beneath the snow before the attacker made it up that rocky hill to the lighthouse door. Hell, before she made it up from the floor.

Stiff with the cold and with the bumps and bruises she'd gotten in her tumble, she could barely move. She rolled onto her stomach and sank her hands into the snow to push herself up. And her fingers ran over something metal . . .

One of the hinges. She was lying atop the trapdoor. It was beneath the snow. So whoever had been waiting for her in the lantern room hadn't come in through the tunnel.

They'd used the door, which rattled before opening. She had nowhere to hide, and she definitely wasn't running up and getting trapped. She had to go out that door . . . through the person standing in front of it. But now the shadow seemed even taller and broader than it had earlier, when it had shone that light in her eyes and shoved her down. Anger surged through her with the memory, helping her to gather her strength, and with all of that and her desperation to survive, she jumped up and rushed forward, crashing into the hard body standing in the way of her escape.

The shadow grunted, then reached out and caught her shoulders. "Edie? Are you all right?"

She smacked her hand against Elijah's shoulder. "No, no, I'm not. Why did you want to meet me here?"

"I didn't," he said. "I didn't send that text."

A gust of wind whipped up, propelling the door against him as it slammed shut. He stumbled forward, nearly knocking her to the floor again. And she knew he wasn't the one who'd shoved her. She was right that that shadow hadn't been as big or as broad.

"I haven't had my phone since the crash yesterday," he said. "I don't know who has it, but its location showed up here. And I saw those texts on my computer, too." In that faint light, he peered around. "We need to get out of here. Are you all right? You were on the floor when I opened the door."

"Someone pushed me down the stairs," she said, her teeth clicking together as she began to shiver uncontrollably.

"Oh my God," he murmured with the genuine concern that made her heart warm. "We have to get you to the hospital. Make sure you don't have anything broken or a concussion or internal injuries."

She would have told him that she was fine, but she really couldn't tell. She was so cold, so numb, that she could feel nothing but that . . . except for that warmth in her heart.

For him . . .

"You're shaking," he said. "You must be in shock." He wrapped his arm around her, drawing her close against him. "Let's get the hell out of here." But when he pushed against the door, it didn't budge. He turned the handle and rattled it, but still it didn't open.

"What the hell . . ." he murmured. "How'd we get locked in?"

"There was no lock," she said.

"There was a clasp, though," Elijah murmured. "Did someone stick a padlock through it?" He pulled his arm away from her and grasped the handle with both hands, shaking the door. But it still wouldn't open.

Then he stepped back and rushed toward it, ramming his shoulder against the thick wood. A grunt of pain slipped out of his lips.

"Don't," she said. "You're going to get hurt."

"But we have to get out of here," he said. "The temperature is already below freezing. . . ."

She brushed her boot back and forth across the floor, shoving aside the snow that had drifted across it until the hinges of the trapdoor glinted in the faint light filtering through the broken windows. "We can get out this way."

"What the hell is that?"

She bent over to grasp the eye hook and pull up the door. But a sharp pain shot through her rib cage, and she cried out. She was more hurt than she'd realized. "There's a tunnel down there," she said. "It'll lead us to the hall."

"That's how you got onto the grounds," he murmured. And he reached around her and pulled up the door. "I don't have a flashlight or even my phone. How the hell are we going to see down there?"

Her hands numb, she fumbled around in the pockets of her parka. "I don't feel my phone. . . ." Her attacker must have taken it, like they had somehow gotten ahold of Elijah's. But she found something, a small penlight. "It's not much . . ." Not like the flashlight she'd brought with her the first time, but she'd left that in the backpack she'd carried the day she'd used the tunnel to trespass. "But if we stay here, we're going to freeze. . . ." Her teeth clicked together again as they began to chatter with the cold that had already penetrated so deeply inside her.

"Okay," Elijah said. "Can you make it down the ladder?"

She had no choice, so she nodded. "We can't both go on it at the same time. The rungs are old and spongey already."

"I'll go first," he said. "Then you can toss the light down and I'll shine it up to help you down." He scrambled easily down the ladder even in that faint light.

She took more time, clinging weakly to each rung, as her body shook nearly uncontrollably . . . so uncontrollably that she lost her grasp and her footing and tumbled down the last few feet.

Strong arms caught her, holding her steady. "Easy," Elijah murmured. "I've got you. . . ."

And she remembered the last time someone had had her . . . when she'd emerged from the other end of the tunnel. "We have to be careful," she said. "This could be a trap. Your grandfather's nurse was waiting for me the first time I went through this passageway."

"Sam Howell must have tipped him off," Elijah said.

"So your grandfather did talk to him?"

"He wouldn't admit it," Elijah said. "But he did tell me other things. A lot of other things, surprisingly . . ."

She shivered at his tone. "What?"

"It's freezing down here. We need to get to the hall," he said. And he shone the light along the rocky walls and floor. The light glittered in the eyes of scurrying little creatures.

And she shuddered again in revulsion. "This way . . ." she said. Clasping her hand over his, she trained the beam down the tunnel. Despite the narrowness of it, Elijah stayed at her side, his arm wrapped around her with his body close to hers, offering warmth and support. Finally, the tunnel opened onto the room she'd found before.

"What the hell?" he murmured. "Where are we?"

She guided the light around the space, showing him the dark holes that opened onto other tunnels. "I followed the one that had a natural incline to it. That's the one that led up to the ravine."

"If we come out there, we'll be out in the elements again," he said. "We need to get you someplace warm and safe. . . ."

"But what if this is a trap?" she asked. "What if we were locked in the lighthouse to force us down here?"

Elijah shone the light around those broken crates until it glinted off something on the ground, some kind of tool. He walked over and retrieved the rusted crowbar he'd found. Then he joined her, handing her the penlight as he wrapped his arm around her again.

She trained it on the tunnel she'd taken just a couple of days before. "That one leads toward the ravine."

"Go to the right of that," he said. "That should bring us out closer to the main building, maybe even under it."

She nodded in agreement, wishing she had figured that out when she'd explored on her own. She started toward it and staggered a bit against his side.

"Are you okay? Can you keep walking?"

She nodded. "I'll be okay. Just keep talking to me to get my mind off how cold it is. Tell me what your grandfather told you. . . ."

Elijah chuckled softly. "With you, the interview never ends. . . ."

It would end if her attacker had their way, if they finally succeeded in killing her. She shivered.

And he began to talk, as if to distract her. "Grandfather's nurse . . ."

"Igor?"

"Theo," he said, as if that was somehow significant.

Her head pounded, and she struggled to focus. "Theo . . ."

"Another variation of Theodore, like Teddy," Elijah said. "He's Teddy Bowers's father."

"I take it you didn't know that?"

"No," he said. "They have different last names. But he must have helped Teddy get the job at the hall as grounds-keeper. Maybe Teddy didn't act alone when he grabbed Genevieve. Maybe they had some kind of plan. Teddy thought he was a Bainesworth."

"And the DNA that would have proved it was lost," she remembered. Over a week ago, the sheriff had shared that with Edie, along with his frustration over it. "He thinks your grandfather made sure it was."

"He swears the only kids he ever had are my mother and my aunt, that neither Teddy nor Theo are related to him. But if they think they are . . ."

"They might have been working together to destroy you and Bode . . ." she murmured.

"They're not the only ones with a secret connection," Elijah said. "I didn't know that Dr. Chase once worked here either, on his summer break between college and med school. Grandfather told us about that after telling us about Theo."

"Rosemary told me about Dr. Chase today," she said. "So, do you think it could be one of them? Theo or Dr. Chase who killed Erika and has been trying to kill us?"

"I don't know," he said. "If Theo believes he's a Baines-worth, he might have killed Erika out of jealousy or something.

But I'm not sure that makes sense. I'm really not sure why anyone would kill Erika." He sighed. "But then, I didn't really know Erika very well."

Edie wished now that she'd researched the personal trainer more, had tried to find out more about her. But because his grandfather seemed to know so much, she asked, "What else did James tell you?"

"Not much else," Elijah said. "Just professed his innocence again. Claimed that all he ever did was try to help people. That he never would have harmed or taken advantage of the young girls, but . . ."

The way his words trailed off had her shining the light around them. Had he heard something? Seen something? Were they no longer alone?

"What?" she asked.

"He said that women are often overlooked . . ."

"Overlooked as what?" Edie asked.

"As murderers."

That shadow had been smaller than Elijah, while Theo was even bigger than him. But Dr. Chase wasn't as tall or broad as Elijah.

She murmured, "I don't know . . ." And she didn't know how much longer she could go on walking. Her neck and shoulders had already ached from the car crash, but now her legs and ribs and head ached, too. At least she wasn't as cold as she'd been, though. This tunnel wasn't as dank and musty as the others either. It was almost as if it had been used more frequently, more recently.

Then the tunnel opened into another room, and in the middle of that room was a bed with straps attached to it. There were other things in it—some primitive-looking surgical instruments. Some old gowns and sheets . . .

And a light bulb dangled from a cord attached to the ceiling above them. It wasn't hewn out of the rock like the other tunnels but looked like the bottom of floorboards. Elijah reached up and pulled the chain, illuminating the space even more. There was electricity here. And an old sink and toilet in the corner, with pipes running down from that wooden ceiling. They were in the basement of some kind of structure.

Or was this a dungeon?

Another ladder led up to the ceiling. But it wasn't as long and rickety-looking as the one in the lighthouse. This one was so sturdy that it looked as if it had been recently placed.

"Where the hell are we?" she murmured.

"I think we're under the hall," Elijah said. Then he looked around and shuddered. "And I don't want to think about what this is. . . ."

The light bulb rocked back and forth over the bed, illuminating the sheets on it, the sheets stained with something that was a dark, rusty color.

Dried blood.

"Was this where Erika was those few months she was missing?" Elijah murmured. "Was this where she was murdered? Right under the hall? Right under my goddamn nose?"

"You don't know that for sure . . ." she murmured. "That might not be blood, and if it is, it could be very old." But she suspected he was right.

"It's past time that I learn all about this damn place," he said, and he climbed up that ladder and pushed against the trapdoor at the top of it. When it opened, steam and heat rushed into the cavelike room.

"Does it open onto a boiler room?" she asked. But then she heard a woman scream. What the hell had Elijah found?

* * *

What the hell is Elijah doing here? Bode wondered as he peered through the windshield at the rental car parked behind a red Jeep at the lighthouse.

Bode knew he shouldn't have let his brother out of his sight. Not after nearly losing him so many times over the past week. But he'd had to go back to his cottage to check on his daughter. . . .

Listening to Grandfather actually tell them things had unsettled Bode, had made him nervous for the safety of his child.

He should have been more worried about Elijah. He should have made certain that a guard stayed with his big brother at all times. Because, after asking Heather to cover for him in the gym, he'd already looked everywhere for Elijah.

That was how he'd wound up here . . .

After checking in Elijah's suite for him, he'd gone into his office. While it was empty, Elijah had left his laptop open to the app that connected to his cell phone. His missing cell.

But it wasn't missing. It was at the lighthouse.

And, suspecting that was where Elijah had gone, especially after he'd read the text messages, he'd rushed out here. Elijah couldn't have sent that message to Edie Stone.

So who had? Who had his phone? It all felt so shady to Bode that he reached into his pocket and pulled out the card he'd grabbed from Elijah's desk, the card that must have been in that yellow envelope with the items Sergeant Montgomery had dropped off. And he dialed the trooper's cell number.

She answered immediately. "Sergeant Montgomery here . . ."

A feeling rushed over him; he didn't know if it was dread or relief. "Sergeant, this is Bode James," he said.

"You've decided to talk to me without a lawyer?" she asked. "Or are you calling to try to cancel that meeting tomorrow?"

"I'm calling you about my brother," he said. "I'm at the lighthouse on the island. Both his and Edie Stone's vehicles are here, but they look unoccupied." The lights were off, and they weren't running. "I think they were both lured out here."

"I'm close," the sergeant said. "I'm at Sam Howell's cottage."

That was closer even than the hall. But Bode still worried that it might take her too long to get here. Where the hell were his brother and the reporter? They'd nearly been killed here once before.

He couldn't wait. So he pushed open the driver's door of his SUV and stepped out. "Hurry," he told her.

"Mr. James, wait for me!" she insisted.

But he was already walking toward the hill on which the lighthouse sat. As he passed the Jeep and the SUV his brother had rented, he confirmed to the trooper, "Their vehicles are empty."

"Get back in yours!" the sergeant ordered him. "You're putting your life in danger."

"I thought you considered me the danger," he remarked. He was fit enough that he managed to scramble up those snow-covered rocks to the top of the hill without dropping the cell. It was serving as much as a flashlight as his connection to the trooper. In its glow, he could discern the door of the lighthouse and the new padlock dangling from the rusted clasp, holding the door shut. Trapping two people inside to freeze to death?

"Elijah?" he called out. "Edie?"

But nobody answered him from inside the lighthouse. Was he already too late? A key stuck out of the bottom of the padlock, but before he could turn it, he heard a gun cock behind him.

"Don't let them out!" a female voice ordered him.

But if his brother was trapped inside the lighthouse, he wasn't leaving him there to freeze. So he turned the key.

And the cocked gun fired.

Chapter Eighteen

Elijah couldn't believe he was back at the lighthouse after so narrowly escaping from it. And he couldn't believe that he'd let Edie return with him before getting medical treatment. But when he'd pushed open the trapdoor to the sauna off the gym and startled Heather Smallegan, the young personal trainer had told them that Bode had been looking everywhere for him. Maybe she had been, too, because she hadn't been dressed for the sauna—she had her coat and her boots on.

Knowing Bode would have looked in the place Elijah usually was, he was certain his brother would have found his open laptop in his office. And knowing how concerned Bode was about him, he probably would have headed out to the lighthouse, too. Once Bruce confirmed that Bode had just driven through the gates and the guard confessed that he'd just realized his weapon was missing, Elijah had borrowed the guard's SUV—like someone had borrowed his gun—and driven off as fast as he could toward the lighthouse, with Edie sitting next to him.

But the minute he'd pulled up behind Bode's vehicle, he'd realized he was too late. The gunshot reverberated off the rocks on which the lighthouse stood. And he saw Bode drop to the ground. He'd left Edie in the passenger seat, but even if she hadn't stayed there, he doubted she would be able to make it up the rocks he was scrambling over, trying to get to his brother.

His heart hammered in his chest and tears stung his eyes. Adelaide couldn't lose her father. Elijah couldn't lose his brother. "No," he murmured. "God, no . . ."

At the sound of his voice, the shooter whirled toward him, the gun shaking in her hand. "How did you get out?" she asked. And when she glanced back toward the door against which Bode leaned, bleeding, Elijah rushed forward and shoved Amanda Plasky down into the snow.

Another shot rang out, and then she rolled over and pointed the barrel toward him. "You don't want to shoot me," he told her, dropping his voice to the low monotone he used when he hypnotized people. But when he did that, like he once had Rosemary Tulle, it was always in the room that was part of his office, with its special lights and music and oxygen.

It wasn't out here in the wind and snow. And usually he was relaxed and in control, not frantic, like he was now.

"We're friends, Amanda," he murmured. "You care about me. . . ."

"I love you," she said. "I loved you from the first moment I saw you. But you never saw me!"

He hadn't. He hadn't seen her as anything other than a highly driven, highly successful publicist. While he'd known she was flirting with him, he hadn't thought she was serious about him. "You were always so busy, Amanda, so focused on your job. . . ."

"Like you," she said. "We have that in common. And so much more. But then that damn reporter started coming around. And you *saw* her."

Edie was impossible to miss, to resist, to not fall for . . .

"I see you, Amanda," he lied. "I see how beautiful you are. How smart . . ."

So smart that he hadn't noticed how fixated she'd become on him, so fixated that she'd become dangerous.

"I see how much you care about me," he said.

"I care more than she does!" she cried, and her grasp on the gun tightened.

He didn't dare look away from the gun barrel. He didn't dare look to see if Edie had climbed up the rocks behind him. "I know," he assured her. "She's just using me to try to get information and records out of me about Bainesworth Manor. She doesn't care about me."

"And you're just trying to get her not to write about it," Amanda said. "That's why you've been paying her so much attention, right? That's what I told her. That you were just playing her for a fool . . ."

He nearly snorted at that. Nobody played Edie Stone for a fool. It was more likely that she had played *him*.

But he doubted anyone could fake the passion that she'd expressed in the back seat of his SUV. And even if she had played him, he couldn't worry about that right now; he was too worried that Bode was bleeding out. And that he might get shot next . . .

Or Edie . . .

That would be the worst.

"You were right," he assured Amanda. "You're always right. . . ."

She released a shaky breath and nodded. "Yes. That's why I know we belong together. I can help you run the hall better than Bode can."

Bode was the hall—more so than even Elijah. If Bode was gone, most of their guests would have no interest in staying there. Except maybe for Morgana Drake and her ghosts . . .

Not wanting anyone else to become one, Elijah stepped closer to where Amanda lay in the snow. "You're going to freeze lying there," he told her. "Please let me help you up. . . ." He held out his hand.

And when she reached for his, he reached for the gun, trying to wrest it from her one-handed grasp. But her finger must have been on the trigger—because another gunshot rang out.

Edie's throat burned from her scream, the one she'd uttered when that shot rang out and Elijah dropped to the ground just like his brother had long moments before. Then Amanda Plasky scrambled to her feet and aimed the gun toward Edie, but before she could fire, another shot rang out, and Amanda dropped back down to the ground.

Elijah had gotten up. And he'd helped Bode up . . .

But Amanda hadn't gotten back up.

Sergeant Beverly Montgomery, standing beside Edie, had killed the publicist with the one shot she'd fired. Then she'd been so furious that she'd looked as if she was going to kill the rest of them.

Fortunately, an ambulance arrived then. Apparently, the trooper had been on her cell with Bode and had heard the shot Amanda fired at him. And so she'd called for the ambulance.

Now Edie was back at the place where she and Elijah Cooke had decided they'd had their first date . . .

At the hospital.

Instead of him waking up to her at his bedside, she awoke to him at hers. Dark circles rimmed his pale blue eyes, and she wondered how long he'd been waiting for her to wake up.

After a CT scan and an MRI, she must have fallen asleep under the warm blankets the nurse had piled onto her. There was also an IV in her arm, running a warm saline solution through her body to raise her temperature. It must have worked because she wasn't shivering anymore. And when she looked at Elijah, staring at her so intently, heat flushed her face and her body and especially her heart.

"Are you okay?" he asked.

"Are you?" she asked.

"The bullet missed me," he reminded her, as he had in the back of the ambulance that had whisked all three of them to the hospital. He had a hole in his jacket, but nowhere in his body.

His brother had not been as fortunate. His shoulder had seeped blood through his jacket and down his shirt to his jeans. "How is Bode?" she asked.

"He'll be fine," he said. "The bullet went through, and they repaired the damage to the tendons. He's going to be frustrated as hell that he won't be able to use it for a while, but he'll recover fully."

"Will you?" she asked with concern.

He sighed. "I don't know. I missed another one. Another killer who was close to me."

Not as close as she'd wanted to be, though. That was what had set the woman off, when Edie had gotten close to him. "Was she a killer, though?" Edie wondered. "You and I survived. Bode survived."

"What about Sam Howell?"

"Why would she have killed Sam Howell?" she asked.

"Yes," another voice chimed in, and Edie peered over Elijah's shoulder to see that Sergeant Montgomery had pushed open her door and joined them. "Why would she have killed Sam Howell?"

"Do you know yet if he was killed or if it was suicide?" Edie asked.

The woman's jaw clenched, as if she was gritting her teeth. Just when Edie thought she would probably refuse to answer, she replied, "The crime scene tech found only his prints on the straight razor, but the killer could have worn gloves."

"He was the one who sent his nurse off to the pharmacy despite how nasty the weather was," Edie reminded her. "It was as if he wanted to get her out of his way."

The sergeant nodded then, albeit begrudgingly. "That could make sense," she admitted. "So maybe you're right, Ms. Stone; maybe Amanda Plasky wasn't a killer."

"I'm not so sure about that . . ." Elijah murmured. Maybe he was thinking about Erika.

"She sure tried plenty of times to kill us," Edie remarked. "Thank you for saving our lives tonight, Sergeant."

The woman nodded, but her shoulders slumped with the burden of taking a life . . . even though she'd saved three. "I had a call earlier that there were lights at the Howell crime scene," she said. "I found Amanda's battered vehicle parked in his driveway. She must have left it there and taken a snowmobile from his shed. That's what she rode through the woods to the lighthouse."

"That's why I didn't see a car. . . ." Edie murmured. "She was clever."

Elijah shuddered. "Too clever. She could have gotten away with it if not for those tunnels. . . ."

"Tunnels?" the sergeant asked.

They filled her in on what they'd found beneath the sauna at the hall. And she gasped.

"You think that's where Erika was murdered?" she asked. "Who else knows about those tunnels?" She narrowed her eyes and studied Elijah's face. "Does your brother?"

"No," Elijah said. "I didn't know either. Edie was the one who showed me."

"Sam Howell told me," she said before the trooper had to ask. "And I have no doubt that James Bainesworth and his nurse know they're there."

"And David would have known," Elijah said with a heavy sigh. "There's no way he could have put in the sauna and not noticed the trapdoor down to that room."

"So you're trying to pin that murder on a dead man just like your brother has been doing?" the sergeant asked.

And Edie remembered what Elijah had shared with her earlier, about what his grandfather had said. "Don't overlook the women . . ." she murmured.

"What?" the trooper asked.

Elijah nodded in agreement. "You're right . . ."

"Amanda was so obsessed with Elijah that she kept trying to kill me, and when he showed interest in me, she tried killing us both. That whole if-I-can't-have-him, no-one-else-can thing," Edie explained.

"But she was obsessed with Dr. Cooke, not his body-building brother," the sergeant murmured.

And Edie wondered if the sergeant was a little obsessed with Bode herself, at least in proving him guilty of some-thing he hadn't done. "Not her. Someone else . . ."

When she'd climbed that ladder and joined Elijah and Heather in the sauna, she'd expected to find the other woman in a towel. Or less . . . she'd screamed in surprise when Elijah opened the trapdoor.

But now she remembered how the young woman had

been dressed. In jeans and a jacket and her boots, and she'd been in the sauna.

She shot upright in bed. "Heather!" she exclaimed. "It's Heather. She knew the trapdoor was there."

Elijah's eyes widened with shock. Then he nodded. "That's what she was doing in there all dressed."

It was probably why she screamed when the trapdoor opened as she was reaching for it.

Sergeant Montgomery looked from one to the other of them, as if they'd both lost their minds. "Who's Heather?"

"One of the personal trainers," Elijah said. "And she definitely has a thing for my brother. She started working at the spa when Erika had to go on bedrest during the last couple of weeks of her pregnancy. If Erika returned from maternity leave, we would have had to let Heather go."

The sergeant's brow creased with skepticism. "And you think she kidnapped and held Erika hostage just to take her job?"

"And Bode," Edie said. "That's why Amanda was trying to kill me, to keep me away from Elijah. Some women get obsessed with men, maybe especially the Cooke men."

"But how would she have learned about the tunnels?" the trooper asked.

Elijah shrugged. "Maybe David. He might have told her. But I don't know. It's at least worth talking to her."

The sergeant nodded, but she sounded grudging when she said, "I'll go talk to her." She turned then and walked back out the door.

Elijah released a shaky breath. "Oh my God, I hope it's over." His broad shoulders lifted a bit, as if he'd lost some of the weight he always carried on them. Then his lips curved into a slight smile, and he murmured, "Well, it's over until you sell your story."

"Is this where you turn the charm back on and try to talk me out of selling it?" she asked.

He tensed. "You don't believe what Amanda said, do you?"

She studied the sincerity on his handsome face, in his beautiful eyes, and smiled. "No, you're not that charming. . . ."

Instead of being offended, he laughed. "No, I'm really not. It took me until date four to get you in bed."

"It wasn't a bed, it was a back seat," she reminded him. "And that was my idea."

"You're not very charming either," he said. "Since it took you four dates."

"That had a little something to do with the overdose on our third one, but . . ." She shrugged. "It doesn't matter."

"Your story does," Elijah said. "To a lot of people. I understand that you have to cover it, that you have to find out what happened to the women and the babies who were born at the manor."

"You understand . . ." she murmured with wonder. But she shouldn't have been surprised. She knew that she'd fallen for him, and this was why. He was so empathetic, so caring, so selfless.

He nodded. "I do understand that those women would like to know what happened to their babies. And the families of the missing girls would like to find out what happened to them. I understand because I don't know what happened to my mother, and I'd like to find out."

"I'll help you," she promised. "And after we find out the truth about the manor, we'll just let those women and babies involved know. I'm not sure it's anyone else's business." Unless she uncovered criminal activity for which the statutes of limitation hadn't already expired, like murder, but Elijah would know that they would have to report that . . . even if it finally sent his grandfather to prison. He might be relieved about that, though.

"You wouldn't go public with it?" he asked.

She shook her head. "Not if it'll hurt you," she said.

His blue eyes widened with shock. "But it could be your Pulitzer . . ."

She shrugged. Because if she got that Pulitzer but destroyed Elijah, it wasn't worth it. She would be successful but alone.

And she was tired of being alone.

"I can't let you make that sacrifice for me," he said.

"Why not?" she asked.

"Because I'm falling for you," he said. "And I want to support you . . ."

"Even if it hurts you?" she asked. "That's why I'm falling for you. You are the exact opposite of your Bainesworth legacy. You are everything that is good and kind and caring."

"You're falling for me?" he asked, and his lips curved into a slight grin.

She nodded, then flinched at the pain reverberating inside her skull. "Down a flight of stairs earlier . . ."

"We'll make sure that doesn't happen again. We'll keep you safe. We'll keep each other safe."

"Hopefully it is all over," she said. "Hopefully there won't be any more danger."

He leaned over the bed and brushed a soft kiss across her lips. "You're the danger, Edie Stone. I knew it even before I met you. I knew you were going to turn my world upside down. I just didn't realize that I was going to fall for you."

She wouldn't have thought it possible either. But she had no doubt they had something real. Something that could last.

* * *

It was all over if Sergeant Montgomery believed the note she'd found in Heather Smallegan's room in the hall. It was the only thing left in her room. Her clothes and toiletries were gone. So was she . . . missing . . . ?

Dearest Bode,
    I'm sorry I killed Erika. She didn't deserve you. She didn't love you and your daughter like she should have. She really left you right after Adelaide was born. She stayed away from you and your baby for three months before she finally came back, and when she was looking for you in the gym, she found me first. She said that I was going to have to leave now. That she was back and wanted her job and her life. I snapped and struck her with the end of a weight bar. Then I dumped her through that trapdoor David Cooke showed me and left her in the dungeon. The coyotes must have dragged her out into the ravine. Please forgive me.

                    All my love,
                    Heather

The confession was enough to close the case, at least according to the prosecutor, who'd refused Mae's request for a search warrant for the hall. But there were still loose ends, like Heather herself. Where was she?

Sergeant Montgomery wanted to find her. Alive.

But she had a feeling that when the woman turned up, she would be dead, like Erika. Both women had written Bode notes when they'd left him. And those notes felt too similar, too coincidental, too damn pat.

Had he orchestrated it all to prove his innocence? Because Heather's note would give a jury too much reasonable doubt for him to be convicted. And he would only go to trial if Mae could convince the district attorney to seek an indictment against him from a grand jury. And he'd refused, but that might have been for other reasons . . .

Personal reasons . . .

And he thought those were the same things that made her doubt that Heather's confession and the note Erika had left were real. The prosecutor thought the same thing Bode James did, that she had a vendetta against the fitness guru.

Maybe she was wrong.

Maybe Bode James wasn't the killer. But she still didn't quite believe that Heather was.

So then there was still a killer out there, running around Bane Island thinking they had gotten away with their crime. But Mae wasn't going to let that happen. She was going to make certain that justice was served if it was the last thing she ever did.

Keep reading for a special excerpt
THE HUNTED
Lisa Childs

The pressures of fame and an obsessive stalker have driven pop star Olivia Smith to take shelter at Halcyon Hall, an exclusive spa on a remote island off the coast of Maine. Yet from the moment she arrives, there are rumors about women disappearing, and stories about the resort's grisly past. Then a note arrives from her stalker, proving that nowhere is truly safe. . . .

It's been twenty-five years since Sheriff Deacon Howell discovered his first dead body on these grounds. Back then, Halcyon Hall was an asylum known as Bainesworth Manor. Others have perished here since, including Deacon's wife. Many locals share his belief that her death wasn't suicide. The difference is, they think Deacon killed her. But he has bigger problems than gossip, because another body has been found. . . .

As Deacon investigates the increasing threats to the singer's life, the danger becomes undeniable. Something evil lurks here—not just in the asylum's grim history, but in the present. And there will be no rest at Halcyon Hall until every sin has been avenged. . . .

Look for THE HUNTED, *on sale now.*

Prologue

A cry rang out, startling black birds into flight. They rose from the pine trees to form a dark cloud in the sky, casting a shadow over the tall wrought iron gate and the three boys who straddled their bicycles in front of it.

Deacon Howell ducked his head down and murmured, "What the hell was that?" A howl followed the cry as coyotes called out to each other.

"What's the matter? Scared?" Elijah Cooke taunted him. The puny kid wouldn't have been brave enough to do that if his cousin wasn't standing right next to him.

David Cooke was already a teenager while Deacon and Elijah were still twelve. But David was dumb, so he was in their grade even though he was older and bigger. Too much bigger for Deacon to fight the two of them alone. Maybe he was the dumb one for coming here.

"I'm not scared," he lied.

Elijah stared at him with those creepy, pale eyes like he could see right through him. Even though he wasn't as big as his cousin, he was somehow more frightening. It had been his idea to come here. So Deacon was probably getting set up, but it was too late to back out now.

Staring up at the tall, iron gates, he asked, "How we getting in?"

A little smirk curving his thin lips, Elijah wrapped one small hand around a piece of rusted iron and pushed. The gate creaked open.

Damn it.

Now Deacon had no excuse and no escape . . . from the curse. That was the legend—that anyone who set foot on the property of the old insane asylum would be cursed. That was probably why the Cookes were so messed up; their family owned the place, so they had no escape either.

Now they were getting him cursed. He drew in a breath of cold autumn air then pedaled his bike after theirs, down the winding drive. The road was overgrown with pine boughs hanging over them, snagging and pulling at their clothes.

The hospital had been shut down before Deacon was born. But he knew what had been done here. He'd heard all the stories about the people who'd been electrocuted and had holes drilled into their brains. Every time one of those branches tugged on him, he felt like it was a hand reaching out to do those same things to him. He shivered and pedaled harder, passing the Cookes, so they wouldn't have time to set a trap for him. He wasn't bigger than David, but he was faster.

He made it to the building first. All crumbling stone with ivy climbing over it, it looked like a castle and was nearly that tall. Mesmerized, he jumped off his bike and let it drop into the thick weeds. As he stared at the manor, the spooky old building seemed to stare back at him, its broken windows like wide, soulless eyes.

Then the manor called out to him in a high-pitched whisper, "Deacon . . ."

The giggles that followed made him realize it was just the Cookes teasing him, trying to scare him. He would show them that he was no baby. He was brave.

He headed toward the double doors at the front of the crumbling stone building. One door had pulled partly loose from its rusty hinges, so he was able to peel it back and squeeze through the opening. His legs shook as he stepped into the building. It was dark and cold and smelled like something dead.

Probably an animal.

Just an animal.

Animals would have been able to get inside just as easily as he had. Easier because they could have gotten through any of the broken windows. Light filtered through those windows, guiding him toward a staircase in the middle of the front room. The steps wound up a few stories to where long branches broke through the ceiling. Ice or lightning must have dropped a tree onto the roof. Staring up, moving toward the staircase, he wasn't watching where he was going until he tripped, falling across whatever his foot had hit on the floor. He reached out to push himself up, and his hand slid over something, or rather, into it. Something squishy and . . .

He looked down at the person lying beneath him, or what was left of the person. Long, scraggly, light-colored hair framed the decaying face that, like the manor, stared back at him with rotted eyes.

A scream burned in his throat, but it stuck there, unable to come out, just like he was stuck there, unable to move. Trapped in a nightmare.

He knew for certain then that he was cursed, just like this poor person had been.

Chapter One

Present Day

The drive wound between the pine trees, the boughs heavy with snow. A thin sheen of black ice covered the asphalt. That was why he didn't press harder on the accelerator: caution and dread. But despite his slow speed, he reached the parking lot and pulled the SUV into one of the many empty spaces.

More than twenty-five years had passed since the day Deacon Howell had discovered his first dead body at Bainesworth Manor. Even though he wasn't that scared twelve-year-old boy any longer, the same sense of dread and doom tied his guts in knots every time he set foot on the property. He opened the driver's door and stepped onto the slick asphalt. Staring up at the massive stone structure with its snow-covered, clay-tiled roof, Deacon wasn't impressed with the renovations that had been completed a couple of years ago. The gleaming windows looked as soulless to him as the broken ones had so many years ago. Though it had been renamed Halcyon Hall and converted from a psychiatric hospital into some kind of fancy treatment-center spa, it would always be Bainesworth Manor to him.

The curse of his existence . . .

If only he could blame this damn place for everything that had gone wrong in his life.

Just as he had all those years ago, he drew in a deep, shaky breath before walking through the double doors that opened automatically to admit him. Now the foyer was all shiny marble and polished wood, and the air was fresh with the faint traces of leather and sage. He still smelled death though—just as he had all those years ago.

Death hung over the manor just like the dark clouds hung over Bane Island, Maine. The manor dominated nearly half of the big island, leaving the village, its outskirts, and some of the rocky shoreline for the locals. The shore was so rocky that few boats dared to dock there, so no ferry ran. It was a four-mile-long bridge that connected Bane Island to the mainland. Since that rickety, old bridge was rarely passable in the winter, the island was self-contained with a small hospital and a grocery store and other small shops.

Deacon was a local—born and raised here. When he'd left, he'd never wanted to come back, but the curse—and his father's failing health—had called him home.

And his job kept calling him out to the hall.

Elijah Cooke stepped out of the shadows, where he always seemed to be lurking—like one of the ghosts that were rumored to haunt the manor. As the director of Halcyon Hall, Elijah was actually running it, though. "What is it this time, Sheriff?"

Deacon had made quite a few trips to the hall during the past month—to help a woman find her missing daughter. He'd found a dead body instead. Fortunately, it hadn't been hers. But not knowing who he'd discovered had made his job even harder.

"You know why I'm here," Deacon said.

Elijah's pale eyes gleamed eerily from the shadows in which he stood. "You know who she is?"

He shook his head.

"What's taking so long?"

"The body was damaged too badly for fingerprinting." The first corpse he'd found here had haunted him since he was twelve. This one would haunt him until he died. And the one he'd found between those two . . .

He would never be free of her either—especially not of her.

"What about DNA?" Elijah asked.

Deacon knew what he was asking but chose to be as off-putting as the shrink was. "It doesn't match Genevieve Walcott's."

"Of course not," Elijah said. "She's alive. Thank God for that." He arched a dark brow. "Or are *you* going to take credit?"

Deacon shook his head. "Genevieve's a smart girl. She saved herself." With some help from her future stepfather, she had escaped the Halcyon Hall groundskeeper who'd abducted her. The woman whose body Deacon had discovered had not been so lucky; she hadn't escaped her gruesome fate. Deacon had found her much too late to save her. All he could do now was make sure she got justice.

Elijah stepped closer to Deacon, lowered his voice to a whisper, and asked, "What about the other DNA?"

"Which of the other DNA?" Deacon asked. "There's so damn much of it now that it's going to take the lab some time to run it all."

Elijah sighed. "You didn't need to get warrants, you know. I do want to know whose body you found."

"How come you didn't report her missing?" he asked.

His mind was still blown over what Elijah had finally

admitted to him. That he was an uncle; his younger brother, Jamie—or as he wanted to be called now, Bode—was a single father. The Bainesworth bloodline continued—maybe even more than anyone had guessed if the other rumors were true. But Deacon, more than anyone, knew not to put too much credence in rumors. He only wanted the facts, like how the mother of Elijah's niece, a personal trainer who'd worked at the spa, had disappeared shortly after the birth of her daughter four months ago.

"She left Bode a good-bye note and resigned," Elijah said.

From her job and from being a mother, according to the note that he had shown to Deacon a few weeks ago.

"Bode thinks it was all just too much for her, and she took off," Elijah continued, in defense of his younger brother. "He doesn't think that body is hers. She'd left months before that woman was murdered."

Elijah was clearly not as convinced. Dark circles shadowed the skin beneath his weird silver eyes. He wasn't getting any more sleep than Deacon was.

"You didn't report Genevieve Walcott as missing either," he reminded him. "Why are you still trying to act as if nothing's going on around here?"

"Whatever was going on—it's over," Elijah said. "The groundskeeper that kidnapped Genevieve is dead. If the woman whose body you found was murdered, then Teddy Bowers must have killed her."

"That's what you want to believe," Deacon said.

"Don't you want to believe that, too?" Elijah asked.

"Doesn't matter what I want," he said. "I have to learn the truth." About everything . . . even that other body he'd found over a year ago. "That's why I asked the state police to reopen their investigation into Shannon's death." Just like the body he'd found a few weeks ago, Shannon had been blond. Genevieve Walcott was also blond. Maybe Bane Island had a serial killer.

"They already ruled it suicide," Elijah said. "Since that made everything easier for you, wasn't that what you wanted?"

"I just told you—I want the truth," he said.

Elijah snorted. "Your truth. You want to blame me and my family for everything that happens on the island—even Shannon's suicide."

"If Genevieve Walcott's kidnapper was telling the truth, your family *is* to blame," Deacon said. "Remember that Teddy Bowers claimed he was a Bainesworth heir. That you and your brother cheated him out of his birthright."

Elijah shook his head. "Teddy Bowers was delusional. If you're just here to antagonize me, you can leave now, Sheriff."

"You call it antagonizing. I call it interrogating," Deacon said.

"I've done nothing to warrant an interrogation," Elijah replied.

Deacon tilted his head and stared skeptically at his old nemesis. "Once again, that's just what you want to believe."

"And once again, you don't want it to be the truth," Elijah replied. "So this conversation is over, Sheriff. The next time you want to come here, you better have a warrant."

Deacon drew a paper out of his pocket. "Look what I happen to have right here . . ."

Elijah cursed. "I don't know how the hell you made friends with the judge."

Deacon wasn't sure either since he had initially treated Whittaker Lawrence, who was Genevieve Walcott's soon-to-be stepfather, with the same suspicion he did the Cookes.

Maybe the difference was that Whit hadn't had anything to hide, so he hadn't gotten defensive. He'd realized Deacon was just doing his job.

"What the hell is this warrant for?" Elijah asked as he took the paper. He read it and shook his head. "No. No. No way in hell!"

Deacon chuckled. Elijah wasn't going to win this time— like he had, with the help of his older cousin, pretty much every skirmish of their childhood rivalry. Deacon wasn't the dumb kid he'd once been—not anymore, not after everything he'd lived through . . . and lost.

How long would she be safe here? How long until the press found her—or worse yet—*he* found her?

She glanced around the conservatory. Although sunshine warmed the room, Olivia Smith shivered as a chill chased down her spine. For once, she was the only one using the room, but she didn't feel alone. She felt creeped out, as if someone was watching her. Anyone could have been standing on the other side of the glass walls, hiding among the snow-enshrouded pine trees. Shadows darkened the snow around all those trees. Maybe one of the shadows was of a person instead of a pine. As Olivia peered outside, she caught a reflection in the glass—of herself, with her clothes hanging on her petite frame, of her dark blond hair tangled around her thin face, of her wide eyes staring back at her.

She wasn't dressing to impress anyone. Because of the winter weather and the holiday season, there were few other guests. That was part of why Olivia had chosen now to attend the exclusive spa. Despite the horrifying history of Bainesworth Manor, she had felt safe here at Halcyon Hall. Until the body had been found . . .

It wasn't even so much the body that had scared her but the arrival of the reporter. Edie Stone was legendary for uncovering scandals and secrets. Olivia had both, and she intended to keep them.

That was another reason why, three months ago, she'd checked herself into the exclusive spa. Halcyon Hall promised their guests absolute privacy. The director, Dr. Elijah Cooke, insisted that would not change despite the discovery of a body on the property. Dr. Cooke swore that a reporter would never be allowed access to the hall and especially not to the spa guests. Olivia was still safe.

Wasn't she?

As she stared out the window, she spied another reflection, of a shadow that moved behind her. She jumped and whirled toward the intruder. "What the hell—"

"I'm sorry," the dark-haired teenager said. "I didn't mean to scare you."

Olivia ducked her head down, so her hair slid over to hide her face, and started toward the French doors that stood open to the hallway.

"I won't bother you," the girl said, her voice cracking with emotion. "Just pretend I'm not here."

That was what Olivia had been hoping the teenager would do—ignore her. But every weekend the girl worked, she found some excuse to seek her out, to stare at her. To stalk her . . .

Olivia had enough damn stalkers. She didn't need one here. Not that she was afraid of the girl . . .

In fact, something pulled at her heart as she looked at the kid. Tears streaked down the teenager's full face, and her body shook with the sobs cracking her voice.

"What's wrong?" Olivia asked even though she really didn't want to get involved . . . with anyone . . . with anything.

She just wanted to be left alone, but something tugged at her heart when she looked at the teenager.

The girl raised her hand to her face and wiped at her tears. "Do . . . do you really care?" she asked, her deep-set, dark eyes widening with shock.

Olivia had done her best to avoid the girl whenever she worked at the spa. That tug on her heart turned into a twinge of regret that she'd been so obvious about her avoidance. She'd been so intent on protecting herself that she hadn't realized she might have been hurting somebody else. "You're upset," Olivia said. "I want to know why."

The girl sniffled. "For the same reason I'm always upset," she said. "Because of *him* . . ."

Olivia sighed. "Because of a boy?" She shouldn't have been surprised. Teenage angst was usually about hormones unless that teenager had grown up like she had. Then hormones had been the least of her problems.

The girl laughed, but the sound was sharp with bitterness. "Like I could ever have a boyfriend with him as my dad. I'm probably going to lose this job because of him—because he's out there fighting with Dr. Cooke right now, like he's always fighting with someone."

"Fighting?" Olivia asked, and her body tensed with dread. "Is your dad violent?"

The teenager nodded.

And Olivia gasped. She reached out now for the girl, closing her hands over the teenager's shoulders. "Does he get violent with you?" She studied the girl's face, looking for bruises. But she knew, from her own experience, that a smart abuser made sure there was no easily visible evidence.

The girl shook her head, sending her long dark hair across her face. Olivia reached up and pushed it back, and the girl flinched as if anticipating a blow. "I'm sorry," Olivia said as she pulled her hand back. She hated people touching her—for the very same reason the girl had flinched. She shouldn't have reached out like she had.

The girl shook her head again. "It's okay."

"What's your name?" Olivia asked. She'd been told it before; the female shrink, Rosemary Tulle, had mentioned it. But she couldn't remember it now—not with so many other thoughts rushing through her head. So many other memories . . .

"Holly," the girl replied, her voice soft as if she was suddenly shy.

"Holly," Olivia said. "You need to report him. You need to tell someone what he's doing to you."

"Report him?" Holly repeated with another bitter chuckle. "To who?"

"The police."

"He is the police," Holly replied. "He's the sheriff."

Olivia held in the curse burning her throat. She didn't want to add to the girl's fear and frustration. "That doesn't make him above the law. We can report him to the state police. Or to that judge, the one dating Rosemary Tulle." Olivia had met him a couple of times; he'd seemed like someone a person could trust.

"That judge is friends with him," Holly informed her. "And he's already been reported to the state police. They didn't have enough evidence to do anything to him."

"They didn't believe you?" Olivia asked, and anger coursed through her. She'd been that girl—the one nobody had believed.

Holly shrugged. "It's not like that . . ." Tears pooled in her dark eyes again. "He hasn't . . ."

"What?" Olivia prodded her when she trailed off. "What hasn't he done?"

The girl, who was much taller than Olivia's five feet, stared over her shoulder, and those dark eyes widened again as she murmured, "Dad . . ."

Olivia whirled around to the doorway and to the man who nearly filled it. He was tall and broad shouldered and so very dark that it felt as if his shadow swallowed all the sunshine in the conservatory. Her pulse quickened with fear racing over her, as that chill had earlier. She locked her legs that were threatening to tremble, and, summoning all her strength, stepped between father and daughter. Between the abuser and child?

"I won't let him hurt you," she promised the girl.

Beneath the brim of his navy-blue uniform cap, the sheriff's brow furrowed. "Holly, what the hell have you been telling people?"

"I . . . I haven't . . ." Her voice trailed off.

A wave of fierce protectiveness swept over Olivia, and she turned back toward the girl. "You don't have to talk to him. Go," she urged her. "I'll deal with your father."

Like she wished someone would have dealt with hers.

She led Holly toward the doorway where the sheriff stood; Olivia stayed between them, so the girl could slip out without her father touching her. He didn't try, though, not with Olivia there. He didn't even look at his daughter, just shook his head as if disgusted.

Shaking with fury now, she barely held onto her temper until the girl was gone. Then she released her anger. "How dare you!" she said to him. "How dare you act as if she's disappointed you."

She knew how that felt, to be belittled and demeaned—to be treated as less than nothing, as nobody. "How dare you!" she repeated, and she reached out again, stabbing his chest with her finger.

The man was like the hall, built out of rock. His chest was a wall of muscle. He didn't budge except for his mouth, which curved slightly upward in a smirk.

She wanted to slap it off his face, but as if he'd read her mind, he cautioned her, "You should think twice before assaulting an officer, Ms. Smith."

Shocked that he knew her name and that she was touching him, she pulled her finger from his chest and stepped back. "I am not the one assaulting anyone," she said.

He narrowed his dark eyes and studied her face. "Neither am I. I don't know what the hell my daughter has been telling you, but I've never laid a *finger* on her."

Olivia stared back at him, trying to determine if the sincerity in his voice and on his face was genuine or just a thin, handsome veneer he showed the world. "Why are you here then?" she asked. "Harassing her at work?"

"I am not harassing her," he said. "I didn't come here to talk to her."

"Then why are you here?" she asked.

"To talk to you."

Olivia's head snapped back as if he'd slapped her. "Me?"

Why the hell did he want to talk to her? What did he know about her—besides her name? What had he learned?

For the first time Elijah understood the satisfaction of balling his hand into a fist and swinging it. Hard. The force of the blow had his knuckles stinging and a vibration traveling from those knuckles up to his shoulder. He could even feel it in his abdomen.

He probably would have gotten hit in return—if not for his brother grabbing the bag before it swung back and struck him. Bode shook his head and cautioned him, "You're going to break your hand if you're not careful."

That was Elijah's problem. He was always so damn careful—always working so hard to control himself and everything around him. But despite his best efforts, his control was slipping.

"If you want to keep punching the bag, at least let me lace the gloves on you," Bode offered. "Or we can spar, if you want."

Since they'd become business partners in Halcyon Hall, they'd been sparring. Weary of the fight, Elijah shook his head.

Bode grinned. "Don't want to take me on?"

Given that his brother was a world-renowned personal trainer, Elijah would have been a fool to try. Bode was the "body" part of Halcyon Hall. A psychiatrist, Elijah was the "mind" part of the treatment center motto of "total well-being for body and mind."

"I don't want to fight with you," Elijah admitted. "Not anymore."

Bode sighed. "Guess we have taken more than our share of jabs at each other."

Elijah couldn't promise that he wouldn't fight with his brother again; they were business partners after all, who each believed his part of the business was more important. But they weren't enemies. Not anymore . . .

"Instead of fighting each other, we need to fight to save the hall," Elijah said.

Bode tensed. "What's happened?"

"The sheriff is here."

Bode cursed. "He better have a damn warrant."

"He does," Elijah said. "He has a court order that allows him to question our guests."

Bode struck the bag now with such force that, despite the heavy weight of it, it swung up toward the rafters of the open ceiling in the cavernous gym. "Damn it! Now the guests, those that haven't already checked out, damn sure will once he starts harassing them like he's been harassing us!"

That was Elijah's fear, too. "And there's no way they know anything about that body. The sheriff found her a few weeks ago, so she was dead before most of them arrived."

But not all of them. Morgana Drake had been here the longest, coming for a few months at a time since the hall had first opened two years ago. She'd been here for six months this last time, so she was more a resident than a guest at this point.

Olivia Smith had checked in three months ago, and she had yet to inform them of her departure date. Given how she valued her privacy, Elijah suspected that would be soon.

"That's not all he's done," Elijah said. "He's having the state reopen the investigation into his wife's death."

"Why?" Bode asked. "Seems like that's going to come back to bite him on the ass more than it will us."

Elijah shrugged. "I don't know why . . ." Except that Deacon probably didn't want to feel responsible or guilty anymore over the loss of his wife. "But if the state police call that murder too . . ."

"We have to make sure none of this hits the news," Bode said, "or all those bookings we have for upcoming stays will get canceled."

That was Elijah's greatest fear. "I know. I'm meeting with Amanda next." Amanda Plasky was the hall's publicist.

Bode sucked in a breath. "You told me first?"

Elijah nodded. "Of course."

Bode raised his arm again, but instead of swinging, he grabbed Elijah's shoulder and squeezed. "Thanks."

A twinge of regret struck Elijah that their partnership had started out so acrimoniously. "We're in this together," he reminded his younger brother.

Never more so than now.

Unfortunately, they were not the only two partners in the hall. They had a silent one—if only he would stay that way . . .

"Do you want to meet with Amanda with me?" Elijah offered, which was something else he wouldn't have done before, just as coming to Bode first wouldn't have been something he'd have done either.

Bode glanced around at the other people in the gym. "Heather should be finishing up soon," he said of the young female trainer. "I'll have her take my next appointment and join you."

Instead of resenting his involvement, as he would have in the past, Elijah appreciated it until Bode added, "Then we should tell *him*."

Dread clenched the muscles in Elijah's stomach, tightening them more than any of Bode's workouts would have. He groaned.

Bode reminded him, "He's the third one in this partnership."

They wouldn't have been able to renovate and reimagine Bainesworth Manor if their grandfather hadn't given them early access to their inheritance with the stipulation that he had a lifetime lease on the property. If they hadn't agreed to his terms, they would have had to wait until he died to start the treatment center, which Elijah was beginning to believe might never happen.

Had the old man made a pact with the devil? Or was he, as so many of the locals believed, the devil himself? If he was ever proven guilty of all the crimes people suspected him of committing, then Elijah and Bode were the ones who'd made the pact with Satan.